TO BE
MARQUETTE

Books by Sharon Dilworth

Two Sides, Three Rivers
The Long White
Women Drinking Benedictine
Year of the Ginkgo
My Riviera

TO BE MARQUETTE

SHARON DILWORTH

CARNEGIE MELLON UNIVERSITY PRESS

PITTSBURGH 2024

Cover art by Tim Lindquist
Find his work at fineartamerica.com/profiles/3-tim-lindquist

Book design by Connie Amoroso

Library of Congress Control Number 2023951324
ISBN 978-0-88748-707-1
Copyright © 2024 by Sharon Dilworth
Printed and bound in the United States of America

10 9 8 7 6 5 4 3 2

for Jim (Rounds) Hautala,
the original Crusoe

I think it was then that I began to think of Marquette as a verb—*to be Marquette* was to be rid of the person I had been and to embrace someone completely different. Up there, everything seemed possible. In Marquette, it was possible to live that close to the natural world—to live that close to beauty.

Project Seafarer, later known as Project ELF, was a top secret government-funded project created during the Cold War in the 1970s that allowed the military to communicate with submarines anywhere in the world, using extremely low frequency radio waves, aka ELF. The short coded, ultra-classified messages were to be used in extreme emergencies, such as a nuclear attack. The first communications lines covered eighty-four miles across Michigan's Upper Peninsula. Plans to develop the project included miles of more lines, all of which were to be embedded in the bedrock across a wide swath of the state's northern wilderness.

1

That first year in Marquette, the ecology studies midterm was in October on Presque Isle Park, a few miles north of campus.

Snow fell. There was no accumulation, but light flakes swirled overhead.

It was a practicum, not something I had done before. We were being tested on our ability to identify the foliage and wildlife of northern Michigan. Dr. Robinson had set it up like a fitness course. Each station had a sample of something we were supposed to identify. We were going out one by one. I was scheduled to go last, right behind Shane.

We were waiting at the burial site of Chief Kawbawgam, the Ojibwa chief, who I knew had lived in three different centuries, from 1799 to 1902. His wife was buried beside him. The sign did not say how long she had lived.

The grave was marked by an enormous white glacial boulder, which had been touched so many times the surface was more like glass than stone. The guys would usually end up sitting on it, until Dr. Robinson reminded them that it was a grave and not a park bench.

Some of the guys finished before half the group had even started. They were winded. They had run the course, and now I would have to do the same. We were competitive like that.

They were talking, all at once. The noise was distracting.

"Careful," Dr. Robinson said. "I'll consider any chatter cheating. I want to know what you know, not what your friends know."

I was nervous, which was stupid. It was just a test, in a class I loved. Plus, I had been studying all week.

My turn. I headed out, notebook in hand, with the miniature pen pushed down into the coil spirals.

It wasn't hard. I knew the three kinds of conifers: pine, fir, and spruce. The white pine had five needles per cluster; the Scotch pine only had two.

The Lombardy poplar tree was next. I knew we'd get tested on that. It was local, and Dr. Robinson pointed it out every time we passed it on the road out to Presque Isle.

It was quiet. The snow had stopped.

There was a shift in the woods, and I felt suddenly alone—isolated from the rest of the class, as if they had all gone home and left me.

I knew I was taking too long. I got flustered trying to hurry. The next station was a white birch bark, which didn't seem right. I had already identified that. I wondered if I had gotten turned around and was backtracking my steps. The path was thick with pine needles, and there were no footprints. I took the next right. The path narrowed, almost disappearing.

I knew Presque Isle. We had been coming out every week since school started. I knew that I should be able to see the lake; it was visible from almost everywhere on the island. But I was deep in the woods and saw nothing but the canopy of trees, the ferns, and the pinecones at my feet.

Something wasn't right. The woods hushed. I felt the shadows of the cloud-filled day.

So I started to run, hoping I wasn't missing a station. If I could get Lake Superior in sight, I would be okay. I kept moving. Dr. Robinson was going out after me to collect the test samples, and I hurried so he wouldn't overtake me. I was taking way too much time.

Then there it was. The huge expanse and the open water. Lake Superior was in sight. Relief. I was right where I should be.

But just as fast, there was something on the ground, something that shouldn't have been there. I couldn't stop. I went down. I hit the ground—smacking into the hard earth.

I felt the blood in my throat, like my teeth were falling out. I closed my eyes and held them shut tight, trying to make the pain go away.

I heard people. The guys were there, so I must have cried out. I was that close to finishing the course.

They said my name, over and over, like a birdcall, where there are no pauses. "Molly! Molly! Molly!"

"Are you alright?"

"Can you talk?"

"Say something."

I swallowed carefully, worried I was swallowing teeth. The blood filled my throat. I did not want to cry in front of the guys, but the minute I tried to speak, the sobs took over. Loud, rasping sobs and I couldn't stop. Dr. Robinson was yelling at them to hurry.

They helped me up. My jeans had ripped at the knee. Cold air against my bare skin.

The guys walked me over to Dr. Robinson. He was in the Jeep, the engine running. I tried to say that I was okay, but I really didn't feel that great, and he drove us down Lakeshore Drive way over the speed limit.

My mind raced. I knew what I had seen. I knew exactly what I had tripped over.

A dark brown stake. Metal. Right in the middle of the path, deliberately, so that I would fall.

It was Shane.

It had to be him because that's how I thought back then. Everything was about me. I didn't even consider another option—that it could have been about something else. Or that the stake wasn't Shane's revenge. I saw what I saw. I knew what I knew, and I believed what I believed, without considering anything else.

Ever since the night of the bonfire, when I had laughed at him, he had been out for blood. Now it seemed he had gotten what he wanted.

A large gash on my chin. I bled all the way to the hospital, secure in the belief that how I saw the world was the way it was.

End of story.

NOW

It's funny what you remember. What you don't.

When I called Charlie to ask him about that first year in Marquette, he laughed. "Are you asking about the weed?"

I hadn't been.

"Isn't that what you want to know? How we got it up there? Because we sure as shit didn't drive down to Detroit every week."

Charlie had a brain tumor a few years ago. He's out of danger now, but he's lost the logic of a conversation that makes sense to both people having it. When you talk to him, you can see the dark crevices of memory loss moving around as if you're in a maze.

"We were always high on something."

That was probably true.

"Dr. Robinson," I said.

The line went quiet. I thought he had hung up. Then the sound of a barking dog.

"Our guru?" he asked finally.

Charlie was in the Pacific Northwest, living in an RV park with a woman who raised chickens and grew her own vegetables. They were only a few miles from the ocean. He had sent me photographs of the peacocks that wandered onto their property. "How do you think they got here?" he had asked.

I didn't want to talk about his animal farm, so I asked him again about Dr. Robinson.

"That's a blast from the past," Charlie said.

"You ever hear from him?" I asked.

"Mr. Nature Man?" Charlie asked. "The Grizzly Adams for the new generation? Our hero who we put on that fern-strewn pedestal? He who knew all the things we wanted to know."

I wouldn't have argued against those descriptions. That's who he was.

"You know where he is? Or heard anything about him lately?"

Dr. Robinson had disappeared—he had left Marquette at the end of our freshman year. Never to return.

"Doc Robinson. Charismatic leader of the lost souls and polluted planet? Looked like a movie star, all that hair and blue eyes, those crazy muscles like he could deadlift a cow. He had that scar on his upper lip. Remember the rumors? That it was from a bear he ran across in the woods. Not sure that was ever proved. Used to make us work on graph paper. We had to buy special notebooks."

Things I had forgotten.

Not what Dr. Robinson looked like. But I had forgotten the scar. I had forgotten the bear story. I only remembered then that we had used graph paper notebooks. It made us feel like real scientists, and when needed, we could draw graphs and diagrams without needing a straight edge.

I could hear Charlie dragging on a cigarette through the phone. When I asked, he told me he had quit smoking years ago.

"The good doctor hated being inside. Couldn't stand buildings. Another rumor, most likely not true, was that he was the son of some wild animal. A panther or a coyote. We used to wonder if he lived in a tent somewhere in those woods."

There were things I needed to know. Things I needed to understand.

"Project ELF," I said. "What do you remember about that?"

"Haven't heard those words in years," Charlie said. He began to talk about the peacocks again. How they lost their tails and left them behind in the brush.

I had to keep him on track. "So you remember it?"

I was at the lake that afternoon and a guy, someone I didn't know, started talking to me about ELF—hence the urgency of the phone call to Charlie. It was an odd and disconcerting encounter, especially right after finding the newspaper article in the library. The one that reported on the demonstration we had all been to that first year. A photograph and quotes about how we felt about Project ELF. It got my mind reeling, and I was suddenly unsettled, without knowing what to do, who to talk to about it.

"Our *raison d'être*? The thing that made us feel useful. Like we were really doing something worthwhile. Us fighting the powers that be."

"But wasn't it?" I asked.

Charlie might have forgotten, but all those protests, the demonstrations, the fights—they were a big deal.

"I'm not sure," Charlie said. "I do know that's what you and the other goofs wanted it to be."

"All those demonstrations, all those protests," I said. "It had to be something."

It *was* something. He was misremembering.

"Think about it—every time anyone talked about it, they always said it was top secret. Every newspaper article described it that way."

"So?"

"So if it was so top secret, how did we all know about it?"

Charlie lit another cigarette. He smoked a lot for someone who had quit. "Only the male of the species is called a peacock. The females are called peahens. A group of peacocks is an ostentation. A group of females is usually referred to as a bunch of peahens."

I didn't think the U.S. government simply gave up on projects. Especially ones that had to do with defense. I didn't think Charlie did either. It was hard to tell if he was being deliberately evasive or if he didn't know what happened to Project ELF. It had been years.

"I'd rather be an ostentation than a bunch of peahens," Charlie said.

He was neither.

"So tell me: what happened to it?" I asked. "This is important."

"We mailed it to ourselves. To a post office box in Marquette. They had no idea what was in the packages we picked up every month. Humboldt Gold. Straight from Northern California." Charlie went off, talking about his failed weed business. "No one up there had any money. And if they did, they spent it on Mad Dog 20/20 and scratch-off lottery tickets."

The dog's barking was louder now. Like Charlie was holding the phone close on purpose.

"We should have been paying attention," Charlie said. "But we were too dumb."

"To what?" I asked. "What should we have been paying attention to?"

Then someone yelling. His girlfriend telling him to get off the phone.

He had to go. "I'll be in touch."

I had so much more I wanted to ask him.

Later that week, he emailed me. *You were in love with him.*

I wrote back. *I liked him. He was the best professor I ever had, but I was never in love with Dr. Robinson.*

It was 3 a.m. on the West Coast, but he answered immediately. The subject line: *I wasn't talking about the good doctor.*

A second email. *Go find out what happened. I'm not much help. Too many holes in my head. It feels important. Even now.*

2

Dr. Robinson talked about Project ELF as if we all knew what it was and as if we all understood why it would be so bad for the region, even though the military said just the opposite.

I had never heard of it but soon realized I was the only one who didn't understand what it was. The others all knew about it. They had opinions on ELF and expressed them with anger, almost outrage. I felt left out.

"It's because you're from Detroit," Finley told me when I asked him to explain it. "If you lived up here, you'd know what it was. It's all anyone talks about. You're either for it: it's going to create jobs. Or you're against it: it's bad for the environment. No one's neutral."

"So, you think it's a bad idea, right?" I asked, hoping he would explain why it wasn't good for the environment. That was only one of the things I didn't get from the class discussion.

"Me?" Finley asked.

"You agree with Dr. Robinson? You think we should fight it?"

"I'm kind of on the fence."

"I thought you said no one was undecided."

"I might be the only one," he said.

He turned to me and smiled. He looked odd, and I realized he was the sort of person who rarely smiled. He worried a lot.

"I may be the only person in the whole world who can see both sides."

He had long bangs that covered his eyes unless he moved them aside. He told me once that his head was too big for his body and that when he was younger the kids had called him Giant Head. "You must have grown," I had said.

He was cute when he smiled. I told him that.

"You too," he said, which felt awkward.

He took me over to the university library, back to where they kept the periodicals. There were comfy chairs, low tables, and lamps—like someone's living room. It was my favorite place to be on campus. It was usually crowded, students asleep, others reading, so I wasn't the only one who admired it.

There was an enormous window back there that overlooked a copse of enormously tall pine trees. I read some of the articles Finley had collected and understood the controversy a bit more, mostly by reading the letters to the editor in *The Mining Journal*. Finley had been right about that. Every other letter was for it; the rest were dead set against it.

I stared out the window and watched the wind bend the trees. It was a small grove of white pines. I knew that now. I knew that their needles grew in groups of five and that the tallest white pine tree in Michigan was 143 feet tall, but I couldn't remember where it was.

I tried to read more about Project ELF. I had a hard time getting past the name. I couldn't be the only one who, every time someone said it, thought of Christmas. Project ELF seemed like it would be festive, like there would be presents and decorated trees. It didn't sound harmful or dangerous or end-of-the-worldish. I saw Lake Superior and heard about the harm ELF would cause to the entire region. Beauty and danger. But it didn't connect for me.

Since soon after the close of WWII and the development and
widespread proliferation of nuclear weapons, it became clear
that the only way to avoid a third world war and the subse-
quent destruction of the entire planet by nuclear annihila-
tion was to practice extensive nuclear deterrence. Nuclear
deterrence follows the assertion that no country would dare
strike another with nuclear weapons while they knew that
country could score a major retaliatory strike. This makes the
survivability of a country's nuclear capabilities of utmost
concern. Any capability that can be easily taken out at the
beginning of a nuclear conflict does not contribute to that
nation's nuclear deterrence, as it does not contribute to the
country's ability to perform a retaliatory strike.

Ballistic missile submarines were, and are still, considered
some of the United States' most survivable nuclear assets, as
the enemy ought never to know where they are, to be able to
destroy them. Land-based assets are much more easily detect-
able, either by intelligence agents working domestically or
by satellite surveillance.

In order for the submarine to contribute as much as possible
to the nation's nuclear deterrence, it must be able to stay in
constant communication with National Command Authority (NCA).
They are the only people who can release nuclear weapons. That
is the president and the secretary of defense, or their suc-
cessors. This is commonly referred to as command and control.
Otherwise, even in the event of unrestricted nuclear warfare,
the weapons aboard will remain dormant. Before the advent of
ELF technology, the vessel would have to regularly surface
or, at best, deploy a buoy near the surface, exponentially
increasing its likelihood of being detected and/or severely
restricting its mobility. As spotted submarines no longer contribute substantially to the nation's nuclear deterrence, it
quickly became imperative to invent methods of communication
that limit or remove entirely the effect of communication on
the vessel's detectability.

Stated in a briefing on the ELF communications system, by the
office of Capt. Ronald L. Koontz, USN, the program manager
for ELF communications, the mission of a ballistic missile
submarine has three main objectives, as follows: "Remain
undetected, maintain continuous communications reception,

and maintain a condition of readiness that will ensure suc-
cessful launch of all missiles if and when directed by NCA."
The development of an ELF communications system helps these
vessels accomplish all three parts of that mission, nearly
anywhere in the world.

3

"The young," Dr. Robinson lectured us the first week of classes, "have never been good at heeding advice."

It wasn't our fault. It was our age—an age of rebellion—a time to question authority, and we shouldn't resist the urge to do exactly the opposite of what we're told. But occasionally we should make an exception and listen.

This was one of those times.

"You're all from Michigan. You've grown up around water. You've been on lakes. You're not afraid of what you know. But beware. Lake Superior is different. It's beautiful. Like nowhere else in the world. But it's also dangerous. Life sometimes presents like that. Beauty and danger at once."

He was getting abstract and could tell that he was losing us. To prove his point, he explained about the freighter that had sunk the previous November. The ballad by Gordon Lightfoot wasn't out yet, and it was the first some of us had heard about it.

"It was a massive ship carrying tons of iron ore, traveling from Wisconsin to Lake Erie. It sank in a hurricane-strength winter storm. All twenty-nine men on board drowned. Some were your age." His voice cracked, and we sat forward. "Don't be foolish. Don't be arrogant. Superior is colder and deeper and more destructive than any of the other Great Lakes."

The past summer, he told us, he was on the beach near Munising and found a bottle with a note inside. He hoped it was a message from the ship, some sort of communication sent out before it sank, but it was a telephone number. Random—no name, but a 906 area code, which was anywhere in the Upper Peninsula, and he just thought it was somehow connected to the ship. He called it every once in a while, but no one answered. He wrote the number on the board, for no apparent reason.

And for no reason that I knew at the time, I copied it into my notebook. I recorded most everything Dr. Robinson said that first semester.

I called the number a few times. No one picked up, and I had no idea what I would have said if they had. It was a message in a bottle. It might have been vital—a real need to communicate something important to someone else. Maybe I would have just listened.

But no one ever answered.

Dr. Robinson said we were going to have to become activists. "As in, take action. You, who have decided this world is worth fighting for." He drew the planet on the blackboard and then wrote *SAVE ME* next to it. "Beauty and danger," he said. "The world was beautiful. What we are doing to the planet is dangerous. We are in peril, without even being aware of how precarious everything is."

But we could help. It was up to us to change things. To make the world a different place.

"It would be great if we could accomplish things by just sitting around bitching about them. But in the end, talk means nothing if there's no action behind it. In fact, talking about it is probably the most wasteful thing you can do. It shows you know there's a problem and you're not doing anything about it."

He advised us to make emergency packs and to keep them handy. "In case you're arrested. And if you take this seriously, you will be arrested.

Rule # 1—Wear comfortable shoes. You never know when you're going to have to run from the law.

Rule # 2—Carry your ID and a stack of dimes for phone calls.

Rule # 3—Prepare a baggie of crackers or gorp (granola, oats, raisins, peanuts). You never know how long you'll be in jail. Bring extra. It's good to make friends in jail.

Rule # 4—Memorize the phone number of a friend or family member who has a car or who can get in touch with someone who does. You will need them if you're released from jail at midnight and the buses are no longer running."

It felt important—a new code.

It felt like a rallying cry, and I was all for it. I had finally found my purpose. I was going to save the planet from unnecessary destruction.

He was speaking my language. I had been looking for a way to save the world from a premature ending since the sixth grade when my teacher Mrs.

Jones told us about overpopulation, acting as if it was our fault. She warned us that we would most likely not make it to the millennium. I counted the years; I wouldn't even be forty. It didn't sound like enough life.

We made paper globes and hung them over our desks. She flicked at them when she walked around the room talking about doom and destruction. "Face masks will become necessary very soon. The air will be so polluted, and no one will be able to breathe." She chewed on a stick that she kept behind her ear. She said it freshened her breath naturally—but it didn't work. "The parks and lakes you love so much will be gone soon. Too many people needing too much drinking water." We asked what we could do, and she said, "Nothing. I'm old. Chances are, I'll be dead. It will be your problem."

I was out-of-my-mind scared. I didn't know what to do but walked around with my stomach in knots of anxiety, dreading the day when the world would suddenly turn dark, the streets would become too crowded, and I wouldn't be able to ride my bike. No one could help, not my mother or my father. No one.

I might have understood that she was a fanatic, a real nutjob, but her predictions scared me into a dull submission. She took away my hope.

One of the kids in the class told his parents that we talked about the end of the world almost every day, forgoing science and math. We got a new teacher halfway through the year. She was young and bubbly and kept stickers in her top drawer. "I know you're not kindergarteners, but I like a reward for a job well done." She had an endless supply—ladybugs, flowers, fish, turtles, and baby chicks hatching from cracked eggs.

Stickers were not going to help the population explosion.

I never believed Mrs. Jones. There had to be something we could do. I vowed then to be responsible. I would do something to change the world, even if no one else would help.

Dr. Robinson admitted that he was so worried about overpopulation that he sometimes felt relief when there was a natural disaster. "Floods, hurricanes, earthquakes. It's not right, but I worry so much about Mother Earth. I don't think she can support many more of us."

It was good to hear him say that. I never told anyone that I did the same thing.

Dr. Robinson saw me smiling. "Do I have a counting comrade in the class?"

I gave a short nod. It wasn't nice, but it's what I did when I saw a headline of a disaster around the globe. I never told anyone because it was ghoulish. Yet the higher the number, the more I thought, *Well, at least it's better for the Earth.*

The others in the class were incensed: "That's sick!" Which is probably why I never shared my reaction to mass death.

"It's also statistically stupid. That sort of thing doesn't change anything."

Dr. Robinson agreed with all the criticism without any apologies. "You're right. You're right. Welcome to the world of humans. We're not perfect. None of us."

I liked how he turned things around. He made it seem like we should be glad we had faults. He validated these things, no matter how extreme.

4

The bonfire was at Shiras Park, on Lake Superior and not far from campus. I was the first one there, but I didn't want to be. Being early made me look desperate or friendless, which I might have been, but there was no reason to advertise that fact. I walked down the beach, halfway to the break wall in the upper harbor up near Presque Isle.

The lake was a surprise. I had not been expecting that. I mean, I knew it was there. I had grown up in Michigan. I knew the Great Lakes. But Superior was like nothing else I had ever seen. Like nothing else I had ever known—deep, deep blue in the late autumn light; vast, the end never in sight; and the promise of the cold that was to come, that at that time of year felt possible. I liked being near it.

It was September. I was in Marquette—in Michigan's Upper Peninsula, an eight-hour drive from my hometown of Royal Oak, outside Detroit. It was as far away from home as I could get and still pay in-state tuition.

I saw some figures on the shore, then the start of the bonfire. I walked back. The light was gone; it was dark now. The guys were all there. The party had started. Most everyone was wandering the beach looking for firewood and kindling. I joined in, glad to be doing something.

Dr. Robinson was the last to arrive. The bonfire crackled; the birch wood was young and wet. Sparks shot into the night sky, then burned out as they fell.

My favorite show when I was a kid was *Lost in Space*. It was about a family traveling the Milky Way, landing on strange planets, encountering all kinds of dangerous elements in the galaxy. They never made it back to Earth in the whole time I watched it. It used to depress me. I didn't realize that if they did, the show would end, and later the show was canceled while they were still out in space. The family's name was Robinson. The father was a doctor.

I couldn't help but think of the show when the professor introduced himself in class the first day. *Dr. Robinson*, I wanted to say, *You're home! You finally made it back to Earth. I've been so worried all these years.*

Dr. Robinson refused the beer the guys offered him. "Got that covered," he said. He had a flask in his shirt pocket, a thick flannel that they all wore like jackets. "But what about Molly?"

Everyone turned to look at me. I got shy and concentrated on watching the embers. Like Tinkerbell dancing around and above the flames. I wasn't sure what he wanted from me or why he had said my name. Except for the three nursing students who were taking it to fulfill their breadth requirement, I was the only girl in the class and usually felt out of place.

"I'm sure Molly would like something to drink," Dr. Robinson told the guys.

Finley was standing next to me. Dennis Finley, but everyone called him Finley, as if he didn't have a first name. He touched my arm. "Do you want something?"

"Okay," I said.

I had brought a bag of pretzels but nothing to drink. I didn't know how a party like that worked. Back in high school, everyone brought their own stuff for the night, but I didn't want to carry a six-pack to the beach while I was alone and without a car. So I thought I would just skip the drinking. But I was just as glad to have something to drink. Like everyone, I was better socially when buzzed.

Finley moved away from the fire and brought back something in a plastic cup. It was sweet smelling, something I had never tasted before.

"Southern Comfort," Finley said.

"It's good," I said before I even tasted it. I was being weird. I told myself to take it easy. "Thanks," I said. There, that sounded normal.

The cup was full, and I took a big drink, which was just as stupid, as it burned the back of my throat when I swallowed. I took several deep breaths to keep myself from coughing it back up.

I didn't know what to do, how to act, or what to say to anyone. I didn't really know any of the guys, but I wanted to. I thought they were so interesting. They were cool. Nature boys. Someone had called them that at the bookstore one day. They were so into the class, so into the outdoors, into nature, the woods, the lake. Like modern-day Daniel Boones, without the coonskin caps.

I stood and took sips of my drink. Finley was tending the fire, so I crouched beside him and pretended like I was helping. He had it under control. It was blazing. I handed him some kindling, and he tossed it on top.

The nursing students weren't at the party. They had early morning rotations at the hospital the next day, and they didn't want to risk hangovers. Two of them were named Sue, and Dr. Robinson called them Sue 1 and Sue 2, like from *The Cat in the Hat*—Thing 1 and Thing 2. He could never remember the third girl's name and sometimes called her Sue 3. She told him that was rude, so he stopped calling her anything. I noticed things like that.

I stood up and took some more sips of my drink. It was helping. I no longer felt like everyone was looking at me.

Dr. Robinson was talking in his lecture voice, the way he spoke to us in class. Loud, with long dramatic pauses, like an actor on stage but without the hand gestures. The emphasis was on the first words of each sentence. "The males are very particular. Mating for them is a careful dance," he said.

I was confused, having missed some of what he had been saying. I thought for a moment he was talking about giraffes. But that couldn't be right. But it was—he was talking about giraffes.

"The male approaches a female once he sees something he likes. He rubs her back, caressing her until she urinates. And then he drinks her pee. With this mouthful, he makes his decision. To mate or not to mate."

He got the reaction he wanted. The guys were laughing. No more party awkwardness. He grinned, tipped his flask to his mouth, and drank.

The guys seemed like good friends, as if they had known each other for years instead of just a few weeks. The second week of class they started calling them themselves the Crusoes, like from *Robinson Crusoe*, the novel by Daniel Defoe. It didn't really make sense—it was the character's name in the book, not a band of guys trying to survive in the wilderness, but that's how they saw themselves.

They loved their nickname. They were modern-day castaways. I don't know if any of them had read the book. I had. It was dead boring.

Someone had told Dr. Robinson about the name. "Wonderful," he had said. He thought a group with a purpose was a great idea. "The revolution needs numbers. The individual will have a Sisyphean struggle. It's always good to have more help pushing that rock up the hill."

I didn't think I was included in their Crusoe club, but I wanted to be. I didn't remember there being any women on the island, but that couldn't have been right. They were probably just left out of the story. I didn't really know what the club was for—did they have secret handshakes and passcodes to enter their clubhouse? I hoped so. That's why I wanted in. I wanted to belong to something.

I drank more Southern Comfort. It burned less going down this time.

"Which brings us to the panda. For the giant panda, mating is what you might call a very slow dance. Frustrating, I'd imagine, mostly because the sexual interest of the female panda lasts, on average, seventy-two hours per year. You heard that right. Seventy-two hours per year. Not like you all, seventy-two hours per day. So it's all very difficult to keep your species going with the odds stacked up against you like that."

When everyone stopped laughing, Dr. Robinson looked over at me. He did that sometimes in class too—called me out, as if my opinion would be different than everyone else's. "What do you have to say to that, Molly?"

The whiskey was warm in my throat, giving me a strange sense of courage. "I say good for the panda."

The fire cracked. Everyone was silent, then some of the guys began to boo.

Dr. Robinson held up his flask. "No, no. Careful, boys. There is power in solidarity. Empathy is a strong emotion. Watch out for that, and know what you're up against."

The wind gusted, and the fire dimmed under the weight of the blowing sand. The guys moved quickly, fanning it back to life.

"Well, I'm off, gentlemen. And Molly, of course," Dr. Robinson said. "I'll leave you all to reach your own conclusions on this wildly and endlessly fascinating subject."

We didn't want him to leave. We wanted to keep him there, but he said it was time.

He tossed the sticks at his feet onto the fire, a burst of light. "Don't stop asking your questions. There are so many things we need to know."

Then he left. I didn't know it at the time, but that would become his charge for us. Always this advice, assuring us that there was nothing wrong in not knowing things.

Not much later, the party broke up.

I walked back to campus with one of the guys—one of the Crusoes named Shane Lebarre. Being with him felt like the icing on the cake of a perfect night.

That was a mistake.

I made a lot of them that year.

Anti-Project ELF protestors to end march in Marquette

August 12, 1977

MARQUETTE, MI (AP)-Protestors against Project ELF in Michigan's Upper Peninsula who have been hiking up from Clam Lake, WI, are expected to arrive in Marquette this afternoon.

Dr. Matthew Robinson, Northern Michigan University professor and spokesperson for the group, said the protestors are trying to raise awareness about the Navy's intention to install a radio station that transmits signals to nuclear missile submarines.

"They've averaged thirty miles a day," Robinson said. "The hikers are trying to inform the general public about the potential environmental dangers of Project ELF."

The protesters argue that Project ELF is a waste of resources and will not bring any new employment to the area. They are also concerned that ELF's electromagnetic fields will harm the wildlife.

Along the two-hundred-mile route, the marchers have been camping in tents and picking up litter on the roadside. A potluck picnic on Presque Isle is planned for tomorrow to celebrate the marchers' long trek.

"We hope the government understands that once people know the dangers of its project, they will know that it is not wanted in Michigan's precious UP," Robinson said.

5

Shane was a fast walker. I had to run and skip every three or four steps to keep up.

He was also a fast talker.

"Quolls," Shane said. "They're really fascinating creatures."

I laughed.

"Well, they are," he said.

We were young. No one used words like fascinating.

He was imitating Dr. Robinson. They all did that. They repeated things he said, acting as if they had come up with those facts and those ideas themselves.

The Crusoes even dressed like him. They wore untucked flannel shirts that flapped behind them when we walked in the woods. They each had a tiny silver hoop earring in one ear, faded jeans, and big belt buckles. I thought of it as their school uniform. Good for hiking, camping, and building bonfires but also practical in the classroom.

I spent a lot of class time looking at Shane. He was that sort—the kind of guy you looked at. He had dark, thick hair that he, sometimes, pulled back into a ponytail with a kitchen rubber band. Still tan from the summer, he wore three rawhide leather necklaces, each with a coin hanging from it. He pulled the coins into his mouth when listening to Dr. Robinson talk.

He was older than the rest of us, though he didn't really didn't act it. Someone said he had been in the service. I wasn't sure that was right. He didn't look like a soldier. His hair was shoulder length, a big mess of curls and tangles. Like the rest of the guys in the class, he seemed interested in spending time in the woods, learning more about nature, and saving the planet—things I didn't associate with guys in the Air Force or Army. Not that I knew that many.

He kept on with his animal mating lecture. I would rather have spent the walk back to campus getting to know him better, even if it meant asking the boring freshman questions: *Where are you from? Why did you choose Northern? What do you like to do? Why ecology as a major?*

Shane was not slowing down. "Quolls are ruthless and usually kill the female during the sexual act," he said and then that long pause. "See, they've been on the hunt for weeks, and when they finally capture a female, they're frustrated and impatient and not very careful. They're violent in getting what they want. Unfortunately, they're so exhausted by their trolling for female partners that they often die shortly after the sex act."

I was out of breath and tired of hearing about the mating rituals of animals I had never encountered and probably never would. "I don't even know what a quoll is," I said.

"You don't?" Shane asked.

It wasn't something I would lie about.

He was annoyed, acting as if I had somehow offended him, but I felt ignored. He wasn't the only one who could tell stories.

"Hey, have you ever heard about the Amazons?"

"The rainforest?" he asked.

"No, not that," I said and rushed ahead, but he pulled on my arm as if to stop me from talking.

"It is too," he said.

"I'm not saying it's not," I said. All that whiskey was making me belligerent.

"It's also the name of the longest river in South America," he said.

"Maybe, but I'm talking about something different. This is an ancient tribe of women called the Amazons."

Shane didn't say anything, so I thought he might be listening.

I wasn't sure I was getting the facts right. A girl in my high school had done a presentation on them for our Women's Day celebration—the first of its kind and not that well attended. Her project had been the only one that was the least bit interesting, and I had been stunned to learn about the tribe.

"They used bows and arrows like men and, to make sure they were proficient in their skills, chopped off their right breasts so nothing could get in the way of their aim. They hated men. And didn't want anything to do with them. A female tribe dedicated to living without men."

"They cut off their breasts?"

"They did," I said.

I was pretty sure the word Amazon translated into man-hater. It wasn't something I would have misremembered, but I didn't want to come off as aggressive or dismissive, or wrong for that matter. I did remember that they each cut off their own breasts. As a ritual. For power. To show their personal strength.

Shane stopped walking. "Why are you telling me this?"

"I'd thought you'd like to know," I said. "They're fascinating, aren't they?"

"Why would I care about them?"

"Why would I care about quolls?" The night had stopped being fun. "Do they even live around here?

"Of course not," he said. "They're desert animals."

It was a Sisyphean task just talking to him. Maybe he was drunk. Maybe it was late. Maybe we were just on different wavelengths, and it was time for me to stop staring at him in class and start staring at someone who at least wanted to talk to me.

His dorm was up on main campus, and by the time we got there, I had to pee so bad I was having trouble walking. "Let me use your bathroom. I have to go," I said and followed him in. My dorm was all the way down the hill, and I wasn't sure I could hold it any longer.

It was a guys' dorm. Nowhere near as clean as mine, the all-girls one. His room smelled like pot and Glade air freshener. I never understood the overuse of that cleaning supply. Glade was used for one purpose and one purpose only—to cover up the smell of weed. If you wanted to catch someone smoking, you could just see who had a can of Glade.

There was only the overhead light, the most horrible light, which showed the floor covered with clothes, most likely flannel shirts, white T-shirts, and jeans.

I went in and peed, keeping my eyes closed so I didn't have to see anything in the bathroom. There was no toilet paper.

Shane had turned off the overhead, but the room was lit by the security light outside. A deep pool of light spilled across the room.

Shane was sitting on the bed. There was only one chair near the window. Books and boxes were piled on top of each other.

"Want a beer?" he asked. He swung open the door to his mini fridge.

I took it to be a sort of apology and accepted it. I sat beside him. "I'll just take a sip of yours," I said.

I didn't expect to make out with him, but we were sitting next to each other on the bed, neither one of us that interested in the can of beer, which was tasteless. His flannel smelled like campfire. So did his hair. So did mine. We leaned into one another, and then we were making out. That was a surprise.

His lips were soft and wet. His tongue was shy at first, then more urgent. It felt great. To be kissed, to have someone's hands on my face and on the back of my neck. After weeks of trying to find a place to be, to make friends, to be positive, it just felt good to do something physical with someone else.

I was going to get going soon, but right then it just felt great to be touched. I kissed him harder, remembering one time in class when he had been leaning back in his chair, trying to balance by putting his head on the wall behind him. He stretched out. His flannel shirt was open, and his untucked T-shirt rode up so far that I could see the dark hairs running down from his navel and disappearing into the top of his low-cut jeans. I had stared then, until he lost his balance and the chair tipped sideways. He had stood up, startling everyone but me because I had been watching.

Shane pulled back. "Don't," he whispered.

I thought I was sitting on his hand and shifted back against the wall.

"Please don't."

I didn't understand why he was whispering. We were alone in the room. There was no one in the other bed. So unless someone was hiding in the closet, we were alone. "What?"

There was a soft puff of air in my ear, his hands were on my face, the smell of wood smoke on our clothes. I pulled back and opened my eyes. There were bits of leaves caught in his curls. I resisted the urge to pull my finger through his hair to get them out.

"Don't fall in love with me," he said.

He moved his hands from my face to my shoulders, holding me there with some resistance, slightly pushing me away. I moved back.

"You shouldn't," he said.

It just started in the base of my throat, a small giggle, then another. It burst forth, really, and just flew out of my mouth, and suddenly I was laughing. Really laughing. I couldn't stop.

I tumbled off the bed, which made me laugh harder.

We had had one miserable conversation.

He stood. He was angry. "You don't know. Girls fall in love with me all the time."

We had talked for twenty minutes. Not even. He had lectured me about quolls for most of our walk. Then he hadn't listened to anything I had told him about the Amazon warriors, so really all we had done was make out for a few minutes.

I was giggling, which even I knew was annoying, but it struck me as hysterical and I couldn't stop.

"It's not funny," he said.

I didn't know what I would love. His curly hair all matted down with fall leaves? His flannel shirts? The coins on the leather necklaces? Those were cool, but I didn't like them that much.

"I know," I said. When I opened my mouth, I laughed, then almost choked myself, which made me gasp for breath, and that made me laugh harder.

"Stop it!"

The door opened, and a second later, someone flicked on the overhead. The room flooded with yellow fluorescent light. I stood. Shane went over to the mirror and fixed his hair. He pulled the leaves out.

"Everything alright?" It was Finley. He tossed his sleeping bag onto the other bed. I hadn't realized they were roommates.

"She's a bitch," Shane said to Finley.

That seemed severe and way over the top. It had been stupid, but there was no reason for meanness.

"Yeah?" Finley asked.

"That's what I said," Shane said. "She's nothing but a big bitch."

"Come on," I said.

He didn't have to be like that.

"Good for the panda," he said. "I'll show you what's good for the panda."

"What'd you do?" Finley asked.

"Me?" I asked.

"I'm going to assume something happened," Finley said.

But I didn't want to tell. It was stupid, and no one else had to know. "Nothing."

"That's not what it looks like." Finley's shirt was dirty from the bonfire, all white and ashy.

"She's not right," Shane said.

It was time to go. I searched through the sheets for my sweatshirt. "Sorry," I said, but Shane was gone.

I didn't want any bad feelings. The bonfire had been so much fun. It was too bad Shane had started acting all crazy.

"See you," I said to Finley. I thought I should say something more, but sorry didn't seem right. I didn't want Finley thinking I was a nutcase, didn't want him telling the others, all the Crusoes, that I was a bitch. That was the last thing I wanted to happen.

"Come on," Finley said. "I'll walk you back. You live in Spaulding, right?"

"You don't have to," I said. I hoped Shane was drunker than he seemed and that he would forget about all this by class on Monday.

We took the shortcut, the path behind the old physical education building. I could smell chlorine.

"Why didn't you stay out on the beach?" I asked.

Some of the guys had planned on camping out on the beach. I thought it sounded great, but I hadn't been invited or included in the plan.

"Police came and kicked us out," Finley said. "Illegal to camp there. It's technically a state park."

"That's too bad," I said.

"Just as glad now," Finley said. "I wouldn't have wanted to miss that scene back there. You going to tell me what was going on?"

"Nope," I said.

Shane would probably tell him. But I wanted to forget it. So I was going to pretend it never happened.

It was hard to see the path, and I walked looking at my feet. It felt like rain.

"I'm getting a dog," Finley said.

"Are you allowed to have animals in the dorms?"

"When I move out," he said, as if he was planning to soon. "An Alaskan husky. That's what I want."

I never had a dog. My mother was allergic to animals, so we didn't have any pets. I liked them but never saw the point really. Most dogs just barked and chewed shoes.

"Girls like Shane," Finley said. "It's not his fault."

"Yeah, I guess not," I said. But it's not what I felt.

I should have peed in my pants. I shouldn't have gone into his dorm. I shouldn't have kissed him. I shouldn't have laughed at him. A whole list of things I shouldn't have done.

"What are you going to call him?" My sweatshirt slipped off my waist. I heard the zipper dragging against the ground.

"Shane?"

"Your husky," I said.

"Got to see him first, then I'll decide," Finley said.

The wind picked up, and we moved down the hill in the darkness.

"I didn't know you guys were roommates," I said.

"Know him from back home," Shane said. "Well, not really. Knew of him. He's a few years older. Knew his brothers. He asked to room with me. Seemed like a good idea. He's cool."

That was not how I would have described him. But I was going to have a normal conversation with someone that night.

"Where are you from?"

"Escanaba," he said.

"Where's that?" I asked.

"You don't know where Escanaba is?"

It wasn't like he said Green Bay or Chicago.

I heard someone calling my name. We stopped walking. They were yelling *Molly* across the open space in front of the row of dorms. Someone was coming towards us.

"A friend?" Finley asked.

It was my RA. She was coming up from the Alibi, the bar on that side of the campus. She and the other RAs went there on Friday nights for happy hour. It started around four o'clock—two-for-one drinks, dancing, and loud, bad rock music. She was quite happy.

"Hey there," I said. I could never remember her name.

"Look at you, Molly," she said. "You're having fun too. Is this your boyfriend?" She put her face up to Finley's. "Is Molly your girlfriend?" He didn't say anything, so my RA insisted. "Is she? Is she?"

"That's enough," I said. She was drunk talking, and I knew she wouldn't remember this in the morning. "Let's get you home."

One shift in the wind and the rain started. Large, slow-falling drops. Finley took off running, disappearing up the hill into the night.

I called after him. "You should call your dog Spot!"

I wasn't sure he heard.

Another wind gust and the skies opened into a downpour.

Candlelight vigil held
in city parking lot

September 29, 1977

MARQUETTE, MI (AP)-A candlelight vigil was held in the parking lot of the Marquette county jail on Wednesday evening to protest the arrest of two activists who were charged with cutting down antenna poles at the newly constructed Project ELF site in Republic. No names were released, pending formal charges.

Matt Robinson, a professor at Northern Michigan University and spokesman for the peace protestors who have frequently targeted Project ELF, said the forty-foot poles were cut down by those arrested using a handsaw.

The Navy transmitter sends messages to submarines equipped with missiles carrying nuclear warheads. The transmitters used in Project ELF, called ELF for the use of extremely low-frequency radio waves, require dozens of miles of aboveground wires strung on these poles. The activists say the antennas are part of a first-strike attack system. The Navy says the antennas are necessary to support a policy of deterrence against nuclear war.

About thirty people, mostly Northern students, attended the vigil. Witnesses indicated that it was a peaceful assembly. "No word on whether those arrested will face convictions or prison sentences," said Matt Robinson.

6

There was sex. There was saving the planet. I wanted both, and I didn't want to do either alone.

Being a member of the class made me think I could have what I wanted. Being with someone and serving a purpose. I was filled with desire that fall. I wanted each equally. I really did. And that feeling of wanting something so badly that I thought I would explode made me restless.

I wanted the guys to like me. I did. I might even have said I was desperate for them to like me. Or at least notice me.

The day after the bonfire and the blowup with Shane, I was particularly impatient. I couldn't find anything to do, and I had that terrible feeling that everyone else was doing something fun and I wasn't.

I wasn't shy. But I wasn't aggressive about inviting myself places. I just had to find out what they were doing and where they were doing it.

Some of the girls on my floor were homesick. They cried at night. Then complained during the day. They missed classes and spent hours on the phone with their parents. They wanted to leave. Some did. Others stayed but weren't happy about being there.

I felt none of that. Moving to Marquette was an explosion of change. The needle moved, and my perceptions were completely altered. Had anyone asked me that summer after graduation if I enjoyed living where I did, if I thought that suburban Detroit was a nice place to have spent life, I would have said sure. I never considered where I lived, what it looked like, or even what I thought about it. It was just home and all I knew. I didn't know places could be so different—that they could change the way you felt.

I was also worried that day that Shane had talked to the others. I worried that he had told them lies about me. I was sure he was capable of it, and I didn't want them to think I was some weird girl. I worried about my favorites. There was Finley, of course, but I had already talked to him. I didn't think he would start hating me. There was Charlie. Like me, he was from downstate, near Detroit. There was Pete. I knew he was from Keewenaw, even further west and north of Marquette, and there was Jon, who was also from the UP. They were so cool with each other. I wanted to be friends with them. I was afraid Shane would ruin all that.

I became more and more restless because there was nothing I could do.

I walked my floor that afternoon, starting at one end and going to the other. Most of the room doors were shut. Boring. I went down to the second floor and walked that a few times too. Nothing going on there either.

The whole dorm felt empty—except for the Peter Frampton playing on everyone's radio. That song, "Show Me the Way," played all day long, and I divided people into two groups—those who changed the station when it came on and those who turned it up and sang along to it.

If anyone was doing anything fun, they weren't doing it near me.

My suitemates put blankets over their windows and slept until 5 p.m., when the cafeteria opened for dinner. They did this every weekend that whole first semester. They were always complaining about being tired, something I found impossible to believe. They just seemed dull.

I went outside, walked up to main campus, and searched the university center. Some kids were playing pool but no one I knew.

The kids in the dorms liked to play cards. They had endless euchre parties. All day long, all night long. They sat around in their dorms drinking schnapps and playing for penny antes. I had never liked games. You won, but then what? It didn't mean anything. It never mattered.

My RA had put up notices about a cupcake and wine mixer with one of the guys' dorms. I hadn't planned on going, but with nothing else to do, I went down to see when it would start.

She had a hangover and had spent the day on the couch in the TV room drinking Coke from a giant plastic pitcher and telling anyone who came in that she was going to throw up.

"The mixer is canceled," she told me. "I'll vomit if I have to stand up. I really will. Don't test me."

She hadn't gone to the store to get the supplies, or I would have asked her if we could have the party without her.

Restless. I wanted to do something.

It had been a day of warm autumn light. The rains had cleared the air, and the sky was all sorts of colors.

I was too shy to call Finley or one of the other guys, even though that's what I wanted to do. I was dying to know what they were doing. They didn't seem the type to sit around and go to cupcake parties or play card games all night. They were probably doing something fun. Something outside, by the lake or in the woods. I wanted to be with them. I could have looked up Finley's number, but there was the chance that Shane would answer, and I thought it better that we wait until Monday to talk. I didn't want to take the chance.

I went back to my room and asked my roommate to take a walk with me.

"Where?" she asked.

"Let's go down to the lake," I said.

"I've got to study," she said. But she didn't study very often. Mostly what she did was sit on her bed and stare at the ceiling. Like she was napping with her eyes open. "I don't want to stay out all night," she said.

There was really no chance of that.

She spent all her time in our room. She went to class and then came right back. She ate dinner, quickly and without enjoying anything, not even the eat-as-many-as-you-want fries or the soft-serve ice cream. She was polite to our suitemates but didn't really talk to them or ask them anything, even though they were friendly to her. We had lived together for weeks now, and I still didn't really know anything about her besides that she was the neatest person I had ever known.

We walked up to the main part of campus. Some people were tossing a Frisbee—a four-person game where one of them kept missing and they would all yell at her. They were barefoot, and I thought the grass must have been cold this late in the day.

We cut through the university center, going the long way around so that we could go by the pool tables. There were a bunch of people playing but no one from class. None of the Crusoes. The room smelled of fried food.

We went past Finley and Shane's dorm. I didn't see anyone outside and didn't want to go in. That would have been weird. I didn't know where the rest of the guys lived. The Crusoes couldn't all be roommates. Or maybe they were. Maybe I didn't know them as well as I wanted to. It was frustrating.

We headed off campus and walked down to the lake.

Janet asked me how long we were going to be, as if being outside and walking down to the greatest of the Great Lakes was a chore, something she had to endure.

I could see the remains of the bonfire. The ashes and leftover piles of kindle. "This is where we had the party last night."

She nodded but was obviously bored—not at all interested in where we were.

I had half expected to see some of the guys. I imagined that they would come back to where we had been the night before. I thought there might be another bonfire and more fun. This time, I would not walk home with Shane Lebarre. But except for a woman walking her dog, the beach was empty. I felt better though. The lake had that effect.

I went down to the shoreline. Janet followed.

I tried to make it seem like we were friends. "What do you like to do?" I asked. "Besides study and all?"

"Not much," Janet said.

"Really?" I asked. "Nothing?"

"And what I really don't like to do is walk around in circles all night."

Which wasn't what we had been doing at all. We had walked down to the lake. She was being rude. She could have asked me questions. I liked to do things. She didn't. She never asked me about where I was from, about my high school, about what I wanted to study. She was really the last person I would have picked to be my roommate.

I said nothing but tossed some stones in the water. They weren't flat and didn't skip, but I kept picking them up and throwing them, hoping one of those round black stones would skim the surface and that the water would ripple, ripple, ripple.

I should have left her sitting on her bed staring at the ceiling. It was the last time I would ask her to do anything.

"Let's go," I said and walked away from the lake.

She must have known she was irritating me. It was like dragging a kid to the dentist. My fault. I had wanted to be with someone if we ran into any of the Crusoes. But I saw that Janet would not have helped endear me to them. They would have found her sullen. Because she was.

I had decided even before I met her that I was going to get along with my roommate. I was not going to be the one to complain about messes, about having friends over, about too-long showers, or about anything. I didn't want to be that person, so I promised myself that I was going to get along with whoever the university assigned me.

Janet finally arrived three days after classes had started. I had no idea why she was late.

I had come a week earlier. I got a ride from the brother of someone I sort of knew in high school. Eight hours in a pickup truck with broken windshield wipers. It rained. He stopped at a hardware store on the other side of Bay City and bought a broom, which he broke in half, then tied to the base of the wipers with some twine. I had to move the contraption back and forth when it rained too hard for him to see. He told me he wasn't much of a talker. "I like to listen to the radio," he said. It stopped raining at the Mackinac Bridge, and I stopped asking questions.

It hit me that I was leaving what I knew and that I was going a long way. I was nervous, the unknown future. I didn't know anyone up there. They could all be like my silent driver.

I spent the week with my RA, whose name I kept forgetting. She was making door decorations. Large bumble bees with everyone's names written in different colored Magic Markers, so we would know where everyone lived. It seemed grade school-ish but might be useful. She played Hall & Oates' *Abandoned Luncheonette* on the tape player, not one of my favorites. They played it over and over on the radio. As soon as one side was done, she would flip it over and start the other side. The speakers on her player weren't very good, and there was a continual echo, like we were in a cave.

I helped cut out the bees. She only had left-handed scissors, so my bees were sloppy. She said she'd finish the rest. "You're going to love it here. It's so much fun. It's just so much fun!" Her enthusiasm was wearying. The opposite of the guy who had given me the ride up. So I didn't know what to expect from Northern, from Marquette.

Classes started. I was glad to be busy. It stopped me from overthinking and anticipating everything.

A few days later, the door opened. Janet and her father walked in.

I was still in bed. It was that early.

"Here we are," her father said. "Here's your new roommate. Janet McAdams."

I couldn't get out of bed. I was wearing a T-shirt, nothing else. "Hello," I said.

Janet stood in the doorway. "Dad," she said. "Stop."

"We're from Pellston," he said. "Just below the bridge. You've never heard of it. No one has."

"Alright," I said. I was uncomfortable.

He wasn't.

"House fire," he said. "Whole house gone. Burned to the ground. Nothing left." He talked like that. Fast, without pronouns or identifying who he was talking about.

I was both confused and uncomfortable but not as bad as Janet.

"She's going to buy everything today. Everything brand new. Never been used. Clothes and all. Lucky her, huh?" he asked. "We thought we'd see what color your things are and then get stuff to match."

I had a blue blanket and yellow sheets. It wasn't like I had spent time thinking about decorations or matching things.

"Where do you shop around here?" he asked.

I didn't know. I had brought everything up from home.

"She's a lucky one, isn't she?" he said. He wore shorts. His legs were tanned. It looked strange on an adult.

Janet dragged him away. I could get out of bed.

They were there when I got back from classes that afternoon.

Her father was arranging bottles of alcohol on my desk. "We'll call this the party room." He wore green shorts and a red T-shirt, looking like a leftover Christmas decoration still on the store shelf months after the holiday.

He had bought everything. Vodka, whiskey, tequila, rum. A long skinny bottle of something called Galliano. "You ever try this?" he asked. "It's the main ingredient in a Harvey Wallbanger. You should make a bunch of those. They'll get you friends." It seemed like a dad thing to say. A dad thing to worry about.

He would be gone soon, I hoped.

Janet was nervous about having alcohol in the room.

"It's college," I said. "I don't think they care about anything but drugs." And judging from the smell of pot wafting from rooms and open windows, I didn't think anyone was policing anything.

It was quieter once her father was gone.

I had a new roommate and a closet full of alcohol.

We were crossing Third Street, and there was Finley coming out of the store on the corner. Bingo. It was like a treasure hunt, and I was on the right track.

"Finley!" I called out.

I was happy to see him. The evening's mood changed like that. He was alone, not like he was doing anything really exciting. But maybe the two of us could find something to do.

"Looks like I can't get away from you," he said.

"Lucky you," I said.

"Is that right?" he asked.

I introduced him to Janet. He said hello. She didn't. If I had had a machine that would make her disappear, I would have used it. If she wasn't going to be fun, then I didn't want her around Finley and the guys. I didn't want them to think I hung around boring girls.

Finley opened a brown paper bag. "Half-priced donuts," he said. "Have some."

I took one. The chocolate icing smeared across my fingers, and I licked it off.

"He cuts the price in the afternoon," Finley said. "They're usually gone by now. I guess the donut eaters must be out of town this weekend."

Finley held the bag out to Janet, but she wouldn't take one. He gave me another one. I didn't want it, but there was something funny about iced donuts on the street on a fall evening. Things that didn't go together, I guessed.

"How's Shane?" I asked.

"Why?" Finley asked.

His gloves had the fingers cut out. It made me think of the movie *Oliver!* It made him look like he was about to pick someone's pocket on the street. It wasn't cold, so what reason was there for gloves, even without the fingers?

"No reason," I said. I wanted to know that Shane wasn't telling everyone that I was a bitch. I hoped he hadn't said anything to the other guys.

Janet pulled on the back of my sweatshirt. "Let's go," she said.

I swatted her hand away. There was no need for that. I wasn't her mother. She wasn't a kid. She had free will. I'm sure she could have found her way back to the dorm. Or she could have waited a few minutes.

"Okay. See you," Finley said.

He was balancing on the curb, walking like it was a tightrope. Half a block down, he stumbled and tripped over his feet into the street. He saved the donut bag from falling.

"That guy's drunk," Janet said. It sounded so judgmental, as if she was accusing him of doing something vile and immoral.

"Maybe," I said. "Who cares?"

"He had bottles in his backpack," Janet said. "Coming out of a store that sells alcohol."

"We live in Michigan," I said. "You can buy whiskey at the grocery store."

"Seems a bit early to be drunk."

"We're in college," I told her. "It's the weekend."

"You sound like my dad," Janet said.

I didn't think I sounded like anyone. I looked down the street and saw Finley with a group of guys. They were too far away for me to see who they were, but I thought I saw Shane. And then I thought I saw some of the other guys from class.

Janet and I went back to the dorm. I felt defeated. Sorry for myself, then stupid for feeling that way. It was only one night.

Janet sat on the bed to study. I went down to the TV room, where some of the girls were making peanut butter cookies. I hung out for a while, but then they started playing cards. More games of euchre. That would go on all night.

Janet had turned out the lights. I guessed she was asleep. I got into bed.

I was asleep when a huge group of drunk kids came running down the hill. I got up and went over to the window. They were loud, screaming drunk.

Janet turned over on her bed. She was awake. "My father did it," she said.

It came out of nowhere. We hadn't been talking.

"He did what?" I asked.

"He burned down our house," Janet said, as if we had been talking about the fire. "On purpose."

"Why?" I asked.

Janet went silent, but I wanted to know. Wasn't that what I was learning from Dr. Robinson—keep asking my questions?

I persisted. "Why would he do that?"

"For the insurance money," Janet said. "He's rebuilding." She spoke in such a monotone, it was hard to believe that she was speaking the truth. It sounded more like she was reciting lines from a book. "Our new house is going to be three times as big as our old one. My little brothers are going to have their own rooms."

"Does your mother know?"

"Does she know what?" Her voice was low, not whispering but guarded.

"That it was your father who did the fire?"

Janet did not answer right away, then quietly said, "She must."

"What does she say?"

"She doesn't say anything. She never says anything. All the crazy things he does. She just lets him."

"Weird," I said.

But it was worse than weird. It was criminal. Janet must have known that. You didn't just burn down your house because you wanted a bigger one.

She turned to the wall. "I don't want to talk about it."

"I thought you did." It wasn't like I had started the conversation.

"I mean I don't want to talk about it if you're going to say things like it's weird."

"I'm sorry," I said. I did wonder if she was telling me this to explain why she had been such a pill on the walk to the lake. Even she must have realized that she was being difficult. I waited for her to accept my apology. "Okay?" I asked. I didn't think I had to say I was sorry again.

There was nothing more from Janet. I doubted she was asleep. But she was done talking to me.

Keep your promise, I told myself. *Don't bother about the small, petty stuff. She doesn't have to be your friend; just be civil. You can live with her without fighting or getting mad.* It felt like a struggle.

It was frustrating to be with all these new people—Janet, the Crusoes, Dr. Robinson. I didn't know them. They didn't know me. I didn't know what they wanted or what they were trying to say to me, what I should say back. It was frustrating. We needed our own Project ELF—our own set of communications lines running through campus. But I wasn't about to champion that.

There was sure to be opposition to that too.

Trespassing Convictions Reversed

Journal Staff Writer

MARQUETTE, MI (AP)-A frequent protestor against the Navy's Project ELF radio transmitter in Michigan's Upper Peninsula has won reversal of trespassing convictions for incidents that happened in the summer of 1976. The Third District Court of Appeals ruled Tuesday that citations against Matthew Robinson of Big Bay, for trespassing at the Project ELF site near Republic, were wrongly amended by a judge, so the convictions must be overturned. Robinson had fought to have the citations thrown out, contending that no ordinance existed for the specific charge written on the trespassing tickets. Later, Marquette County Circuit Judge Robert Courchane agreed that the county ordinance did not conform to state laws.

7

Dr. Robinson was organizing a protest for Saturday morning at 9 a.m. in downtown Marquette. "I hope you'll show up," he said. "Numbers make an impact and a difference."

He read us a letter he had received from the state senator's office: "The people of Michigan owe it to themselves and to the nation to take a long, unemotional look at the need for Project ELF before they stymie a project that is vitally important to our nation's safety."

He must have been doing some letter writing. I hadn't seen his name on the opinion page, but I'm sure he wrote in.

The Crusoes had their own protest. "It's too early," they told Dr. Robinson. "Way, way too early. It's the weekend, and we're in college."

I hoped they were just kidding around. I couldn't wait to go. My first real protest.

Dr. Robinson had everything planned out. We were to meet downtown. We were to stand together. We were to show our opposition. We were to bring signs and to wear red bandanas like armbands over our jackets. It would connect us as a group. "Power in numbers!" someone yelled, and Dr. Robinson agreed.

"Don't forget your emergency kits," he said. "Jail might be inevitable."

I was thrilled. I was going to prove Mrs. Jones wrong. I could do something about the world. I could at least try to save it. I didn't feel naïve. It didn't feel futile. Not at all.

Saturday morning, I slept in and almost missed the demonstration. It was dumb because I was awake at 6 a.m., but that was too early, so I turned off the alarm and stayed in bed. I woke up a few minutes before the protest was to start.

I was out of breath when I got to the post office. Dr. Robinson was there, surrounded by all the Crusoes. The nursing students weren't there. They said Saturday mornings, when they weren't at the hospital, were sacred, and they were not to be disturbed. The guys looked like lumberjacks, dressed in their flannel-shirt uniforms.

I went up and stood next to Finley.

"Did you run here?" he asked.

"Why would I do that?"

Now it felt stupid that I had rushed. People were just hanging around. Nothing important was happening yet.

"Teacher's pet afraid of missing his big show?"

"You think *I'm* the teacher's pet?" I asked.

Dr. Robinson definitely favored the guys. Charlie, Pete, Jon, Finley—those were the ones who knew everything, the ones he called on when he asked for identifications, the ones who hung around after class. He treated all the Crusoes like his buddies. He never acted like I was part of the group. He addressed me separately, calling them guys and then singling me out—Molly—as if I was different, not quite on the same level. They were the experts. I was the neophyte.

Finley was tough—I had a hard time trying to figure him out. Usually he was nice, like he wanted me to be his friend, maybe even something more. Then sometimes his teasing overstepped into meanness. Like I wasn't even his friend but someone he had to tolerate.

It was not the day to worry about my feelings. We were there to do good, not to be petty or personal. We were supposed to be concentrating on saving the world. I had to forget the other stuff.

Some of the protestors had made signs: *KEEP THE UP FREE FROM ELF. SAVE OUR FORESTS! DON'T KILL OUR WILDLIFE! SAVE THE PLANET!*

Dr. Robinson had a megaphone that looked like it had come from a cheerleading squad. He taught us a call and response. It took some time to get used to it. It sounded like random yelling, and our words got swallowed in the air, but we finally got our timing right.

"NO PROJECT ELF!"

"PROTECT OUR PLANET! SAVE MOTHER EARTH!"

We chanted for a long time. It sounded less like a song than like screaming, which most of the Crusoes were doing.

The crowd grew. It was fun to make so much noise. It felt good to yell our heads off. The shoppers and other people on the street stood and watched, and it was like being on stage.

But after a while, that got tiring, and the yelling got weaker, less enthusiastic. My vocal chords felt like they had gotten a workout. The crowd was getting bigger, and people started pushing, everyone trying to move around the small space.

Dr. Robinson then had us make a line so that it would be difficult for anyone to get onto the steps up to the post office. They would have to move around us.

"Lock arms and hold tight," Dr. Robinson said.

It was like a game of Red Rover, making a solid wall of bodies.

Shane was standing near me, and instead of taking my hand, he bowed out of line and walked to the far end so that he wouldn't be anywhere near me. I was going to have to talk to him. I thought I had apologized enough. But he was a good grudge carrier. We were too small a group, and I had to do something to correct it. I didn't like confrontation, but this was my fault. He was being stubborn and ridiculously egotistical.

We locked arms and held tight.

A few minutes later, a policeman in uniform pushed his way through our human barricade. Dr. Robinson motioned for us to drop our arms. It had been a short stance of solidarity.

"Not again, Matt," he said.

"A peaceful protest against something that could be dangerous," Dr. Robinson said. "Dangerous to us and the Earth."

"ELF's got nothing to do with the city," the policeman said.

We grouped around Dr. Robinson, wanting to hear what he was saying to the law.

"It's got everything to do with the people who live in this city," Dr. Robinson said. "This is much more important than commerce."

"Are you sure about that?"

"You should appreciate what we're doing here," Dr. Robinson said.

"Oh, I do," the policeman said. "You've made your point. So now you can go home."

"We've got lots more to achieve today."

"You're going to get these kids arrested."

"They're not kids."

"So you're going to tell me this was their idea. To come here on a Saturday morning?" the policeman said.

We hadn't seen Dr. Robinson challenged like this before.

"I'm not making anyone do what they don't want to do."

"I should arrest you for brainwashing innocent children."

"They're hardly innocent."

People were leaving, moving away from the post office steps. The show seemed over. The Crusoes were complaining about being hungry. They did that—they were always hungry, always on the lookout for food.

"I'll give you half an hour, then let's clear out," the policeman said. He held out his hand as if making a deal with Dr. Robinson.

Dr. Robinson did not extend his.

Another guy came up. "Anything for me that hasn't been said?"

He had a small notebook and two pens, one in his mouth, the other in his fingers, which he twirled like a miniature baton. Finley told me he was a reporter from *The Mining Journal*.

"You know where I stand," Dr. Robinson said.

"What about the students?" the reporter asked. "Do any of them want to say something?"

"Ask them," Dr. Robinson said. "They're capable of thinking. Some of them can even speak."

"Let me guess who they'll sound like," the reporter said. He turned to me. He had ink marks on his face—tiny blue lines around his lips. "You," he said. "Can you tell me why you're here this morning? I'm going to assume that because you're with this guy, you're not in favor of the project."

I was caught off guard, and the first thing I did, uncomfortable at being the center of attention, was laugh. He looked at me, not impressed with my awkwardness.

I didn't want to come off as an idiot, so I said the first thing that came to mind. "Beauty matters," I said. "I think it should last. Forever."

He stopped twirling his pen. "What's that?"

"It's what I think," I said.

"So say it again," he said. "I'll get it this time." He flipped open his notebook.

I took a deep breath and began to talk without knowing where I was going with my thoughts, nervous that I wasn't speaking in full sentences.

"I've never been in such a beautiful place. We shouldn't let anyone destroy it. Beauty should last forever." I felt more confident the more I talked. "I'm young. I don't want to live in a world that's been destroyed by big business or by the government. Not when there are other solutions."

The reporter asked my name, my age, and where I was from. He wrote it all down in his tiny notebook.

The policeman was still there. "You've trained them well, Matt. They're like seals in the zoo."

Dr. Robinson was looking at me. "That's all her. And seems like it's from the heart. Also quite original. Nothing to do with me."

I hoped it was original. We had been reading Baudelaire in French class, specifically his poem called "Beauty." It was about dreams being carved in stone. At least I didn't say that.

Finley was standing behind me. He was so close he stepped on the heel of my shoe and lifted it off. "That was good," Finley said. "Did you just come up with that?"

I was happy to have said something that hadn't sounded idiotic.

"You'll be in the paper," Finley said. "Famous."

"Famous in the UP, which means nothing." That was Shane. He was looking at me. He held up his hand, a peace sign, then he turned his fingers around and stuck them up his nose.

I wasn't sure what that meant. He looked like a pig.

"Good job, good job," Dr. Robinson congratulated us. "You should be proud of yourselves. And not one of us arrested."

It was my first demonstration. Everyone else seemed bored with the whole thing, but I was really thrilled. I tried not to show it. It didn't seem cool to be so enthused. I wasn't sure what we had achieved, but it felt like we had spent the morning doing good, and I wanted to do it again. I felt like I had found what I had been looking for, without knowing that I had been looking for something. I had a purpose. A real purpose in life.

Beauty lasted, but so did other things. Like anger. Resentment. All that lasted too.

And with beauty came danger. I just didn't know it yet.

Vandals ruin yearlong study

By Jenny Lancour
Journal Staff Writer

CRYSTAL FALLS—A research project designed to study the effects of Project ELF on the environment lost a year's worth of work after the research site was vandalized.

The Iron County Sheriff's Department is still investigating the incident that occurred in October. Navy Lt. Charlie Walker, commander of Project ELF, said a solar panel at the site was unbolted and placed on the ground; rain gauges, air sensors, and perimeter stakes were removed from the ground; and steel bands measuring tree growth were also removed.

The action "totally shot the whole project for an entire year," Walker said. Walker said the project is one of about twenty geared towards establishing a database to compare with future studies on the environmental effects of the low-frequency antenna system expected to become operational soon.

While loss of material was estimated at about $200, Walker said lost money already spent on research ranges from $30,000 to $90,000, adding that total losses have not been determined.

8

The Department of Natural Resources had a plan to reintroduce moose to the Upper Peninsula. I didn't know they were gone. I assumed there were moose, wolves, elk, and even reindeer up north.

Their disappearance wasn't a mystery.

"It's not like they just got tired of the view and decided to go west," Dr. Robinson said.

The first reason they left was excessive logging. Moose were plant-eating animals, not carnivores as their size might suggest. They were slow-moving animals and needed trees to survive.

Then there was a huge problem with brain worms, which killed off many moose in the last century. They were parasites that got in through the ear canal, then burrowed into their brains. Once inside, they would multiply, and after a while there would be hundreds of microscopic creatures in the moose's head. Brain worms eventually killed them.

"Then of course there's unregulated hunting. That killed the heartiest of the survivors." Dr. Robinson abhorred hunting. He often wrote the word on the board and then would cross it out with several long chalk marks. "No one really needs the meat," he always said. "Not anymore."

He looked around the room. Some of the guys had grown up hunting, and they disagreed with Dr. Robinson that it was unnecessary. They had argued with him the first few weeks of class, then stopped. I didn't know if they had really decided it wasn't such a great thing or if they just didn't want to argue with a professor.

"Of course, that would be the exception," Dr. Robinson said. "If someone did hunt because otherwise they'd go hungry, then even I would have to agree that it was essential. But I'm not sure how many of these guys are doing it for any reason except the need to kill something." He turned to the Sues. "I wasn't being sexist with that. I don't know any female hunters."

"I could introduce you to some," Sue 1 said.

"I'll look forward to that," he said.

Dr. Robinson was optimistic about the reintroduction of the moose. He had spent the summer working for the Department of Natural Resources, and they had tested conditions to determine where the best place would be to bring the moose back to northern Michigan.

I raised my hand. "How are they going to get them here?"

"What's that, Molly?"

"The moose," I said. I couldn't think how they would get fifty moose to the UP.

"Jesus Christ." Shane slapped his hand on the table.

Dr. Robinson looked over. "Shane? Everything okay there?"

"This is stupid," Shane said.

"Is that right?"

"If you ask me," Shane said. He looked around the room, checking to see who agreed with him.

I couldn't watch.

It was the first time he had attacked me in class like that, and I was mortified. I wanted to leave, to bolt out of my chair and get out of there. I should never have asked such a stupid question. I looked at the table, praying, I mean really praying, that I would not cry. I got hold of my breath, but my palms were damp, and I could feel my face burning.

"Well, why don't you explain it to Molly?"

"Do what?" Shane asked.

He stopped grinning. That was something.

I thought we should move on. I didn't have to know the answer to my question. I was sure the Department of Natural Resources had it all figured out. I could learn later. Or never. It wouldn't affect my life one way or another.

"Answer her question," Dr. Robinson told him. "Tell her how they're going to get the moose into the UP."

He moved back and forth in front of the chalkboard. He grabbed a piece of chalk and tossed it across the room towards Shane. It missed by a long shot and landed in the center of the tables. Someone crawled under and put it in front of Shane.

"Come on, then," Dr. Robinson said. "Show us. Draw it on the board if you will. Let us see how they're going to bring them in."

Shane didn't move. He stared straight ahead. Not looking at anything, just fixed on the far wall.

The mood had changed. I didn't like being the center of attention.

Dr. Robinson waited. Nothing happened. No one moved. It was uncomfortable.

Finally, Dr. Robinson spoke. His voice was low, even lower than normal, not whispering, but we had to strain to hear. "A stupid question might be *What is a moose?* A stupid question might be *How does a moose walk?* Another might be *How do you spell moose?*" He went over and picked up the chalk pieces that he could reach from that side of the table. "But there is nothing stupid about asking how the moose will be introduced to the region." A really, really long pause. "You want to know why?"

No one answered.

"Because I haven't any idea. I have no clue how they plan to do it. I never asked."

There was some tension released when he opened up his backpack and shoved in his books and papers. It seemed class was going to end early.

"Don't humiliate each other," Dr. Robinson said. "The world will do that for all of us."

He left.

Silence for several minutes. Then we left too. I didn't stop to talk to Finley. I didn't want to be blamed for this.

The Sues smoked cigarettes in the space between the double set of doors on the lower level. They had class across the way and tried to get in at least two cigarettes before they went in. I followed them down that day. I felt better with them than with the Crusoes, who were sure to take Shane's side. I'm sure they all thought I had asked something useless.

"He better watch himself," they complained.

They weren't talking about Shane. They were mad at Dr. Robinson.

"He's too much," Sue 2 said.

"It's always something," Sue 3 said.

"His preaching is beyond the pale."

"These tantrums have to stop."

The chalk throwing had been dramatic. But he didn't have tantrums. He cared about what he was teaching us. That made him the best teacher I had ever had. He was that different.

"Shane wasn't very nice," I said.

I wasn't used to self-pity, but the Sues didn't seem to think anything had happened except Dr. Robinson overreacting.

"Shane's a kid. They're supposed to be dumb. He's the adult. He should act like one."

They snubbed their butts on the bottom of their shoes, then flicked them into the air when they got outside.

A few days later, Dr. Robinson came to class and handed me a piece of paper. It was a memo from the DNR that explained that they planned to airlift via helicopter at least fifty moose from Algonquin Provincial Park in Ontario, Canada. At the bottom, in all caps, he had written: *DON'T STOP ASKING YOUR QUESTIONS, MOLLY.*

The Sues were wrong. The scene in class wasn't about Dr. Robinson. This wasn't about testosterone or out-of-control tempers. It was about me. And Shane—me and Shane.

I had to do something. I had to get him to stop being angry at me. I wasn't sure how.

I had said I was sorry that night. I had tried to apologize in class a few times. He usually ignored me, acted like I wasn't there, like he couldn't hear me.

One time, Pete had tried to help. "Shane, I think Molly's talking to you." Pete stepped in front of him so that he had to stop moving away.

Shane looked over. All innocent and pretending he couldn't hear me. "Is she?" he asked, then slipped past Pete and left the room. No big deal that I was trying to say something.

Pete had shrugged, and I gave up. I wasn't going to force Shane to be nice to me.

But enough was enough.

I knew Finley had a gym class. He took hockey in the new sports center, which was a trek from main campus.

I went to their room. I knocked softly. I felt myself chickening out but did not leave.

I heard someone moving around. If it was Finley, he was skipping class. If it was Shane, he was doing some cover-up. I listened for the hissing sound of the Glade spray.

"It's open." It was Shane.

The room was even dirtier than I remembered. I couldn't tell what it smelled like. Maybe weed. Maybe just guys living for weeks without ever cleaning.

He was sitting on the bed but stood immediately. "Get out," he said.

His flannel was unbuttoned, and he wasn't wearing a T-shirt. I saw his bare chest. It stopped me, not because I was attracted to him but because it felt like I was invading his privacy, whatever he had been doing before I arrived. I had to do this. I had to at least try and make things better.

"Wait," I said.

"I'm not talking to you," he said. "Never again."

Never ever again? I wanted to tease, but I had experience and knowledge that it wasn't a good idea to joke around with Shane. He took himself much too seriously for that kind of sarcasm.

"I just wanted to say again that I'm sorry," I said. I was going to get it all out, get it all over. "I shouldn't have laughed at you. I shouldn't have been mean."

"Get out, you little prick tease," he said.

I hated that word. Nothing was more disgusting to me. Guys in my high school had used it to describe girls who wouldn't sleep with them, who wouldn't give them blow jobs. They said it because if a girl didn't want them, then they were teasing them sexually, and that was the problem. It always meant that there was something wrong with the girl and that the guy had been doing nothing more than trying to have sex, which was normal. There was no equivalent for a boy, nothing a girl could say back.

Besides, laughing at Shane's ridiculous demand that I not fall in love with him did not make me a prick tease.

I had tried. But there was a limit.

He was standing right in front of me. He had taken a hit of something. The weed wafted around the room. I grabbed his crotch and squeezed as hard as I could. I got mostly denim. But he yelped and then bent in two.

"That's a prick tease," I said.

He told me to fuck off.

"Now you'll know what one looks like when you see one," I said. "They're really fascinating creatures."

I left.

9

Another weekend, another protest against Project ELF.

"Numbers are important," Dr. Robinson said. "The more people, the greater the impact. We have to let them hear our protestations."

Dr. Robinson encouraged us to go but stressed that it was not mandatory. He may have sensed a lack of enthusiasm. Not for the demonstration or the cause. No one liked the time and that they were on the weekends.

"Don't they ever want to protest at night?" someone asked.

"They want to disrupt the city and its residents," Dr. Robinson explained. "They do it at night, and they would only disturb the flyboys."

He was talking about guys from the Air Force base who came in on weekends in packs. They were easy to identify because of their buzz cuts, so different from the college kids or the guys from Detroit. I didn't know if there were women on the base. I thought there had to be—there were lots of women serving in the armed forces, but if they were on the base, I had never seen them.

Dr. Robinson was enthusiastic. "Come on, guys," he said. "We have to carry on keeping the wolves at bay."

I expected a crowd like the last few times, but when I got there—right at 9 a.m.—the streets were quiet. There was a short line on the steps of the post office, and not knowing what else to do, I stood with them until I realized they were waiting for the doors to open. I went to the top step and looked around.

There was Finley, standing against the stop sign on the corner.

I went over. "Where are the others?"

He was wearing a red knit cap; it was low on his forehead and just about

covered his eyebrows, making it look like he was hiding. He didn't say anything, so I asked him again.

"What gives you the idea that I know things?" He was cranky.

It was early. I didn't take it personally.

"Because you do," I said. "You almost always know everything."

"Do I?"

He did. Not always, but I didn't mind asking him things because he
never made fun of me.

"Are we in the right place?"

"Have to be," he said. "Marquette's not that big."

But it wasn't just one intersection. With little chance of getting arrested,
I opened my bag of gorp. I didn't offer any to Finley. He would have to talk
to me nicely before he could have any.

I didn't really think the guy from the newspaper would be back. I'm
sure he wouldn't interview me again, but because I had liked the way Dr.
Robinson had reacted to my comment, I had come prepared. I actually
worked on my statement. Taking notes from class discussions, I put a few
sentences together. I had it in my coat pocket but didn't want Finley to see
it. I had tried to memorize it. *The natural world is a connected web: You pull
one thread, and the whole world is destroyed.*

It wasn't original. I had put it together from class notes. Things Dr.
Robinson had said. I liked to think of things being so fragile. It made sense
that we were there to protect it. My purpose had grown tenfold since the
beginning of the school year.

Two police cars pulled up a few feet from us. Four or five men in uniform
rushed out and moved down the street, almost running. The mood was
different this time. It felt ominous.

A long line of protestors came around the corner from Front Street. The
woman leading the parade was dressed in all black with a cape, a large hood
pulled around her head. She looked like death, minus the scythe.

Dr. Robinson was still not there. Neither were any of the other Crusoes.

The four police walked alongside the protestors, moving with them up the
steps as if they meant to go into the post office. It was all done in complete
silence, and I realized they had planned it this way.

One of the policemen spoke through a megaphone. He demanded that
the protestors clear the area. The protestors refused, then the police brought
out handcuffs and took the woman in black and a few others away. The
group dispersed.

No one was paying us any attention. We were just spectators that day. I thought Dr. Robinson would have been disappointed had he seen us.

The wind kicked up, and we moved, planting ourselves in front of the corner store. The display window was filled with furniture, packed with tables and chairs and all kinds of lamps.

The guy working there came out. He was wearing a red apron, the strings untied and hanging down by his sides. He had a broom and swept the alcove free of the leaves that had gathered, pushing them into the street.

"Can't loiter here," he said.

We certainly weren't doing that. He seemed to think differently.

"You're scaring off my customers," he said.

That didn't seem true either. But he had a broom and didn't seem like someone we should fight. We walked down the street towards the lake.

"Was that normal?" I asked.

"How many of these do you think I go to?"

"More than me," I said.

"I don't think so," he said. "I'm not exactly a cheerleader for this cause."

"You told me you were on the fence about it," I said, as if to remind him of his position on Project ELF.

The protests were important. Not something we should miss. Dr. Robinson made it sound like without them, the U.S. government was going ahead with Project ELF. According to him, the government didn't really care if the public was behind it. They would install their communications lines when no one was looking. They would get away with it unless people knew what was going on. The protests also served to educate. "Make our presence known. Get the word out. We will not be deceived."

"What are you doing?" Finley asked.

I thought he was accusing me of following him, so I stopped. "Nothing," I said. I thought Shane must have told him about my crotch grab and he was mad at me.

"I mean, are you busy?" he asked. "Do you have something you have to do?"

Maybe I was wrong. Maybe Shane hadn't told him.

"No," I said. "Not really."

I found the weekends at the university long, with not much to fill them.

I knew the guys did things. They were always talking about what they had done. They went camping and fishing and for long hikes in the woods. I didn't know how to get in on those activities. I wasn't the sort to just invite myself and couldn't quite get myself to ask if I could come along or just ask what they were doing. I didn't know how to tell them I wanted to do what they were doing.

"I need to take care of something," he said. "You want to come with?"

It was just what I wanted to hear. "Where?" I asked. I didn't know if I was wearing the right clothes for a long hike. It might be muddy. But maybe not.

I looked at Finley. He wasn't dressed for a hike either. He wore red Converse high tops. The laces shot. He had taken a pen to the white rubber part on the toe and drawn stick figures.

Maybe they were planning a hike up Sugarloaf Mountain, which we had done once with the class and wanted to do again. From the top you could see Superior and the Huron Mountains. The leaves were changing color, and the reds and oranges and yellows were beautiful.

"Just something I need to do," he said. "Shouldn't take long."

I didn't care if it took all day and all night. I liked being with Finley.

I said sure. Anything was better than going back to the room where Janet would be cutting her toenails off the side of the bed. That's what she did on Saturday mornings. She put Kleenex on the floor and cut her nails one at a time, the clippings shooting off onto the tissue. I couldn't complain; she caught the nails, but I hated being there when she did it. It seemed like something she could do in the bathroom.

Finley owned a VW. At one time it might have been yellow, but it was like the color had drained out of it and now looked almost a dull beige.

Inside, it looked like a garbage can.

He saw my hesitation but wasn't embarrassed. "I know," he said. "I've got to clean it."

"They have trash cans at McDonald's," I said.

He ate an enormous amount of fast food. Hardee's, Burger King, but mostly McDonald's.

"They're never there when I'm there," he said.

"At least two in every parking lot. They're bright yellow."

"Yellow?" he asked. "Is that right?"

"Almost glow in the dark."

I pushed aside the wrappers and plastic straws, the milk cartons. At least pop cans didn't smell. Rotten milk was wretched.

We drove out on 550, the road to Big Bay. We had been there with Dr.

Robinson and the others when we had climbed Sugarloaf. We passed that turnout and drove further on. Finally, he slowed at one of the huge silver mailboxes and pulled in.

I was done asking Finley where we were going. Sooner or later, I would find out. The day was fun even if we hadn't protested anything. Even if we had missed or gotten mixed up about the demonstration.

We bounced along; the road was unpaved with all kinds of deep ruts. I held onto the dashboard.

"Must be a bitch in the winter. Have to have your own plow. City's not coming down this every time there's a snowstorm."

It was a large log cabin, built out of dark wood. The front door was painted red, and the whole place was surrounded by white pine trees. We parked several feet from the house.

The place was quiet—no cars, no one around.

We got out. The wind hit us right away, and my hair went all over my face. I held it back in my fingers, searching my pocket for a rubber band.

We walked around. There was a large patio-porch on the back. Everything faced the lake. We were in a cove right on Superior. It was the most beautiful house I had ever seen. I wanted to live there. To sit on the porch in one of the chairs that were covered in sand and sit there and look out towards the blue open waters of Superior all afternoon.

It was magical.

I saw someone near the water's edge. Maybe two people, but then one of them waved and I thought I was wrong. It was just one person. They waved again.

Finley waved back. I didn't. They were standing beside a lean-to tent structure. They stood and waved. We waved back. A few minutes later, the figure came up the path through the tall grasses growing in the sand.

"Hello," she said. She looked us over.

I waited for Finley to say something, but he was just standing there looking at her. It wasn't a comfortable few minutes.

She was slightly out of breath. "He's not here," she said.

I got nervous, feeling guilty—like we had been caught doing something wrong.

"Up in Houghton for the weekend. Back tomorrow," she said.

"Hello," Finley said. "How are you?"

"I assume that's why you're here? To see him, not me?"

We were at Dr. Robinson's house. This was his wife. I stood behind Finley, as if I could hide myself.

"I was here last week," Finley said. "Doing some work."

"You moved the loom?"

"That was the other guys," Finley said. "I helped with the stones here."

"That's right. I remember you."

She was barefoot. It was not warm enough to go without shoes, but the sun on the rocks seemed to please her, and she purred, not like a cat but like a larger animal. Nothing subtle or silent about her appreciation.

"Look how he's got you working," she said. "You're students, not free labor. I don't think he knows the difference."

It felt like a mean thing for a wife to say about her husband, even if she was smiling. Maybe a joke, but it felt rude. Finley reacted the same way.

"He paid us," Finley said.

"He bought you beer," she said. "Not exactly handing out paychecks."

It was the first I had heard about the guys working at Dr. Robinson's house. They were good with their secrets. The Crusoes and their club—*No girls allowed!* might just as well have been posted on the proverbial door. The anger flicked through me. I wanted to get out of there. Quickly.

Finley had other ideas.

"This is Molly," Finley said. "She's in the class too."

I said hello.

"This is Ms. Wyatt. Not Mrs. Robinson," Finley said. "She's not like the song."

I was lost.

"Simon and Garfunkel." He sang a few bars.

My parents had the album. It was from a movie, I knew that much, but not what we were talking about. It was Finley being weird.

"Well, it's not like he's going to ask you to do any work," she said to me. That laugh again—so high pitched and mocking. "You don't have enough muscle on you."

She didn't look like a wife. She looked like a hippie, someone left over from the sixties, with her long skirts and multicolored hair, the bleach washed out. She had silver bracelets on both wrists and a large ring on her index finger—two snakes intertwined, the head of one ending above her knuckle so that she had to hold it almost straight.

I didn't know what we were doing there. But it didn't seem right. Finley knew it too. That's why he hadn't told me where we were going. I wouldn't have come.

"I thought he wanted us to help him move some things," Finley said.

This sounded, even to me, like a lie. Finley didn't seem embarrassed. He stood there smiling at her. She had tiny gold stars at the corner of one of her eyes. Two little stickers, the kind I used to get on my math homework at school.

"Did you?" she asked.

"I thought he had more," he said.

"More what?" she asked. "You thought he had more what?" She was mocking Finley.

He was flustered but pretending not to be. "More stones," Finley said and then he laughed as if it was funny, which it wasn't.

She didn't think it was either. She stared at him.

Finley kept talking. "More things he wanted to be moved."

"Not that I know of," she said. "I'm sure he'll let you know when he has more. We do want the path finished before winter. Though I don't know why, do you? It's not like we're going to use it in the snow."

Finley was up to something. Acting all weird. I wanted to go. We didn't know her. Dr. Robinson wasn't there. There was no work for Finley. It was a nonsensical charade—some sort of Finley game that he had roped me into by not giving me enough information.

"He'll be back tomorrow," she said. "I'll tell him you came by."

Please don't, I said to myself. *Please don't mention this at all.*

"Thanks," Finley said.

She ran up the steps and pulled out two green bottles from a milk crate by the back door. They looked like wine but didn't have any labels.

She saw me looking at them. "It's homemade. From some flowers I grew over the summer right here near the beach."

I didn't know how one made wine. I thought it was all from grapes.

"Sorry I can't ask you to stay. I have to be careful of losing the light," she said. "I'm painting the lake."

It was early afternoon. The sky was cloudless. Losing light didn't seem like something she had to worry about. It sounded like something an artist would say, and I wondered if that's why she had said it.

"We have to go," I said.

I pulled on Finley's windbreaker. It wasn't zipped, and it slid off one shoulder.

Finley seemed to hesitate. I could just see Dr. Robinson coming back early and catching us there. That's what it felt like, like we were doing something we shouldn't. If caught, we would be punished.

"Come back. Come back soon." She went back down the path to the shoreline.

Finley kept standing there until I pushed him.

"Let's go. Now!"

He didn't move fast, but he finally started walking away.

He stopped when we got to the other side of the house. "Where is she?"

"On the beach," I said.

"Can you see her?"

"Sort of," I said.

"Don't let her see you," he said.

He made me step around the side of the house and look out. I could just see her hair in the wind.

Finley went to the back windows and looked in. He put his face right up to the panes, just where it didn't belong. I was horrified.

"What the hell are you doing?"

"Keeping an eye out," he said.

"For what?" I asked.

"For anything."

He tried the door. It was not locked. "Come on," he said.

"No way," I said.

He disappeared inside.

"Finley," I called. "Stop it. Get out here!"

I got louder. I guessed he was stealing something. He had come to take something from Dr. Robinson. I went over to the car and put my head in and searched until I found the horn. It wasn't too loud, but he got the message.

He came running out. "Are you crazy?"

"Are you?" I asked.

We got in and drove away. If he had stolen anything, it wasn't large enough for me to see. So I wasn't sure. It might have been something small, a wallet, some jewelry. That didn't seem like something Finley would do— steal from Dr. Robinson. That couldn't be right.

We went back out to the main road, the drive even bumpier than on the way in.

"You know he doesn't have a television," Finley said. "All the way out here, nothing to do, and he doesn't have a TV."

"Is that why we came out? So you could see if he had a TV?"

He didn't answer me. "She has a giant loom in the living room. It's so big there isn't room for anything else—not even a couch or a chair. She's got a spinning wheel too. Makes her own yarn."

"That's the reason we were there then? Because you think his wife is a witch?" I asked. "She didn't really look like one."

"What does a witch look like?" he asked. He was definitely avoiding giving me an answer.

"They wear black robes and have large pointy hats. You've seen them before. On Halloween, they walk the streets asking for candy," I said. "Now tell me."

"It was nothing," he said.

We made it out to the main road, and Finley waited for a truck before turning.

"We were out here last week doing work, and we smoked a couple of bowls. I got home, and I couldn't find my hash pipe, so I thought I left it out here." The words came tumbling out, a real confession.

"You thought you left your hash pipe?"

"It's stupid," he said. "I know."

"That's why we were there?" I asked.

"Like I said. Dumb, dumb, dumb. Let's just forget it."

The sun came in, warm through the windshield. I stared at the colors of the passing trees. Red, yellow, orange, the green of the pine trees. The parking lot to the summit of Sugarloaf, a popular destination, was full, with the overflow cars parked along the road. Finley slowed as we passed to let a trio of hikers cross in front of us. They had packs on, so maybe they were going further than just to the top of the mountain.

Finley drove to a part of town I hadn't been to and up against a low, dark building with a Christian cross on the door.

"Is this a church?" I asked.

He laughed. "You really are from another planet," he said. "This is St. Vincent de Paul's. Tell me you've heard of it?"

I saw the sign then, but it didn't mean anything. I nodded. I got tired of not understanding things.

We went inside. It was a resale shop. Old clothes.

"We're going clothes shopping?" I asked.

"It's time we get you some boots," he said. "You can't wear those all winter."

I was surprised he had noticed what I wore. Most guys wouldn't. I had just been thinking about winter boots. There was a bus that went out to the mall, and I thought I would have to go one day, without knowing if there were any shoe stores out there. We didn't really use winter boots in Detroit. We just wore our shoes and avoided being outside on really snowy days.

Inside was a long, large room with clothes and books and toys piled everywhere. It wasn't very clean, and the smell of mothballs was so strong I could taste it in my mouth. Finley and I were the only customers.

There were several old couches along one wall, and on one of them some-one was sleeping. He was the only person there, so I guessed he was working. He had a home-knitted afghan pulled over him. He did not move when we walked by. Light snores, like soft music playing in the background.

Finley knew his way around and took me to the back, where the shoes and boots were in barrels according to shoe size. He dug out shoes—sneakers, rubber boots, old-fashioned high-heeled party shoes. I tossed them back into an empty barrel.

"Eureka," he said. He pulled out one mukluk. "That should fit."

I took it and held it up to my foot. Maybe. It looked about right. It took him another ten minutes to find the matching boot.

The shoe bins were marked—a handmade sign: *$5.00 a pair; Single Shoes—Free!* In small print: *Establishment decides if the shoes are matchless. No arguing!*

Finley said he was paying. "My treat," he said.

A guy had never bought me clothes before. I said he didn't have to do that, but I didn't have any money, so technically he did if I was going to take them with me, something I really wanted to do.

We left the money on the table by the cigar box—another handwritten sign: *CASH ONLY.*

We left.

I balanced on the hood of Finley's car to see if they fit. I thought they were too small, but Finley said they were just right.

"They take some getting used to," he said. "But you'll need them in the snow."

The wool was damp or maybe just cold from being in that cavernous space for all that time. They smelled like old dog. Most likely, the odor would fade.

"Walk around," Finley said.

"Here?"

"No one will see you if you fall."

I didn't think I was going to fall, though they did make you walk funny—like one of those kid's toys—Weeble Wobbles—dolls that were weighted at the bottom and never tipped over.

I made a large circle, trying to get used to the weight difference and the balance. Finley sat on the back bumper of his car, and I joined him.

I was really happy to have them. They made me feel like one of the Crusoes. I had one plaid shirt, and I wore it sometimes. No one accused me of copying them. But I thought it was obvious. When no one said anything, I wore it more often. And like them, when it got too warm, I tied the arms around my waist and let it drag down my legs.

"Hey, let's not tell any of the others that we went out there."

"Why not?" I asked.

"I knew you were going to ask me that," he said.

"Then you should have an answer all ready for me," I said.

"I just don't think anyone needs to know."

He picked up a rock and threw it over to a nearby tree, one that I could not identify. Its leaves had dropped, and I didn't recognize the bark.

I held up my foot, the boots were untied just how the guys wore them. "Are these a bribe for my silence?"

"If I say yes, will you keep quiet?"

"You're my friend," I said. "You asked me not to say anything. I can do that."

"Is that right?" he asked.

"Sure," I said.

"Then give me back the boots."

"I think I'll keep them," I said.

I leaned in and gave him a kiss. He pulled back. I guessed we weren't going that way.

I was surprised. Not that I thought I was so great or so attractive, but I had thought Finley hung out with me because that's where we were heading. But I was wrong. It felt like a rejection, and I might have been hurt, but the more I thought of it, and I did, especially when I got back to my room that day, the more I realized that I wasn't sure I really liked Finley—like that. I know I would have fooled around with him. I would have slept with him if he had wanted me, whether or not I wanted him. I liked him enough. That's how I thought things worked. But it was nice not to have that hanging over us. I had yet to figure out desire.

My mind raced. I tried not to be hurt. Finley was looking at me.

"What?" I asked.

"You'll keep quiet then?" he asked. "No talking with the guys?"

"I thought we had closed down that subject?" I asked.

The boots were warm. My feet were sweating. I couldn't wait to test them in the real cold weather.

"I'll keep quiet," I said. "If you tell me the truth."

"About what?" he asked.

"The hash pipe," I said.

"I did," he said. He tried. But he was a terrible liar.

"That was bullshit," I said. "That's not why we were there."

I didn't know how Dr. Robinson felt about drugs. But he wasn't stupid. The guys smoked. You could smell the pot whenever they showed up anywhere. It wasn't like they smoked out in the open, but they didn't exactly keep it a secret. I didn't think Dr. Robinson was the kind to be shocked by a hash pipe after having the Crusoes over all afternoon.

I didn't think I was challenging him because he hadn't kissed me back. I wasn't that vindictive, or at least I didn't think I was. I told him I wanted to know the truth.

"Let's go somewhere where we can be alone," he said.

We were in a deserted parking lot. I wasn't sure how much more alone we could get.

He must have realized how that sounded. "Let's get something to eat."

I was hungry. "Alright," I said.

We drove into Marquette and went to a place called the Tip Top, a place I had walked by several times.

We sat in a booth, where people had carved the table so often it was nothing but names and numbers and hearts and drawings of faces and several body parts. I traced them with my fingers, the wood surface gone to carvings over the years.

"It's an old bar," Finley said.

He was right about that. We were the youngest in the place by about twenty years. That's how it looked. Ancient.

"So, what's the deal?"

"It's not easy to explain," Finley said. He looked around as if afraid of someone eavesdropping.

"Okay," I said. "Start talking now, and maybe you'll finish by the time I have to go to bed."

The bartender came over, and Finley ordered something. I was too hungry and too impatient to read the menu, so I just said I'd have the same.

Tuna melts with fries.

We drank whiskey and soda waters. The ice machine was broken, but the bartender brought over a perfectly round snowball in a large cup.

"From last winter," he said. "Found a whole bunch in the freezer. Can't remember why I put them there. Who's the smart one now?"

The snowball was frozen solid. We took out forks and knocked against it, breaking off bits and pieces and scooping them into our drinks. We played with the melting snow until it was mostly water.

We ate, pouring ketchup on everything because it all tasted of grease. The bread was soft and stuck to my fingers.

The bartender brought over another round of drinks and said they were on the guy at the bar. He had won the scratch lottery and had bought the entire bar a round. That was a first for me.

"This has got to be top secret," he said.

"Top secret?" I asked. "Are you for real?"

Finley's sandwich collapsed as he ate. The tuna was falling out of the ends, and the whole thing exploded into a mess on his plate.

"I'm not going to tell you if you're going to treat it like a joke."

"Treat what like a joke?"

He reached across the table and took my hand. I hadn't been expecting him to touch me.

He whispered, "I think I'm being followed."

He was talking so low it was hard to hear. I leaned closer. He did not back away.

"Are you doing something illegal?"

"Not any more than anyone else."

"Then why are you being followed?"

"I'm pretty sure it's the CIA," he said. He whispered the last word.

I looked at him blankly. That was the very last thing I expected to hear him say. "Up here?" I asked.

We were a long way from Washington, D.C., and that sort of thing.

"You might have seen them."

I looked around. There was no one who looked like they worked for the government. But I'm sure if they were trying to blend in, they would have looked like someone from the UP. And that's who was in the bar—a bunch of regular-looking guys drinking beer, watching some hockey game on the overhead TV.

"The UP seems a strange place for the CIA," I said.

"They're everywhere," he said.

That was hard to believe.

But he wasn't joking. At least I didn't think he was. There was something convoluted about what he was saying. It didn't make sense.

"Why are they interested in you?"

"Because of ELF," he said.

I didn't understand. "Why you?" I asked.

"Because of the protests," he said. "They're watching me because I'm participating in anti-government protests."

"They're not exactly anti-government," I said.

We had talked about this in class. It wasn't illegal to protest. It was our right to show how we felt about something.

"The government and the military want Project ELF. If you disagree, that's anti-government."

His reasoning wasn't right. It lacked sense for one thing. We were American citizens. We had the right to peacefully gather and demonstrate. I didn't think anyone in our group had been violent or done anything more than carry signs and chant out protests against ELF.

"Why not all of us?"

He took the crust of his bread and wiped his plate clean.

"Think about it," he said but didn't give me anything more, and when I thought about it, I came to a dead end of confusion.

The bartender came over with the bill. Finley shook his head, letting me know that he didn't want to talk.

I waited, then asked, "Are you telling me we're all being watched?"

"I think we might be," he said.

"Why didn't you just tell me?" I said. "Why are you being all Encyclopedia Brown, acting all weird."

If we were all in trouble, what was the point in being so secretive?

"I wanted to talk to Dr. Robinson first."

It was the first thing he said that made sense.

"Do the others know?"

"No one knows," he said. "And I don't want them to know."

"But they should," I said. "We have to tell them."

"Not until I know more," he said.

"Know more about what?" I asked. "They shouldn't be targeting you. You're not any more guilty than the rest of us."

"Slow down," he said. "There's no reason to be so upset." He reached across the table and put his hand on top of mine and petted it. It was an old person's gesture. "For now, can it be our secret?"

I waited to see if he would tell me anything more, but he waited for my response. I nodded.

I felt like I was missing a beat. Things felt off. Like everyone else was doing this, and I was doing that. Things didn't fit—I thought we were all having fun while learning how to save the planet from eventual despair, and Finley thought he was in trouble with the U.S. government. Nothing fit.

I was going to keep my eyes open—just to be sure I wasn't missing something.

At least now I had cool boots for the winter.

10

Madame taught us a French expression—*entre chien et loup*—which was how the French described dusk. The time when it was impossible to distinguish between a dog and a wolf because of the fading and changing light. I went down to the lake often at that time. Classes were done. It felt too early for dinner, and I liked being outside in the grayness. It was always dark when I got back to the dorm. I loved walking into the bright light of the cafeteria, feeling tired from the walk, my cheeks red from the winds. I liked having somewhere to go—a destination like the lake. It was always different, but it was always beautiful.

Moving to the UP showed me that where I had lived before was ugly. Or worse than ugly. It was a ruined landscape. Those were Dr. Robinson's words, but I took them on. I had grown up in a place that had been destroyed—gas stations and cars and strip malls—miles and miles of nothing but concrete and flat roads. The trees gone. The landscape nothing but stores and fast food restaurants. I dreaded the thought of returning.

That first year, I walked about, whispering a mantra that even then I knew was strange: *I want to stay here. I want to stay here forever.*

One night, I was over by the ore dock near Presque Isle. There was a ship at the dock. I looked at the lights, way overhead, tons of different colors that showed me how massive it was. I heard the men, then saw them all standing by the phone booth. There was a light in the booth, and the guys standing there were shadowed.

"What you doing?" It was a man. Standing right beside me. Close.

I stepped back. He was too close. I hadn't seen him, hadn't sensed him coming to me. He put out his arms. Trapping me there. He pushed up against me, and I felt his hard-on and panicked. Heart pounding, I was in flight mode. He held tight.

I fought back. Frightened.

I didn't see the two men who approached. But they grabbed the guy from behind and pulled him away, locking his arms in a bear hug.

I stepped back. I bent in two, trying to get my breath back.

"You okay?" one asked.

They were wearing dark parkas, fur-lined collars around their hoods, so I couldn't see their faces. I thought they were part of the ship crew. There was no one else out there. I assumed that's where they had come from. They looked official, something about the way they were dressed, the way they acted. Full of authority.

I stepped back and tried to get everything in place. It was hard because there wasn't much light left in the sky. Night had come in.

A runner went by. He passed quickly, then doubled back. It was Jon.

"Molly?"

I breathed, no longer petrified. A Crusoe. I felt like I was being rescued.

"Hey, Jon," I said.

He stopped running and came over.

"What's going on?" he asked.

"I'm not sure," I said.

"Did that guy grab you?" he asked. He told me he was over by the running path. He had seen what had happened. "Didn't know it was you," he said. "Not until I got close."

The two guys in the matching blue coats were gone. Not anywhere in sight.

"You okay?"

"Yes. Now I am," I said. I had dodged something creepy. I wanted to get away from there.

He sensed it. "Let's go," he said. He was wearing all black—shirt, jogging pants, and a wool cap.

"I don't know if I can keep up with you," I said.

"You can't," he said. "Come on, we'll walk."

We walked along the path just up from the lake. Headlights passed every few minutes. I could hear his breath. Hard, from running. Then I realized that it was me. I was breathing that hard.

He reached for my hand. I was wearing mittens. He held it all the way until we got to the new physical education building.

"I'm going to shower here," he said. "You want to wait for me?"

"No, I'll head down to the dorms," I said.

"You'll be okay?" he said.

"Yeah, yeah," I said. "Thanks."

"Anytime," he said.

He hesitated, and I thought he might walk me back.

"Hey, who were those guys?"

"In the parkas?" he asked.

"Yeah," I said.

"They looked like they were from the DNR," he said.

But the guys who worked for the Department of Natural Resources usually wore brown. Maybe they changed it up in the winter, but they usually wore the ugly brown shirts and pants that the guys made fun of and used as a reason that they didn't want to work for the DNR. Dr. Robinson called them superficial, and they all had agreed.

Jon was staring at me. "You sure you're okay?"

"I think so," I said.

"Alright. See you soon."

He gave me another hug. His running gear was wet.

I walked back to my dorm. I wanted not to be a girl. I really wanted not to be caught in situations like that. A dog was harmless; a wolf was not.

It wasn't fair. I hadn't done anything.

I thought about Finley calling me sheltered. I would not have argued with that description. Back at the upper ore dock, I had just been taking a walk. Nothing to fear. Just admiring the beauty of the lakeshore.

One moment, I had just been standing there watching the lake; the next, someone was changing all that into danger.

THE MINING JOURNAL

Letter to the Editor—
KNOW THE FACTS BEFORE YOU SPEAK

October 10, 1977

People around here think they know the facts,
but they don't. They don't have the information they need to take a stance against the
Navy's proposed installment of Project ELF.
They should know a few things: The Soviet
Union has an ELF system in operation, and both
France and Britain already have plans to build
similar communications lines of their own,
according to the U.S. military defense program coordinator, who has recently criticized
the civil rights protestors for their stance
against Project ELF being built in Michigan's
Upper Peninsula. Of course, they claim to be
against the project without understanding many
of the facts. They complain that the communications lines will make locals sterile—something that has not been scientifically proven.
Nor is there any solid research done to show
that animals could also be affected, though the
deer population could use some sterilization
to keep the numbers down. The number of traffic
accidents would be brought down by limiting
these numbers. People are afraid of war. But
they should be more afraid of what happens
when we are not ready for war.

Eric Kramer
Negaunee, MI

NOW

A phone call in the middle of the night. Someone whispering. I thought it was a crank call. A deep breather getting off on a woman's voice. But they had other ideas, and before I could hang up, I heard, "The Russians?"

"Charlie?"

He hushed me, though we were thousands of miles apart. Certainly no one there could hear me except him?

"I was thinking about the Russians," he said.

"Why?"

"They wouldn't have wanted the U.S. to have a system in place like ELF."

I supposed that was true. I didn't know much about the Cold War. I tended to think about it in such literal terms. I pictured a long red theater curtain dividing the world. I imagined someone opening it when the Berlin Wall came down.

"So what are you saying?" I asked.

"Do you think they might have done something?"

"Like what?" I wanted to hear him say what he was thinking. It was important that someone put my fears into words.

"Do you think they got rid of them?" I asked.

"Do you?"

The problem with trying to be a detective is the resources. You have to know where to look once you know what you want to find. I was having trouble with all the questions I had.

You walked around in your life, and things looked normal. Just like they always did. But I felt the shift. Something had jarred my sense of normalcy. I had to know.

11

That following week was the midterm and accident on Presque Isle.

Dr. Robinson drove me to the hospital, telling me the whole way not to worry if I bled on the T-shirt he had pulled from the back seat. "Tell me if you're going to faint," he said. "Or be sick."

I wasn't sure there was any warning before one fainted. I didn't think it worked like that. "I've never fainted before," I told him.

"You know, I don't think I ever have either," Dr. Robinson said.

It hurt to talk. I shut my eyes. The ride was bumpy and uneven. Dr. Robinson swore, then apologized, then drove faster.

The doctor pulled away the T-shirt I had been clutching. "We'll get you cleaned up and put in a few stitches, and you'll be good to go."

It felt strange to be with my professor in a hospital room with doctors and nurses. There was something personal about it. Me sitting on the table while the doctor made me open my mouth, shone a light in my eyes.

Dr. Robinson sat on the window sill, facing out. I don't know what he could see. From my point of view, it was just the pine trees.

"There's an escalator in this hospital," he said.

I nodded to show him that I was listening. I couldn't think of any way to respond to that kind of statement. Most hospitals I had been in had escalators.

"It's the only one in the whole UP," he said. "When it was first installed, people came from everywhere to see it."

The light shifted again. The day was over.

"They couldn't keep them away. Everyone wanted to ride it. Up and down. It drove the hospital staff nuts. Everyone out in the front entrance having a good time. Like a state fair, some sort of carnival ride. They decided they would charge money. A dollar up, a dollar down."

"Did that stop them from riding it?" I asked.

"No, I think they came, but it bothered the hospital less when they knew they were making money."

"Do they still come?"

"I think everyone in the entire UP has ridden it a few times by now," Dr. Robinson said. "We can go see it if you'd like."

"That's okay," I said.

"I forgot you're from downstate," he said. "You've probably been on lots of escalators."

I didn't want to come off as jaded, but it was hard to be enthusiastic about an escalator. I strained to look interested.

The two of us sat there. It was awkward. I didn't feel good.

"You don't have to stay, Dr. Robinson," I said.

"Call me Matt," he said.

I didn't think I could do that.

He saw my hesitancy. "I call you Molly."

It wasn't quite the same thing. The doctor came back. That felt even weirder.

Dr. Robinson knew the doctor. They talked fishing for several minutes before he gave me a shot to numb my chin.

"We'll give that a few minutes, to make sure you don't feel anything," he said. He left the room.

"Guy thinks he's another Hemingway," Dr. Robinson said.

"The writer?" I asked.

We had read *For Whom the Bell Tolls* in high school. I hadn't loved it. I didn't remember any fishing in the novel, but maybe I skipped over those parts.

"He used to fish around here," Dr. Robinson said.

I guessed we were still talking about Hemingway. I knew that he was from Michigan.

"Did you read *The Big Two-Hearted River*?" Dr. Robinson asked.

It seemed important, so I said I thought I had. I hated when I told people what I thought they wanted to hear. I did it often.

"In the story, he called the river the Big Two-Hearted River when it was really the Yellow Dog. That's right down the road from here."

My pants were wet where I had fallen. The room was cold. I tried to burrow further into my coat.

"You know why he did it, don't you?"

I had no idea. This time I didn't pretend I did.

"He knew all the best fishing spots. But he didn't want anyone else to find them," Dr. Robinson said. "He didn't want other people ruining his paradise."

I tried to smile. I couldn't quite move my face muscles the way I was used to. I was completely numb.

His nervous conversation was making me feel worse. "Really," I said. "You don't have to stay. I'm fine."

"I'll make sure you're okay. Take you back to campus."

Dr. Robinson stretched his arms overhead. Something fell out of his pocket. It hit the floor and sounded like it would break into a million pieces, but it was thick and metal and was not going to break on a tile hospital floor.

It was the stake, the one I had tripped on. With that, I knew what had happened out on Presque Isle.

Dr. Robinson had pulled it from the ground and stuck it in his jacket pocket.

I think maybe if I hadn't been in such pain and so worried about getting stitches, I wouldn't have said anything, but the amount of self-pity I was feeling was suddenly overwhelming.

"He's been mad at me since the night of the bonfire party on the beach," I said. "The beginning of the semester."

"I don't understand," Dr. Robinson said.

"Shane," I said. "He did it deliberately."

"Shane Lebarre?"

I tried to nod, but it was hard to move my head. "He hates me," I said. I was going to tell him the whole story. Right then. I had to tell someone. The only person I had ever talked to about Shane was Finley, and he shut me down every time. "It's been going on for a long time. He got upset about something, and now he can't let go of it." The words weren't coming out right, but it just felt good to tell someone about Shane. I had been holding it in for so long. "I thought he was over it. I thought he would forget it. It was just one stupid thing. Who carries a grudge like that?"

"I don't think that's right," Dr. Robinson said.

Shane had been out for blood, I told him. "No, he meant for me to trip," I said. "Maybe even to kill me." I could hear how dramatic I sounded. I sounded full of self-pity and off, like I was out of my head.

Dr. Robinson wasn't reacting the way I thought he would. He didn't seem to believe me about Shane.

"You took a wrong turn," Dr. Robinson said. "I was right behind you. You circled around yourself. You were a bit lost."

I remembered that part. I had doubled back on the path. That's when I lost sight of the lake.

My tongue was numb. It had thickened where the shot had gone in. I didn't want to drool, so I stopped talking.

"I'm not sure that's what happened," Dr. Robinson said. "Best to get you home. No reason to worry about all that."

Dr. Robinson didn't know.

Then he came over to where I was sitting on the exam table. He turned over the stake and showed me: *PROPERTY OF U.S. GOVERNMENT.*

This was further proof.

"Shane was in the service," I told him.

"I don't think this has anything to do with Shane and some kisses he gave you," he said.

He didn't know the extent of Shane's anger. He was capable of revenge. I knew him.

"In fact, I don't think you were the target."

"I wasn't?"

"I think I might have been."

"You?" I asked. I felt fuzzy.

"I think that's enough of all that," he said. He must have been tired too.

We both got quiet. The light in the room shifted. It felt like we had been there for days.

It was dusk when we walked out of the hospital. I had missed my two afternoon classes. Dr. Robinson took the name of my professors and said he would get me excused.

Madame Graves, my French teacher, was coming in just as we were walking out.

I was surprised they knew each other. They were just so different. Madame was from France and curled her hair into sausage rolls. She wore calf-length straight skirts and white ironed blouses and lots of gold jewelry. She talked quickly in both languages and seemed out of place in Marquette.

She didn't seem the kind of person who would want to hear about the pollution of the Great Lakes or about glass and can recycling to help save the planet from people tossing their used stuff anywhere they wanted.

She clapped her hands, as if applauding us. "I had no idea this was the place to be in Marquette."

"We had an accident," Dr. Robinson said.

"I can see that," Madame said. She was flirty and happy, not the kind of mood you'd think someone would be in when they were doing a hospital visit. "You should be careful."

"Presque Isle isn't exactly the wilderness," he said.

"But obviously dangerous."

He introduced us.

Madame smiled. "Molly and I are old friends. *Les bonnes amies.*"

"*Oui,*" was all I could think to say right then.

Dr. Robinson asked about her mother.

Madame said it was nothing serious. "She likes the attention they give her when she comes here," she said. "You better get your patient home."

We weren't that far from campus.

Dr. Robinson honked at the car in front of us. "That's my wife's car," he said.

It was red. Something compact. American made.

"It's not like I'm wrong. Look, I can read her license plate. She's driving." He waved. "But when I ask what she was doing in town, she'll tell me she wasn't here."

"Why?" I asked.

"She likes her privacy," he said. "She guards it like it's something precious that I'm trying to take from her."

"Ms. Wyatt," I said.

"That's right," he said. "Did I tell you that?"

I think I said something, but it might not have made much sense.

"Are you one of those too?" he asked.

"I'm what?" It had been such a long day. I was so tired and just wanted to put my head down and close my eyes. I was done trying to communicate, but he was my professor and I wanted him to think I was smart.

"A feminist," he said. He said the word like it was dangerous or maybe just distasteful.

Either way, I wasn't going to claim it.

We were by my dorm. I pulled out my room key. The lanyard was fraying. I would have to make another or risk losing my keys.

"I know you all like to talk, but I think it's best for the class if you don't say anything."

"About your wife?" I asked.

"About the stake," he said. "Can it be between us? Our secret?" He held out his hand.

I guessed he wanted me to shake it. So I did. "You can trust me. I'll keep quiet."

"Let's do that then," Dr. Robinson said. "Let me take care of everything."

The day had started to feel surreal, like things happening in a dream.

I got out and dragged myself up to my room. Even my clothes felt heavy. It took me a long time to get up the three flights of stairs.

I took off my wet clothes, leaving them in a heap on the floor. I put on a dry shirt and underwear and got into bed. I was warm for the first time in hours.

Janet picked them up and hung them in the shower. "Some guy came by," she said. No more information, like a name—just an accusation.

I slept, until Janet shook the bed.

"He's back," she said.

"I came to see if you were still alive," Finley said.

I was glad to see him. I sat up, punched the pillows behind my back. It wasn't like I was going to get up and go anywhere. "I got stitches," I said. I lifted my chin to show him the bandage. My skin was tight and sore.

He came over to look. "That looks nasty."

He sat on the bed. I pushed against the wall. There wasn't much room.

"Otherwise you're okay?" he asked. "Nothing damaged?"

"Just feel lousy," I said.

"It was a nasty fall," he said. "Next time, you've got to watch your big feet."

"Next time, I won't run," I said.

"Got something medicinal. Just what the doctor ordered."

He opened his coat and took out two flight-sized bottles of Irish whiskey. I had never seen them outside of an airplane.

Janet was at her desk, her back to us. Finley offered her one. She said no right away. A few minutes later, she took her books and left.

"That your roommate?" Finley asked. He opened my bottle and passed it to me.

Who else would she be?

"You've met her before," I said. The night after the bonfire, when he was handing out half-priced donuts on Third Street. I guessed he had forgotten that.

"She seems grim," Finley said.

I laughed. It was true, but it wasn't nice.

"She's quiet," I said. I was glad Finley was there. It would have been boring to sit in the room all night with Janet studying at her desk.

"Dr. R. took you to the hospital?" Finley asked. He had taken off his shoes and was leaning against the far wall. More comfortable. His socks were wool, gray with red stripes around the ankles.

"No, he pushed me out of the Jeep halfway into town," I said.

The first bottle was gone. I loved the way the whiskey shadowed the room, making everything softer, everything more fun. I didn't even care about Janet.

"Did he stay with you?" Finley asked.

"While I got the stitches? Yeah," I said. Then because I didn't want it to seem like he had given me special attention, I added, "It didn't take long."

"Was he mad?"

"At me?"

"Why would he be mad at you?"

"Why would he be mad at anyone?" I asked. I was buzzed. My tongue felt too thick for my mouth.

"That's what I'm asking," Finley said. "Was he?"

It was strange that he had asked me about Dr. Robinson. Finley was my friend, but I had promised, and I didn't want Dr. Robinson to think I wasn't someone who could be trusted.

"Jon took the midterms to his office," Finley said. "We didn't have yours though."

"Think he's going to have a redo. You could have all cheated after we left," I said.

"But we didn't," he said.

"I'm just telling you what he said."

"Is that what you talked about?" he asked. He was definitely looking for an answer to something that was bothering him.

"Why?" I asked.

"I want to know," he said.

He took out a cigarette, but I told him Janet would have a fit if he lit up in the room.

"We talked about Hemingway," I said.

"About fishing?"

I could feel my whole body relaxing. I thought he would kiss me. Alcohol changed things.

Janet came back in. She dropped her books on the bed. One fell to the floor. "When's he going to leave?"

I could feel her unhappiness, but it wasn't any big deal. We weren't doing anything. He was just there.

I must have fallen asleep first. I woke once. He was still there. I liked the weight of his body on mine. It was warm, and I moved closer. He didn't wake. If my chin hadn't been so sore, I would have liked it more.

I didn't hear him leave. But the next morning, he was gone.

Janet was up. And she was mad. "I had to sleep in my clothes," she said. I didn't see how I had anything to do with what she wore to bed.

"I didn't want to change into my nightgown with a boy in the room."

"He wouldn't have seen anything. Not in the dark," I said.

She could also have used the bathroom.

"He was so loud when he left." Janet had a list of things she was unhappy about.

I wasn't going to fight with her. "Yeah, sorry."

"I don't like that kind of thing," she said.

"What?" I asked—and then because I was feeling rough, "Having friends?" It wasn't nice, but it slipped out. I hated being told what to do. I hated being criticized.

Janet was quick with a comeback. "I may not have friends, but at least I'm not a slut."

"A what?" I didn't need clarification. I had heard her. But I asked for it anyway.

She did not repeat the insult.

"You think I'm a slut because Finley fell asleep on my bed."

She was right there. She must have known we hadn't had sex. She would have heard. We were a few feet away.

"Him. The guys in that class you're always talking about. Your professor."

"What?" I was so angry I could feel it rushing through my body.

"Your Dr. Robinson. Precious Dr. Robinson. Do you have any idea how much you talk about him? All the time. All day long. That's all you do. Talk about him. Dr. Robinson says this. Dr. Robinson says that," Janet said. "I don't want to hear about some stupid science professor just because you're obsessed with him."

I walked out. I ran down the hall and pushed open the doors. I ran halfway up the hill to main campus and realized I hadn't taken my lanyard with my keys. I didn't like being without them. For all I knew Janet would lock me out later. I went back. Janet was on the bed, her face buried in the pillow. She might have been crying. I thought to say I was sorry. But didn't. She shouldn't have called me a slut.

A prick tease, then a slut. I was doing something wrong.

From *MOMENTS IN THE UP—REFLECTIONS*

PROJECT ELF = PROJECT ELVES

The U.S. Navy was confused by the reaction to Project ELF. They had assumed the residents of the Upper Peninsula would embrace the project enthusiastically because of the promised employment opportunities. They never imagined there would be any pushback.

But the connection between Project ELF and nuclear war was made when the proposal was introduced, and the people of the UP questioned the impact of the project on their land and their protected wilderness areas. They wanted guarantees—they wanted to be assured that no harm would be caused by the installation of the communications lines.

The government did not share confidential information with civilians, but they tried to alter the notion that the project had anything to do with "the bomb." Which was not altogether true. Some might have even called it a lie. The messages communicated in the system would be warnings of nuclear war. Included in these missives would be the coordinates of the destruction followed by instructions that would allow the ships to move to safety. Every submarine had points of safe return—that is to say, they knew in advance of their missions, locations where they could escape—if and when these sorts of geographical positions would be needed.

The residents fighting the installation in Michigan's Upper Peninsula correctly equated the project with the Defense Department. Many, incorrectly, believed that the project would include some sort of top secret control panel where bombs aimed at the Russians would be launched. It was for this reason that they were against the project. They feared retaliation and believed that the Russians would deliberately target the location from which the bombs were sent. The protests gained support from antinuclear protestors throughout northern Wisconsin and the Upper Peninsula of Michigan. The government attempted to correct the misconceptions, but they did not get very far, and support for the project waned considerably.

SUPPORT ELF signs were defaced and redecorated—SUPPORT ELVES!

In December and the Christmas season, these signs seemed ubiquitous, showing up on every storefront and in some bars, where the patrons used them as dartboards.

Two high school students dressed as elves, who had been hired by Michigan Bell to help pass out gifts at the annual Christmas gift giveaway, were reported to have been harassed and attacked outside the Michigan Bell Building on Front Street. They claimed the perpetrators were Project ELF protesters. Later, the incident was rereported: the ELF protestors did not attack the elves; they simply mocked their costumes.

12

Janet's name-calling got under my skin. I spent the morning feeling bad about myself. I skipped sociology and walked down to the lake. It was one of those perfect autumn days. The sky the same color as the deep blue of the water. I took off my socks and shoes. The top of the sand was warm, but as I buried my toes in, it got cold. The temperatures dropped at night. I could feel winter in the wind.

I tried sending messages out across the open water. But I wasn't sure who would receive them. I didn't really know who I wanted to communicate with; I just wanted someone to hear me. To hear what I had to say. Things had gotten confusing—slipping out of control. I needed grounding.

I went to see Dr. Robinson during his office hours.

I had to give him back his T-shirt, which I had washed in the sink in the laundry room, then paid for a whole twenty-minute cycle to dry it. It didn't look great, but it was his, and I wanted a reason to be there.

The faculty offices were in the basement of the library, divided by departments. I walked to the far end, to the science wing.

Dr. Robinson was standing in the doorway to his office talking with Madame.

"Molly," Dr. Robinson said. He held out his hand.

I wasn't sure if I was to shake it. I didn't do that sort of thing so I gave him a small wave, keeping my hand in the pockets of my ski coat. Madame smiled. Her lipstick had smudged against one of her front teeth, but otherwise she was dressed like she was going to a party. She wore opaque black nylons.

She said something, in French of course, and I thought she was calling me blessed, then realized I was translating it wrong. She meant injured.

"I was coming to talk to you," I said to Dr. Robinson.

"Sure," he said. "What's up?"

I couldn't say anything to him with Madame standing right there. But even if she hadn't been, I wasn't sure why I was there or what I wanted from him. I wanted him to tell me I wasn't a slut and that I shouldn't let someone call me names that weren't true or that I should ignore someone like Janet because she was just angry and lonely. I wanted him to tell me that Shane had only called me a prick tease because he was angry and didn't know what to do with his emotions. I wanted Dr. Robinson to tell me that I was a vital part of the group. I wanted him to assure me that I was going to do great and important things. I wanted him to reassure me that the planet would be okay and that I would be one of the reasons we would survive. I realized he wasn't going to do any of that. But that's what I wanted.

There was a notice about the Michigan bottle bill on the wall next to his office door, and I asked where he thought we were on that. If it passed, it would allow the state's residents to return bottles for ten cents and cans for five cents.

"We're going to get a victory there," Dr. Robinson said. "Even the trolls are on board with that." He was talking about people who lived downstate. People who lived south of the Mackinac Bridge. Technically I was a troll. But he talked like he had forgotten that.

"That's good," I said.

I shoved the T-shirt into my coat pocket, a huge lump. I did not want Madame to see it. She would get the wrong idea.

"Come during office hours," he said, and they walked away.

I could have pointed out that these were his office hours, but I didn't want to come off as a smart aleck. I waited there.

Dr. Robinson's office door was covered with photographs. Some were black-and-white, and those were mostly winter scenes. Tree branches against snow, making all kinds of shapes and shadows. The rest were of Lake Superior in all seasons. Bright fall leaves. Great waves coming up over the break wall in the lower harbor, the spray crashing against the rocks. The tape holding them in place was yellowing and curling under. I picked at a piece, and the photograph tilted. I tried to retape it, but the stickiness was gone, and I couldn't put it back.

"He's not here."

I turned around. It was Shane.

I hadn't heard him coming down the corridor, but there he was, all dark curly hair, freckled cheekbones, and smirky smile.

"Dr. Robinson's not in his office," he said.

He stood so close I could smell his toothpaste. This felt dangerous.

"Yeah, I know," I said.

I looked at the ground and waited for him to leave. For a few seconds, I thought he might hit me. I took some steps back. But he didn't move. Just stood there and stared at me. It took me a few minutes, but I realized he was smiling.

"What?" I asked.

"What what?"

"What do you want?" I expected him to call me names again. I wasn't going to break down or react. I was done with that.

"You okay?" he asked.

There wasn't anyone else in the corridor. He had to be talking to me. Unless he was talking to himself.

"Molly?" he asked.

Night and day. It was like he had transformed into something new. Someone completely different, something I hadn't met before. It made me feel creepy.

"Why wouldn't I be?" I asked. *Caution*, I told myself.

It felt like a setup, like a bucket of water was going to land on my head. That, or a can of paint. I looked up. Looked around. It seemed we were the only ones in the hallway, but I couldn't be sure. Didn't any of the science or ecology professors keep office hours? I thought they were all irresponsible. We were undergraduates and needed guidance and mentoring.

"You look funny," he said.

Maybe he had some sort of weird animal that he was going to let out of a cage, that he had trained to attack and kill me.

"Differently than I normally do?" I asked.

I remembered some of the stories told at the bonfire that night. I remembered that male dolphins sometimes separated the females from their families and denied them food until they agreed to mate.

Get control. I could run. He had those heavy boots on. I could probably outrun him.

"I don't know," he said. "I don't look at you that much."

Fair enough.

It was time to get out of there. He had stuck a stake in the ground, deliberately to hurt me. He was not a good person.

"I wanted you to know that I was right," he said.

It was like he was talking in code, and I wondered if it was possible that he was telling me something. Maybe in his weird way, he was talking about the CIA or the government officials who were following Finley. He might have been trying to explain that to me. I stayed. I wanted to know more about this.

"No matter what you think," he said.

"What is it that I think?" I asked.

Did he think I knew something? Did he think I had some knowledge about what was going on?

"Girls fall in love with me," he said. "They can't help it."

So, that again. I should have known it wasn't anything to do with me. He must have found a new girlfriend. That's what it felt like. Like he was bragging, about to show me the hickeys on his neck, proud that someone wanted him in that way.

It made me doubt the CIA story even more. If he and Finley were worried about being followed, being watched or trailed, it didn't seem to be bothering Shane.

"Women love me," he said. "You were dead wrong."

His arrogance was something I could almost reach out and touch.

It was too bad that he was so off his rocker. He was really cute. Attraction was a weapon. He knew it too. He licked his bottom lip when he talked. His thick, lazy tongue moving back and forth, all pink and wet. He knew what he was doing. I looked away.

"They do," he said.

I had promised Dr. Robinson I would let him take care of Shane. It was too soon to break that promise.

"So you were wrong," he said.

That was enough talking to Shane. I walked away.

He followed. "Did you hear what I said?"

I went into the bathroom and sat on the toilet for a long time. I wanted to make sure he wasn't hanging around out there waiting for me.

He wasn't. I was safe.

I had learned my lesson. I didn't trust Shane. I had a gash on my chin that reminded me he was a loose wire, someone I should stay as far away from as possible.

I walked out into fierce winds. Winds so strong they felt like punishment.

THE MINING JOURNAL

Letter to the Editor—
ALL IN FAVOR OF PROJECT ELF—STAND TALL

These tree huggers are trying to keep jobs
from people who need them here in the Upper
Peninsula, where unemployment rises every
year. They should be ashamed of themselves.
They worry about the animals PROJECT ELF might
harm, but scientists have no proof of any
damage beyond sterilization. This seems a very
small price to pay for families to have food
on their tables and heat for the long winters.

Patricia Gallivan
Ishpeming, MI

13

The winds got worse, gathering force over the next few days. The noise sounded like engines, airplanes continually landing. There were times when I thought the windows were going to bust out.

They brought down the power lines and cut the electricity to the entire university. The dorms went silent; all radios and record players stopped at once. Then came the cheers, as if losing lights was something to celebrate. The rumors that classes would be canceled started immediately. Things died down. It was 4 a.m., but at 7 a.m. when the electricity still hadn't been restored, it was official; classes were canceled for the day. The dorms erupted, and the parties started immediately.

I had a few drinks with the girls on my floor. I walked around outside, but the campus police advised me to go back inside. "It's not safe," they told me. "There are wires down all over the place." Electric company trucks pulled up outside the dormitories and parked every which way.

I called Finley's room, but Shane answered both times. I gave up on that.

I took a nap. Had another beer with my suitemates who were running a euchre championship. I considered learning the game but wasn't sure anyone there would be willing to teach a beginner.

The radiators went cold. The rooms lost heat quickly.

I put on my ski coat, with an extra sweater, long underwear, hat, and mittens. That made it tolerable. But I was bored. Most of the Crusoes lived in the lower campus dorms, and I went to search. The entire student population was playing cards. They seemed entertained. Happy. Most of them were drunk. A lot were asleep, buried under piles of blankets and sleeping bags.

There was no food service in the cafeteria that day. But around noon, sandwiches were set out on trays, and we were told we could take as many as we wanted. They were individually wrapped—peanut butter and jelly, turkey and cheese, gobs of yellow mustard seeping through the thin pieces of bread. I opted for peanut butter. The trays emptied quickly. Next came milk crates full of apples and oranges. Those were less popular but tasted better.

The day's light faded, the rooms taking on a grayish tint, then suddenly it was night. The shadows were gone—it was dark, cave-like. Things got even more dull—the only sounds from my wing, the sound of shuffling decks of cards, girls screaming about not being able to see anything.

I could still navigate the hallways, so I continued to wander. Looking for something better to do than sleep or read by my flashlight, which kept flickering as if the batteries were low.

Everyone had their doors open, and the flashlights and candles made it possible to see while I roamed around.

I found Pete and Jon in the cafeteria.

"Molly!" they cheered when I walked in.

"We've been looking for you," Pete said.

"You have?" I asked. It felt great to hear that. I was so happy to see them.

"We called your room a thousand times before the phones stopped working."

They had other supplies—candles in coffee cans, a camping lantern up against the window. They had crackers and cheese in a can. They had liquor and cafeteria plastic cups. Their faces were flushed.

"My roommate isn't great with messages," I said. "She's not good with much else either."

Jon laughed. "I know that story."

To be fair to Janet, since the electricity went off, I hadn't been in my room much. There wasn't anything to do there, and studying seemed like a waste. It was too bad. The day would have been so much better if I had been in the room when they called.

"Girls playing euchre?" Jon asked. "It's all they do. Like they have a disease—and the only thing they can do is play that stupid fucking game."

They started laughing. It was not as funny as they were making it seem.

"Are you guys high?"

"Very," Jon said. That cracked him up.

"Really guilty," Pete said. "Started early this morning. Before sunrise. Longest high ever."

"I can tell," I said.

"You want a hit?"

Pot made me sleepy, and I was tired of the feeling of fatigue. I was excited to find them and didn't want to dull that sensation. They had a bottle by the window, and I said I'd rather have a sip of what they were drinking.

Pete got me a cup from the rack and poured something into it. "No ice," he said. "We came down searching for it. But if there was any, it melted long ago."

"So," Jon said.

"So?" I said back.

We all laughed. I was more into it this time.

"Can we ask you something?" Jon asked.

"Okay," I said. I waited.

Nothing from them.

"What?" I asked.

"What?" Pete said.

I didn't think we had to keep repeating that word. I waited.

"You know what Doc Robinson would say? Don't stop asking your questions!"

That made us laugh. Them more than me. They thought it was really funny.

"Okay," I said. "Ask away."

"What should we ask you?" Jon asked.

That got them laughing too. I drank. The drink tasted like medicine, but after a few sips I got used to it.

"What do you want to tell us?"

"What do you want to know?" This was fun, what I had been wanting to do all semester. Just be with them.

"Do you think about sex all the time?"

I took a sip to give me time. Then answered. "All the time? No."

"We do," Jon said. "I mean I do. I think Pete might too."

"You do?"

"All the time."

"That must be hard," I said.

"Exactly," Pete said.

It took me a minute to get up to speed. I groaned. "I meant difficult," I said.

"But interesting that you chose that particular word."

They laughed, high-pitched stoner giggling, which seemed even funnier than what they were saying.

"Dr. Robinson does," Pete said.

"He does what?"

"Thinks about sex all the time."

"How do you know that?" I asked.

"Isn't he always talking about it?" he said.

"Technically animal sex," Jon said. He turned and made some sort of shadow puppet with the light of the lantern. A rabbit, something with ears.

"Just the one time," I said. "Or have there been more discussions?"

"Not with us," Pete said.

Charlie walked in. He had just woken up. He had red marks on his face where he had slept against the pillow. "Is it morning?" he asked. "Is there any coffee anywhere?"

"Who takes a four-hour nap?" Pete asked.

"Fools who get up at four in the morning." Then he turned to me. "Where did you come from?"

"I live here," I said.

"So not just a myth then?" he asked.

I mumbled something stupid because I wasn't sharp or clever when I was around them. I would think of something I could have said hours later.

"We knocked on about fifty doors," he told me. "We couldn't find you anywhere. These bozos were sure you lived in Spaulding."

I knew so much about each of them, and they weren't even sure where I lived.

I knew that Pete was from up north. "The end of nowhere," he had said. "Calumet." Pete and Jon had known each other in high school. Not the same one but not far away. Pete told me once he had grown up in a crowded house. We had been talking about dorm rooms, and he said it was the biggest room he had ever had. He had shared a bedroom with his three brothers, his grandparents had the other room, and his parents slept in the converted living room. His sisters had the attic, which was okay in the spring and fall but pretty bad in the summer and winter.

I knew Jon was from Ontonagon. His father was a park ranger on Isle Royale, an island in Lake Superior off the western end of the Upper Peninsula. The entire island was a national park—nothing but wilderness. There were some structures in the park but no houses. Jon had spent his summers there. After Dr. Robinson, he was the one who could best identify the animal trackings, the bark on the trees.

And of course I knew Charlie was from downstate, a troll like me. He was from even further south, downriver from Detroit—Wyandotte—or, as he called it, *the ugliest place on planet Earth.*

Another difference between male and female or maybe just the difference between them and me. At least, they didn't know how much I knew, how much I remembered about them. That was my secret; they never had to find out.

"Why didn't you just ask someone?" My last name was easy enough—Grey—but even if they couldn't remember it, there weren't that many Mollys on campus.

"That would have been smart," Jon said.

"Too stoned," Pete said. "We were paranoid to talk to anyone."

"Strangers answered the door. We said your name, then walked away."

I wanted them to have been looking for me before they were stoned but was still glad they had made the effort to find me.

I handed him the cup.

He took a long drink, then handed it back. "No more of that shit. I've got to sober up."

He was so cool it was intimidating. I was not used to being so close to him. I looked over and saw him staring at me. I looked away. When I looked back, he was still staring at me.

He wore a long underwear shirt and jeans. They were frayed at the bottom. He was barefoot. He saw me looking at him and shrugged like I had caught him doing something he shouldn't have. Something about so much skin showing.

"Is Molly telling us her secrets?" Charlie asked.

"She's tight-lipped on all that," Pete said.

That would prove not to be true. For now, though, I didn't know what they wanted to know. I kept thinking about Charlie's bare feet. The way his toes curved into one another.

"Do I have any?" I asked.

"You must have some," Jon said.

"One or two at least," Charlie said. He pulled my ponytail. Not hard. Teasing me.

"Lie if you don't," Jon said.

"What do you want to know?" I asked.

"Everything," Pete said.

"I'm too shy," I said.

"Drink more," Pete said.

The candles dripped over the sides of the coffee can and onto the table. We were all playing with the wax. I made small little balls, and Jon and I played table hockey, all of them falling onto the floor until we gave up. I thought they were asking me something specific.

"You mean the CIA?" I asked.

"The what?" Charlie pushed into me.

I didn't mind him holding me like that. "The CIA?"

"What about them?"

"Someone said they might be following them. Maybe following us," I said. Even as I said it, it sounded far-fetched, but it got their attention.

"Who told you that?"

"Finley," I said.

"And let us guess," Charlie said. "He heard it from Shane?"

"I guess so."

"Odd birds from Escanaba," Charlie said. He put his hands in front of his mouth and whistled. A duck call, long and steady—piercingly loud.

I had just taken a drink of the vodka, and when they started laughing, I did too. It sprayed out of my mouth. It felt so good to hear them run down Shane. I was going to tell them the whole story, everything that had happened between Shane and me, when the electricity flickered on. The cafeteria filled with light. I was immediately disappointed.

We could hear cheers from the dorms, wild screams as if they had won something. It went out a minute later, then after a few minutes it came back on and stayed on. The flood of overhead lighting broke the mood. We abandoned the conversation. Jon blew out the candles, splattering wax across the tabletop. We stood up to go.

We would have classes the next day for sure.

"Next time, don't hide," Jon said. "We're not smart enough for games. We tend to lose."

Pete gave me a bear hug good night, both arms wrapped around me, my head against his chest where I could hear his heart. He whispered in my ear, "When we get to heaven, I'm going to introduce you to my granny. She's going to love you."

"Who?"

"My grandmother," he said. "She got there a few years ago."

I had not been expecting that. It was sweet and original and what I liked best about the guys. They were like that. So different from the guys I knew back home. The Crusoes were not afraid to be out there with what they said and what they did. I didn't know many people like that.

It was too bad about the power being restored. I had liked the shadows, the long gray pockets of flickering light, the way the darkness made it easier to talk.

Things being normal, working properly and all that, was fine, but it wasn't always fun.

14

My first real boyfriend was named Keith. We met the summer after tenth grade at a summer arts program at the YMCA near my house. I had signed up to take lifeguarding classes, but they never found a certified teacher, so they offered us space in the art classes—drawing, painting, ceramics.

Keith was the best in the class—drawing, clay making, painting, papier mâché—anything we were assigned he did the best. I was one of the worst but had really wanted to be a lifeguard at one of the country clubs in Birmingham or Bloomfield Hills. Anyone could see he had real talent, just as they could see I had none. He might have felt sorry for me, but one day he came over and helped me finish a drawing assignment. We were supposed to draw a car—as large as we wanted. Mine looked like it could hang in a kindergarten classroom. His was abstract—full of shadows, made from smeared pencil marks. You would not have known it was a car, but it looked so cool. The teacher hung it up on the only windowless wall, and we looked at it all summer.

We went to the same high school that fall and started hanging out. We started fooling around after a few months of driving around suburban Detroit. It felt like the next logical step.

I had never slept with someone, and my inexperience seemed to bother him.

"Have you ever done this before?"

"Done what?"

I had made out with guys before. Starting in junior high. Mostly at the skating rink. We would get to the rink and put on our skates, then we'd circle around the rink about twenty times. There would be a huge group of us, and then one of the guys would pull on your jacket, and you'd go over to the bleachers by the snack shack and start kissing. It was always cold. We kissed; they'd put their hands under our coats and maybe under our shirts. But it wasn't like there was much privacy, and like I said, it was cold.

We spent time in Keith's basement. He had set up an art studio down there. Two card tables filled with pencils and paints. We used to go down there saying he was going to draw me or that we were going to make art, but we never did anything. He wouldn't have painted or drawn anything while I was there. We usually went right to the couch, a ratty old thing that smelled like old dog.

His mother didn't work, and she was always home.

"She's not dumb," I said. "I'm sure she knows what we're doing."

"She doesn't care," Keith said. "Just ignore her."

It was hard. His mother wore shoes that clicked against the wood floors above. She walked around the house—back and forth, back and forth. But I liked Keith. I wanted him to like me back. I had read somewhere that in all relationships there was one person who loved the other more than they were loved. We didn't talk about being in love, but I thought that was true of Keith and me. I was more interested in him. He was happy to have sex, but I thought it seemed like it didn't necessarily have to be with me. I blamed it on my lack of experience. But we were sixteen. How much experience was I supposed to have?

A couple of days later, Keith said he couldn't take me home. He had to stay and work on an art project. I didn't think anything of it. But a few more days passed, and I hadn't seen him.

I called him a few times and finally he said he had time. We went up to the Ram's Horn, a diner where everyone from our high school went to eat fries and smoke cigarettes, drink endless cups of coffee.

"I think we should be friends," he said.

"We are friends," I said.

"I want to stop the other stuff," he said.

We had just gotten started on that stuff. I had thought we both liked it. It was just so good to fool around like that with someone like Keith. Someone who liked me, who I could trust not to make fun of my inexperience. I had thought he liked doing it for that reason too. He knew I liked him, knew how much I admired his artwork and how much I liked being with him.

"We should stop fooling around."

I didn't know how to talk about sex, and his saying he didn't want to do it anymore made me feel like there was something wrong with me. I was hurt by this rejection but in a way that I had never been, and I was bothered but pretended I wasn't. I acted like it was no big deal.

"Okay," I said.

"It's okay?"

"Sure," I said.

The waitress brought our fries, and Keith poured salt on them. Then ketchup.

That's all we said. Other friends came over, and I got a ride home with someone else.

I waited a week. He didn't call or come over. I missed him. I was bothered that he didn't want to sleep with me. I felt like we had just started something. I wanted more of a reason.

I went to the art room.

I smelled the pot right away.

"Are you getting high?"

"You don't have to announce it to the world," he said. He was stoned and laughed at my disapproval.

The art room was down a long corridor, far from the main office and the other classrooms, but it was still part of the school.

"Where's your teacher?" I asked.

"She's cool," he said.

The art teacher was new—she had started in January with the new term. She was young and looked like you'd expect an art teacher to look. She wore her hair up in a bun held together by paint brushes, and when she came to the cafeteria at lunch, some of the guys would imitate her hairstyle, sticking anything they could in their hair.

The room reeked. If anyone came in, they would know right away that someone had been smoking.

"She allows you to toke here?" I asked.

"What are you, some kind of narc?" he asked.

"It's not that," I said. But I wasn't sure what it was. I just knew I had to get him to see things the way I saw them. "You'll get kicked out. They will expel you for smoking pot on school grounds." Cigarettes were okay, drinking was tolerated the first few times, but weed was out.

"No one comes down this wing," he said. "Especially when classes have finished."

"But they could," I said. "It's not like it's locked or anything."

Our school was filled with kids who didn't want anyone to have what they didn't. They were that petty. And they were always talking on everyone else. That was a favorite pastime of students in that school.

Keith called me a worrywart. Then he showed me what he was making: gigantic animals that all looked alike except for the size—all different—a cow, a sheep, a pig, and several chickens.

"We're making a whole farm," he said.

"Why?"

It all seemed childish. He was talented, and this just seemed like cut-up newspaper sections covered in wet glue. They looked like I could have made them.

I didn't see him for a while. I didn't call. Let him smoke pot with his teacher if that's what he wanted to do. I pretended I didn't care that we were no longer friends.

A few weeks later, though, I went to the art room to see if he would help me. Maybe it was an excuse, but it was valid.

I was the head of the ecology club, and we were organizing our big spring event: Recycling Day, when we would collect scraps of metal and cans. I wanted signs and thought Keith could make me some. My handwriting was illegible, and he could make them look fun.

I could hear them. They were in the supply closet, not even trying to be quiet.

"Keith?" I said.

The farm had grown. There were dozens of the papier mâché animals scattered all over the room. There was a wood structure, like a lean-to that I guessed was going to be the barn. I touched the creature on the table. It was wet. My hands were sticky with glue.

Keith came out of the supply closet. The teacher said something, but I couldn't make it out.

I expected him to be stoned, but then I smelled it. I knew that smell.

I had been so stupid.

"Jesus, Keith," I said and backed away because the smell was so pungent, so male. "That's gross. That's so gross."

He was surprised by my anger. So was I.

"It's no big deal," he said.

But it was. Sleeping with a teacher was a huge deal, and he knew that. The other students would go crazy if they found out.

The teacher was still hiding in the closet.

"You better watch yourself," I said.

Keith was too pleased with himself to listen to anything I had to say. He seemed to think of it as a big joke, and that made me even angrier.

He said he had it all figured out. Besides, it wasn't my business.

Keith had everything figured out alright—until that spring, when the art teacher got fired. It seemed that Keith was not the only one she had been fooling around with. The others weren't as discreet as Keith.

Keith was shattered. He came over as soon as he learned she had been fired. He didn't even try to hide the fact that he was crying. We were in the backyard, but he was making so much noise my mother came out. She stood there, wanting to know what the problem was.

"Just school," I said.

"Did he flunk out?" she asked.

"Something like that," I said.

"You should tell him there's always summer school."

"Good idea," I said.

She was happy to have solved that problem.

Keith was over a lot before I left for Marquette. He bought bottles of Lambrusco, and we sat in the backyard and drank. It turned our teeth blue, and then we'd walk to Woodward Avenue and go to the Dairy Queen for vanilla ice cream cones.

One night he kissed me.

I pushed him away. "Don't," I said. I didn't want him to touch me like that.

"Why are you being so mean?" he asked.

Things had changed. Or maybe I had changed, which seemed more important, at least to me.

"Don't you want to fool around?"

I didn't. That was why I had pushed him away.

"You sure?" he asked. "We could go back to the way we were before. Sleeping with each other and all."

"No thanks," I said.

I wasn't the same person. Neither was he. It was better just drinking wine and eating soft-serve. I hadn't really forgiven him for lying to me about the art teacher, his arrogance, the way he treated me. I didn't have the same feelings about him. And that made a difference. Keith was a friend, but he had been mean to me. Something I couldn't forgive entirely. I wanted to really like the person I was having sex with, and I didn't really like Keith anymore.

Besides, for most of that year, I had been hanging out with my next-door neighbor.

Alejandro was a foreign exchange student from Chile and was living with our next-door neighbors, an older couple who had no children. They were sponsoring him through their church. He went to the Catholic school in Birmingham a few miles north of us. He came home from school on the bus, wearing his light blue button-down shirt and his mandatory tie hung around his waist or as a headband. He carried his books in a net shopping bag that his host mother had given him, and it dragged on the sidewalk. We had been introduced at a neighborhood barbecue.

I was coming home from school.

He was on the porch and waved. "How are you?"

I went over, and we started talking. He asked me several times how I was. I told him fine, just fine. Really fine. I told him I wished I was taking Spanish but was studying French and had been since sixth grade—and I still couldn't speak.

He told me French was the language of snobs. He flicked his nose so I would understand.

"Let's go," he said.

"Where to?" I asked.

"Where to, where to, where to," he said.

I didn't know if he was imitating me or if he didn't understand the question. It didn't matter.

We walked down the street. He caught my hand and began to play with my fingers. It seemed silly and fun. There was an empty lot at the end of the street and then, beyond it, the railroad track. Alejandro acted like he had been there, like he was leading me somewhere special. The lot was overgrown with weeds and tall grasses. Alejandro picked two or three of the flowers— the Queen Anne's lace—and handed them to me as if offering a bouquet. The bees, even in fall, hovered everywhere.

He suddenly stopped and faced me. We were head-to-head. I took a step back, but he pulled me into him and kissed me. It was a tongue kiss, full of spit and tongue. I hadn't been expecting that.

He had been playing soccer and smelled like boy and laundry soap. His host mother washed his practice clothes every night, he told me later.

He put one of my fingers in his mouth, and I felt a pull in my lower stomach.

We kept fooling around but waited to have sex, and when we did, we were in his bedroom, not in the empty field of Queen Anne's lace and broken bottles.

His host parents worked every day. They took the train up from downtown Detroit and walked from the station. There were only so many trains, so it wasn't like they could come home early. But I was always gone by 5:30 every afternoon, just in case. We were never caught. Everyone thought it was such a good thing that I was helping the foreign exchange student with his homework.

We had all that time together. All that time alone.

Alejandro found everything fun. "Happy?" he asked every time after we slept together. "Is Molly happy?"

"I am. Are you?" I asked.

"I am. I am. I am."

We took off all our clothes. It felt grown up. Not like we were in high school.

"I am new to sex," Alejandro told me.

"Me too," I said.

"You are pretty to sex," he said.

"So are you," I said.

That made him laugh, and he clapped. "Yes. Yes. Yes."

One day I asked him to walk across the room, naked. I wanted to look at him.

He did. Several times. Back and forth, showing me some of his soccer moves. All naked.

"You like me," he said.

"I do," I said.

I did. I liked the muscles in the calves, the way his hair grew darker as it went down in between his legs. I liked his back, the way I could still see the outline of his bathing suit even after months away from the sun. I liked his face, his nails, which he cut square. He wore a necklace—a gold chain with a cross on it. "I never take it off," he had said. I liked that too.

He was so easy.

"No brother?" he asked.

"Do I have a brother?" I thought that's what he wanted to know. "No, I don't."

He flicked his penis. "Then you would know this," he said. "I have two brothers. All I see are these."

Even if I had a brother, I wasn't sure I would have seen his penis. My friends with brothers didn't talk about seeing their genitals.

Sex was fun. We were careful. We used condoms. One day he showed me a box, a shoebox in the closet where he had put all the used condoms so that his host mother wouldn't find them.

The last time I saw Alejandro was at his going-away party. His host parents invited the whole neighborhood and a bunch of kids from his school. They had strung up Christmas lights along the back patio. There were coolers filled with beer and pop, and the host father worked the barbecue. There were plates of deviled eggs that no one was eating. Later, one of the little kids knocked them off the table, and the neighbor's poodle ate most of them.

"I will never forget you, Molly," Alejandro said.

"That's sweet," I said.

I thought I should offer to write, but I didn't know what I would tell him in a letter. I got weepy all of a sudden. I knew I would never see him again. And that made me feel both old and sad.

He bent forward and took off his necklace, the gold chain with the cross hanging from it. "Here," he said. "This is for you."

I didn't want it. It was religious, and I wasn't. I wouldn't wear it. Besides, it was his, and I didn't want him to give it up.

"I can't," I said.

We didn't mean that much to each other.

I handed it back.

"It's yours," I said. I knew he was relieved. "I will never forget you." I didn't need a gold necklace to remember him by.

I had had a lot of sex with Alejandro, but it was never a relationship. What we had was fun. It wasn't anything more.

Sex was tricky. It was always tricky. I didn't know how to balance what I felt with what I wanted. I felt attraction. I wanted a relationship.

There was the desire to be part of their group, to be one of the Crusoes.

There was the desire I felt when I got near them. The way they looked, the way they smelled, the way they acted. I was divided. To be one of them. To be with one of them.

I knew if any of them came onto me, I would sleep with them. I knew that about myself. I wanted to be admired, to be liked, to be desired. If they wanted me, I would want them back.

NOW

I sent Charlie an email and asked him to send me anything he could remember about the late seventies in Marquette. I wanted to know more about Project ELF. Charlie had always been political and smart; he would know about it.

My inbox was suddenly flooded with emails from Charlie.

For someone with memory issues, he was not short on things he thought he remembered. None had anything to do with Project ELF.

I clicked on the first one: *ICE FLOE PARTY* was the subject line.

In the email: *You were there.*

Nothing else. No other details. Nothing about ELF. Just this.

I wasn't. I would have remembered going to an ice floe party. That was something I wasn't likely to forget, no matter how long ago.

I wrote back: *Not me. Must have missed that one. What about Project ELF? Project Seafarer. In the end, what happened?*

He responded: *We were all there. All the Crusoes. Even Shane. It was out 550. Out by Wetmore Landing. It must have been in November or early December. The lake was frozen. We hitchhiked out. At least I did. You probably got a ride from some guy who was in love with you at the time. Some guy with a truck and a deer rack.*

He was confusing me with someone else. I wasn't looking for a trip down memory lane. I needed to know. He wasn't my only source of information. I was looking everywhere else. But I thought he could have helped me.

But he insisted. *Of course you were there!*

The details came next: *The party was on a small lake out 550. They dragged everything out in sleds. Remember? Firewood, cases of beer, hot dogs. No buns or ketchup, just packages of frozen hot dogs, which, if I had to guess, were all stolen from the cafeteria.*

A fire on a frozen lake? How would that work?

That's what I remember.

Maybe it was a dream.

No, no. It was real. The fire may have been an exaggeration, but the rest happened.

It wasn't that far-fetched. We were always having parties out in the woods. That whole year, no matter the weather: Wetmore Landing, Sugarloaf Mountain, Presque Isle, anywhere on Lake Superior, McCarty's Cove, Pictured Rocks.

I think we made out that night.

I think we didn't.

No, you were there with your hunter.

You make things up. You did back then. You haven't changed.

The party was fun—that's no lie.

So reckless of us. A party on a piece of ice in Lake Superior. A miracle we didn't all die.

Everyone lived. We all went back to campus. There was talk of being suspended, of some guys getting kicked out, but I'm not sure the administration ever knew about it. And if they did, what could they prove? That Marybeth Grill had an epileptic fit at a party? She'd had them before. I went to the hospital with her once. She bit off my hand. I thought I was the one who needed medical attention.

Who was Marybeth Grill?

Art student. Used to model for my life drawing class.

You took art classes?

I guess I must have.

Did you ever draw anything?

Almost never went. Except when Marybeth was modeling. Then I was front and center.

I definitely didn't go to a party on an ice floe in the middle of a Michigan November. I don't think Charlie had either. But it was a good story.

The Crusoes loved to talk. They loved to entertain themselves. They were always outdoors, camping, hiking, snowshoeing, cross-country skiing. They passed the time with their stories. Always, always talking and telling each other things, defining themselves, inventing themselves. All that.

I liked making out with you.

I thought back to his email, the one he had sent weeks ago.

Who was I in love with?

I thought he was going to tell me he didn't know what I was talking about. But he remembered.

You know.

Charlie was from downriver, south of Detroit. One of three of us from downstate. His mother worked for Ford. His father lived in Canada with a woman who had no hands. She had lost them in a snowmobile accident.

Charlie's grandfather lived in the UP. Charlie had spent several summers up near Sault Ste. Marie, and the first time we talked, he said he was from there. Later, he explained why. He said he hated Detroit. Hated being from there. Hated cars, hated freeways, most of all hated car factories. His biggest fear in life was that that's where he would end up—on the assembly line putting parts on cars and collecting overtime on the weekends. He also told me that his grandfather was an Ojibwa and lived on the reservation, then later said his grandfather fought with everyone and had moved off the reservation but lived close by. Later, he said his grandfather wasn't an Ojibwa but had been married to a woman who was. Then, once, he told me his grandfather didn't work, had never had a job, and spent a lot of time in the woods, drunk and railing against the world. "He's convinced everyone is working against him. Even people he doesn't know. Especially them."

The Crusoes were great with their stories.

That's what I thought the ice floe party was. One of Charlie's stories. I liked it. But didn't believe it.

But that's what we did all the time back then. We took risks. With everything, with everyone. It was our age. An age of rebellion, and we thought we were the first. The first to do just about everything, the first to have those kinds of thoughts.

We wanted to be reckless and sometimes were.

15

Dr. Robinson thought we should see the destruction.

"Witness it all," he said. "The good, the bad, and the ugly. It's the only way to appreciate what you have and what, one day, you might not."

We all knew about the fires, even me. For once, I didn't have to have Finley explain it to me.

They had been burning for months down at the Seney Wildlife Refuge. But some days they were visible in Marquette. A thick gray line would appear on the horizon, something that didn't look right. You knew it wasn't clouds. The odor of charred wood hung over the city. Most days it was just a hint, like burning leaves, but other times it felt like there was real damage happening somewhere nearby.

The fires had started in early July.

The Crusoes who had been in the UP over the summer remembered the storm.

"Thought there was going to be a tornado. *The Wizard of Oz* in our own backyard."

"My mom made us spend the afternoon in the basement. Stupid, really, because it flooded and we all get wet."

"At least you didn't get blown away."

"No one got blown away. There wasn't any tornado."

But there was lightning, which had started the burning. It wasn't unusual for sparks to ignite a fire, especially after a dry spring with thick undergrowth. What was unusual was the way it raged: nature out of control. It was quick, spreading in every direction at once. They tried to stop it but couldn't. Long lasting and damaging—the DNR had never handled anything like that before. Some said they thought it would burn the entire UP down to nothing but ash and waste.

The trip was optional, but Dr. Robinson promised it would be worthwhile.

"You may not get another chance to see a disaster like this up close. I guarantee you'll learn something."

On Sunday morning, we all met in front of the student center.

Dr. Robinson had one of the university's vans. It was dark green with a yellow wildcat—its mouth open, its claws in attack mode—painted on the one side.

We argued over seats, who would sit where. There were four rows, but no one wanted to sit in the way, way back. Someone suggested we draw straws, but no one had any. Pete had a toothpick in his jacket pocket, but he said it might have been used already.

Dr. Robinson threatened to assign seats.

He looked over the group, then turned to Finley. "Where's Shane?"

"Not sure." Finley pulled up his bandana, covering his mouth and nose.

We had been told to bring them. The air quality wasn't good down in the refuge, and Dr. Robinson said the smoke might bother our throats. Most of us wore ours around our necks, like kids playing cowboy.

"Aren't you his roommate?"

"I didn't talk to him this morning," Finley said. "I'm not sure he's coming. The trip isn't required, is it?"

Dr. Robinson shook his head, then asked, "Should we wait?"

"It's cool. We can leave."

Right then, the car that pulled into the circular drive was honking like crazy. It was the Sues. All three. They usually didn't go on the weekend field trips. They were too busy with all their requirements for the last year of nursing school. Dr. Robinson said that was more important for them. The rest of us were majors and therefore had different obligations.

"We're here!" Sue 2 said, and the way she said it all sing-songy, like a cartoon character, made everyone laugh.

They had finished an exam at the hospital the day before and decided they would come with us.

It was sometimes odd to be the only girl when we went places on the weekends. But I had gotten used to it.

Sue 2's car was a big old Chevy. Even the color, a deep maroon, was old-fashioned. Much of it was rusted out; there were holes in the exterior.

"It was my grandfather's," she said. "He died."

"I'm sorry to hear that," Dr. Robinson said.

"Oh, it was years ago," Sue 2 said. "I've had the car since high school."

Dr. Robinson looked confused. He held up the van keys like he was ringing a bell to get everyone's attention.

"We should get started," he said. He directed us to get in. "We don't want to get there too late. The days aren't that long this time of year."

The Sues told me to come with them.

"Girls' car," Sue 3 said.

All three of them were loud.

"That's okay. I can just go with the others," I said.

But they wanted me with them.

Sue 1 caught my sleeve and pulled so hard, she almost pulled my coat off.

"Yes!" Sue 3 said. "We need a girl car."

That got them going. "Girl car. Boy van!" They chanted it several times.

The Crusoes found it funny. Dr. Robinson was impatient to get going. So rather than make us wait, I said sure. I'd go.

I felt like I was with the cheerleaders back in high school who used to drive around the building on pep days and scream out senseless things. Our sports teams were called the Oaks, and it was hard to get excited about people yelling about trees.

We followed the van through town to the highway.

"You don't really like all this rah-rah Earth Day, save-the-planet stuff, do you, Molly?" Sue 3 asked. She was sitting in the back with me.

I did, but the way she asked the question told me she was going to make fun of me if I said yes, so I just nodded and looked out the window. We were driving by the prison, a maximum-security facility. There was a large sign by the road: *GIFT SHOP*. It struck me as odd to sell souvenirs at a prison. I was curious what they sold.

"Molly loves all this ecology crap," Sue 1 said. "She's under his spell. They all are. The pied piper could lead them anywhere, and they'd follow."

I couldn't remember if the pied piper got the rats or the children in the village to follow him. A line of rats seemed gross. But I didn't like being called a child either.

"Molly!" Sue 2 shouted from the front seat. She was driving, and it didn't feel safe to have her screaming her head off when she was supposed to be paying attention to the road.

We followed the van for a while, but a semitruck passed us, staying in the other lane and driving alongside us, which made me nervous. It finally pulled in front of us, and we lost sight of the van.

They were drinking from a large silver thermos, the kind that looked institutional, like it had been taken from the hospital.

Sue 3 passed it to me.

"That's okay," I said. "I don't really drink coffee."

I had forgotten her first name and felt like Dr. Robinson, thinking her name might just as well be Sue.

"That's okay," she said, pitching her voice in a perfect imitation of me. "It's not coffee."

I took a long sip because for a minute I thought it was juice, but the smell as I opened the top should have tipped me off. I swallowed my mouthful and then had to clutch my throat to keep from throwing it back up.

Peppermint schnapps.

The whole thermos. No 7UP, no coke or tonic—just alcohol. Sunday morning. A rough drink of choice.

"Okay, Molly," Sue 1 said. "The time has come. Tell us." She was in the passenger seat, playing with the radio.

It was Sunday. There were a lot of churches on the AM stations.

Then the three of them started in like a choir, demanding that I spill my guts. "Tell us. Tell us. Tell us."

"What do you want to know?" I asked.

"Which one are you sleeping with?" Sue 1 screamed. "What else?"

I was sitting right next to her. Shouting seemed unnecessary.

Keep your eyes on the road, I communicated to Sue 2 in my mind. I communicated it several times. I thought my determination to keep us safe was what was keeping us from crashing.

"Nobody," I said.

"We do not believe that. Not for a second!"

"You have to be doing something with one of them," they said. "All these guys. All of them so cute and friendly. What do they call themselves? The crew club."

"The Crusoes," I said.

"See!" Sue 3 shouted. "There's your proof. She even knows their secret code name."

"It's not a secret," I said. "Just what they call themselves."

We had talked about the novel in class.

"You've got to be having sex with at least one of them."

They were a chorus of demands. One louder than the other.

"Tell us. How many are you sleeping with? One? More? Three? Spill! All your secrets." Sue 2 turned around to look at me in the back seat, something else that seemed not only unnecessary but dangerous.

"We see you hanging out with Finley. You're always with him," Sue 1 asked. "You keeping your shoes under his bed?"

It was something my mother would say.

Sue 1 was dead set on finding some music. It was a lost cause, but she kept trying. Static, static, static, the low voice of a preacher.

"He's a friend," I said.

"That's how it starts," Sue 2 said.

It wouldn't have mattered how I answered; they were talking to themselves. I could have admitted to sleeping with all of the Crusoes, and they would have had the same reaction.

Finally done playing with the radio, Sue 1 put in a tape, Bob Dylan's *Highway 61 Revisited*. She played "Like a Rolling Stone." Only. There were other songs that could have been played, but as soon as it ended—and it was a long song—she would hit rewind and play it again. I didn't mind at first, but she kept playing it, and by the time it started up for the sixth or seventh time, I asked her to play something else. She strummed her air guitar, concentrating, as if she was the one making the music.

I thought we had been driving for about a half hour. I wished we would go faster.

"Promise us it will never be Dr. Robinson," Sue 2 said.

"Dr. Robinson!" I said and started to protest. I hoped they weren't going to accuse me of being in love with him. I had had enough on that subject.

"Because I want him!" Sue 2 said.

"She loves him," Sue 3 said.

"I do, I do," Sue 2 said. "But he won't have me."

"You're crazy," I said.

"He's got a wife he's in love with, and he won't make the world go around with me."

"Don't you have a boyfriend?" I asked.

"I'd leave him in a second if Doc Rob would give me the sign," she said.

They were buzzed—it was hard to take them seriously.

We missed the turn into the Seney Wildlife Refuge. It was clearly marked with a large sign, yellow lettering—*TURN HERE*—but Sue 2 was talking and zoomed past it like she was going to drive straight down to the bridge. I told her she had missed it, and she slapped the steering wheel and made a right turn onto the berm. Gravel went flying. The Sues went flying. A semi coming from behind honked a long, low warning. She made a U-turn right there, and we turned in.

The guys were hanging around. Most of them were wearing their bandanas, making them look like a band of outlaws.

I got out of the car. I would have screamed if everyone hadn't been standing around.

"Everything okay here?" Dr. Robinson asked. He had obviously heard the truck.

I shrugged. "Glad to be alive," I said.

He saw them struggling to get their things together. Maybe he smelled the schnapps. "Did they drink all the way here?" Dr. Robinson said.

"Pretty much," I said.

"Girls," he said, as if they were drinking because of an absence of a Y chromosome.

In my experience, guys drank way more than girls. But that morning, it looked like the girls were winning in that division. I was just glad to be out of the car and not to have been run over by a semitruck carrying a load of timber. I would not be driving back with them. I would make sure of that.

The Sues were dancing around the car. The thermos had to be almost empty by now. They had been drinking from it since we left Marquette.

Dr. Robinson said he'd deal with them. But he walked the other way, so I wasn't sure what he planned to do.

The Sues were yelling about having to pee. They started up the path.

Pete came over. "Hey, Molly, tell them there's a bathroom in the visitor center."

I stopped them from going too far away. "Bathroom inside," I called after them. I might as well have been shouting into an empty box.

Sue 3 already had her pants down and was crouched behind a skinny tree. "Don't look!" she cried out, which of course just got everyone's attention.

I was embarrassed for them, though they seemed to be having a great time, like the whole thing was a party.

I walked into the visitor center.

There were stuffed animals in a circle on the table in the center of the room. Creatures one could find in the refuge.

Pete was there. He smiled when I came in and gave me a hug—that smell of musk I associated with all the guys.

"Look at you," he said.

"Yeah?" I asked.

He had been hugging me ever since the night of the windstorm. But he was shy when it was just the two of us—always more talkative when there were others around.

"You're always so clean," he said.

"I am?"

"I love the way you smell."

He put his face up into my hair. I had washed it the night before with my suitemate's shampoo, something in a green and purple bottle with no label. It took hours to dry. I slept on it wet, and even the next morning, it was damp.

"I want to shower at your place one of these days."

I didn't think he was serious. "My roommate's afraid of boys."

It was fun to flirt, but we came to a dead end and turned to look at the table.

"Taxidermy," Pete said. "My uncle does these sorts of things. You should see the stuff he has in his garage. Eyeballs, pelts, teeth."

I had just been about to say that I thought that sort of thing was creepy. But I wasn't sure if Pete admired his uncle or agreed with me. I went neutral. I was better talking about taking showers in my dorm.

"I didn't know there were such things as river otters," I said.

They looked like seals—their skin sleek, their faces all squished together.

Pete turned the red fox to face me. The specimens weren't mounted or glued to anything. They were posed and looked ready to escape.

"This is the one you have to be afraid of," he said. "They're thieves. They'll rob you blind. Any food and watch it. It'll be gone in seconds if you've got these guys sneaking around your campsite."

I liked that he knew that. It seemed smart, the kind of thing Dr. Robinson would have warned us about.

The woman working at the center came over. She wore a green apron that was covered with a white substance like flour or sugar, as if she had been cooking.

"Please," she said. "Two fingers when touching the animals." She demonstrated.

Pete moved away and let me deal with her. She straightened out the red fox, putting him back in his place. She wasn't happy.

"There are too many of you," she said.

"Too many what?" I asked.

"To be in here," she said. "There have to be limits. People are moving things around. I can't keep track."

There didn't seem to be that many of us actually in the visitor center, but I said I was sorry anyway.

Finley was standing a way off, in the back corner. He looked harmless— his back to the woman. He stood in front of a laminated topography map on the wall, studying it as if looking for something specific.

"Hey," I said.

He didn't turn, just kept looking at the map.

I didn't need to be ignored. "What's wrong?"

"Let's not have all your questions today," he said. "I've got enough to deal with here." Like he was in charge of reading the map and tracking our hike in.

He was in a mood. He wasn't the one who had spent an hour with three nursing students slugging back peppermint schnapps.

"Why?" I asked. "What's going on?"

"Do you ever listen to what people tell you?" He walked away.

I didn't push it. I used the bathroom, then went outside and joined the others.

Dr. Robinson pulled up his bandana and spoke through the cloth, making it hard to understand him.

We followed a well-worn path. A low wood fence started it off but ended as we moved away from the parking lot. Signs at the start warned us not to stray. The land was protected, and we were to be careful where we stepped. They wanted to minimize the damage made by our footsteps.

The Crusoes sprinted ahead, the Sues lagged behind, and I ended up walking with Dr. Robinson. The path narrowed, and he walked in front of me. The landscape looked like the moon. There was no green, no living trees, no living anything. Just the torched earth. Like the remains of a campfire— one that extended for miles. Ugly, gray, brittle earth.

"It's quite something, isn't it?" He stopped to pick something up off the ground, a rock or a twig. He pocketed it.

I didn't imagine the refuge to be so flat, so gray, so endless. I liked to be near Superior, and from where we were, we couldn't see the lake. The sky seemed heavy that afternoon. It was the first time I felt claustrophobic when walking in the wilderness. The day felt weird; everything was not the way it should have been.

Dr. Robinson turned. I was right on his heels and bumped into him.

"The refuge covers 100,000 acres. All of it protected," he said. "It's incredible for the study of wildlife and their forms."

I thought it might be better to catch up with the others so they could hear about the refuge. But he seemed oblivious that I was the only one hearing all his facts.

"The refuge protects migratory birds. You can find all sorts of surprises here. Loons, swans. Every once in a while, a bald eagle will fly by, but that's rare. Very rare. The last time one was reported, the park ranger had a heart attack."

I laughed.

"I think he died, so I'm not sure how funny it was," Dr. Robinson said.

I had thought he was making a joke.

He stopped again. This time, I was looking up and didn't run into him.

"Do you read poetry?" he asked.

"Only in French," I said.

"That's very sophisticated."

It wasn't. I wasn't at all sophisticated. "No, I meant I only read it for class," I said. "For French class."

"I never read it. Not when I was your age. But I find myself drawn to it these days."

"I mostly just have to look up every other word, and even then, I don't understand it," I said.

"I don't think it's much different for me," he said. "But I want it to matter. I read it and want the words to make a difference in my life."

"You do?" I asked.

"Very much," he said.

We mostly read Rimbaud because Madame said he reminded her of her youth, her *jeunesse*. I found it cryptic, even when I translated it word for word. Even when I read it in English. I liked it when Madame explained the poems to us. But I didn't think it made any difference in my life.

"The fountains mingle with the river, and the rivers with the ocean, the winds of heaven mix forever."

"That sounds nice," I said.

"Shelley. He wrote it a hundred years ago," he said.

A lot of the poetry we studied in French class was old too. I thought that was part of the problem. Life had changed. People had changed too.

"All those writers, those great minds, those artists, the best of their times. All those creative endeavors that reflect years and years of thought and struggle. All of them working on the problem of love and none of them having a solution. None of them."

The bandana made breathing more difficult, and I pulled it down and took a few deep breaths. I could taste the smoke.

"So how does someone like me have a chance?"

"Someone like you?" I asked.

"Someone who grew up in a cabin in the woods in the Upper Peninsula of Michigan, the middle of nowhere. All those years, living with a grandfather who never said the word love. How am I going to tell someone what's in my heart?"

The question sounded desperate, and so I took it to be rhetorical. I waited for what he would say next.

"You think love is yours, that you can have it. People tell you it's all possible. You can love and be loved. But it doesn't work like that. Not that I've ever seen. It's just heartache. And loss. Always. At least with me."

He walked slower and slower. We were hardly moving forward. I could hear the Sues. They seemed to stay away from us, deliberately staying back so that they wouldn't have to listen to the lecture. I could have used some help with Dr. Robinson. The Sues would have had something to say about love. I wasn't sure what love was. I just knew I hadn't been in love with anyone. Yet.

It felt like something I would learn one day, but right then I was limited. I had nothing to offer him.

Dr. Robinson took his bandana and wiped his face. Rather than retying it around his mouth and nose, he shoved it into his pocket.

We came to a wood bridge that went over what in the spring might have been a river but was mostly dry now. The guys were standing on the other side as if they had been told to stop there.

"This looks good," Dr. Robinson said.

The guys took out their field notebooks. I pulled mine from my backpack. We stood ready for note-taking. The Sues were not there, but that seemed for the best. That much peppermint schnapps and I didn't think they would care about what had been saved and what had been lost in the fires.

We waited for the facts and figures that were sure to come next. The air was heavy; the acrid smell hung on us all, so thick we could have touched it. I pushed my bandana closer to my mouth and tried to breathe through my nose so I couldn't taste the smoke.

We took soil samples and collected samples of the ash. Charlie thought he found a pile of dead birds, and we all went over to see, but it was just the pattern of the ashes on the ground.

Dr. Robinson read off a list of the wildlife that had inhabited the area before the fires. "It will take years to get it back to where it was."

We waited to hear more.

"Just years."

I wasn't sure, but I thought he might be crying. His voice was thick and sounded like he was speaking through a long tube. He used his bandana as a handkerchief.

Dr. Robinson nodded when he saw that we were all looking at him. "People worry," he said. "That our lands and islands have all been discovered. That there will be no more explorers. That discovery is a thing of the past. Some of us weep to have been born in the wrong century, that we've come too late to the wonders of the world. That's why we preserve our land. That's why you have to see what will happen. Populations cannot be controlled. Not in any meaningful way. The horizons of our world are vast, but only if they are protected from those sinners who want to do nothing but turn a profit. Our world is precious. Treat it like a gift."

His words were better and stronger than anything I had read in French class. Anything I had read, ever. I was crying, the tears flowing down my face. I didn't worry. I could blame them on the fires.

"You are the stewards of this world," he said. "It is your responsibility. You must grasp hold of that notion. Understand what that means."

I put my hands together, then—because I thought it looked like I was praying—I put them in my pockets.

"Keep what is precious. Which means you must protect it. You are charged with taking care of it. Things that are important in our lives need our attention. You are the stewards of the world. You must do something. You cannot wait. In twenty years, it will be too late. The tides will have turned, and you won't be able to do anything."

I had memories of my sixth-grade teacher and her doomsday prediction. But Dr. Robinson was not preaching the end of the world. There was a way out of the despair. It was us. We had to do something.

"It's connected," Dr. Robinson said. "It's all connected. That's what most people don't understand."

We did. We understood. We knew this.

This was his refrain. Something he had said to us and something I thought should be our anthem. Something we all should sing. Together.

"The entire natural world," Dr. Robinson said. "It's an intricate web. Not only beautiful but awe-inspiring." He spoke louder. "But you pull one of the threads, you destroy one, and the whole thing is ruined. Once damaged, you can't bring it back. It's gone. Ruined, completely destroyed. That's what the world doesn't understand."

I wanted to be up to these standards. He set the bar so high, and I wanted to show him that I could do it.

I repeated his words in my head. Silently saying them over and over again. A mantra before I knew what that even was. I repeated it several times as we walked and looked at the burnt landscape: *I am the steward of this earth.*

I wiped the tears from my face.

Dr. Robinson didn't want the Sues driving home. "None of you are sober enough."

Sue 1 said she was good. But she slurred her words, so it was hard to believe that this was a wise decision.

"Next time, one of you should abstain," Dr. Robinson said.

They protested their soberness, like every drunk in the world not wanting to admit that they were three sheets to the wind. "We're not drunk. Not at all. We can handle our liquor!"

"You'll get a DUI and spend the night in jail. Or worse, you'll drive off the road and kill yourselves or someone else." Dr. Robinson said he'd drive their car home.

They didn't protest for long. Sue 2 handed over the keys. Then she crawled into the back seat. She put her head against the window and fell asleep.

Finley volunteered to drive the van back to campus.

"You got a valid driver's license? You sober? You're not too tired?" Dr. Robinson went through his list of questions quickly, not even giving Finley time to answer. Eventually, he handed Finley the keys.

The guys complained even before we had left the wildlife refuge parking lot. We were going to miss the Sunday meal at the dorms. They served a lunch/dinner combination until 4 p.m., then shut down until Monday morning. The Crusoes, who were always hungry, said they were starving.

Finley said he'd stop at a place he knew. "It's called the Crossroads."

"As long as you don't take us down to Escanaba," Pete said.

"You wish," Finley said.

"Been to that pit hole," someone said. "Never want to go back."

"On a summer's day? No better place in the world."

"You gotta get out more. At least get to Wisconsin."

I was sitting in the way back between Jon and Charlie. There wasn't a lot of room, and I was aware how close we were sitting to each other. Jon's leg pressed against mine. He shifted, trying to get comfortable.

"Sorry, "I said.

Something moved, a dark shadow coming from the middle row. It went to the front, then seemed to come to the back. It was a bird flying in the van. That's what it looked like.

Everyone acted like we were being attacked—screaming and flailing arms. Finley screamed at everyone to settle down, like he was our father and we were fighting in the back seat.

It wasn't real. It was stuffed. The Canada Goose from the taxidermy table. No one confessed to taking it, but one of them had. That woman would go crazy when she discovered it was gone. There really had been too many of us.

"Do we have any homework?" Jon asked.

I thought he was talking to Charlie, but he dropped his hand to my neck. Like an electric shock, I tried to turn, but we were packed in, and it was hard to turn to look at him.

"We're in the same soc class," Jon said.

"I don't think so," I said. I would have known if one of the Crusoes was in one of my other classes. I wouldn't have missed something like that.

"I never go," he said. "It's too early." He put his arm across the back of the seat. "Almost never. I've been a few times. I get the notes from a girl in my dorm. But I saw you there once. You sit in the first row."

It was a large lecture class—maybe fifty students in a big auditorium. The teacher was a bit dry. He lectured, speaking in a low voice, so I sat up front to avoid falling asleep. Most of the other students slept.

"What was that crap he was talking about the other day?" he asked. "About the Three Stooges?" Jon asked.

I knew exactly what he was talking about. It was the most interesting moment of the class so far. "Dr. Barnes thinks there's only one difference between men and women."

"That's it," Jon said. "He said there's only one difference between men and women."

That got everyone's attention. They stopped playing with the stuffed goose, and the van quieted.

"Has he ever seen any women?"

"Doesn't sound like he's ever talked to any."

They bombarded me with their thoughts. Jon put his fingers in his mouth and whistled, an ear shattering noise to get everyone to shut up. Instead, they began to complain about their eardrums being damaged.

"Hey, I'm driving!" Finley yelled. "Shut the fuck up."

"Is that what you call it?" Charlie shouted.

Jon elbowed me. "Tell us," he said.

"As far as this professor is concerned, there's only one difference between men and women," I said. "He says men love the Three Stooges, and women think they're stupid."

The van went silent. I could feel them anticipating a punch line, but that was it. I had thought it was a joke when the professor said it too.

"That's his big secret?" Charlie asked. "The Three Stooges?"

"I don't know if it was a secret," I said. "He said it in front of the whole class."

The guys thought it sounded ridiculous. Charlie said he had never heard anything so stupid.

"Sounds like a nutjob," someone said. "Is he an easy grader? I should have taken that class."

He wasn't. In fact, he was just the opposite, which had made it so funny when he said that he had reduced all the differences between males and females to this one thing. He called it his amazing discovery of the sexes.

"The Stooges are great."

"I think they're stupid," I said.

No one heard, so I said it again.

"No, you don't," someone said.

"Yes, I do."

"Then you haven't watched enough of them."

"Or I'm female," I said.

That got a laugh from someone in the second row.

After the professor told us his thoughts about men and women, I did a bit of research on my own. Nothing formal. I asked the girls in my dorm and then asked some of the guys in my French class when Madame was late one morning. The French-Canadian hockey players didn't know who they were, but the other guys in the class loved them. None of the girls I talked to liked them even a little.

"Is that what we're debating?" Jon asked. "Whether or not Molly's female?"

He put his face up against mine. I could feel the prickly hair on his chin. Then I felt his tongue on my cheek. He licked me.

"She's a girl alright," Jon said.

It was a strange thing to do, but it jolted me, and I felt the buzz of desire race through my body. I wanted him to do it again.

I waited, holding my breath, feeling that strange warmth in my stomach. It wasn't specific. It was wanting that surprise touch again.

He didn't.

Then we were there.

It was a one-story, long, low building that looked industrial. The neon *OPEN* sign was lit. Steady red. The parking lot was big enough for fifty cars, but there were only two. The van made three.

It was not a popular place, so I wasn't sure why Finley had picked it. It looked like it had closed long ago, like the sign was a prank and we would find nothing inside but spiderwebs and dust.

The bar was one large room. A long bar on one side and then an even larger room with tables and chairs—so many but all empty. The bartender knew Finley. They shook hands—a grown-up thing to do.

"You boys here to eat?"

I guess he didn't see me.

"It's going to take me a minute to fire up the grill."

It wasn't the sort of place that had a menu. There were burgers and fries, and that was about it. He had cheese but nothing else to put it on.

He poured out a few pitchers, then disappeared into the kitchen.

I asked Finley how he knew the place. I figured there was a moratorium on the no-questions request from earlier in the day.

There were baskets of peanuts on the bar. The guys dove in, cracking open the shells and tossing them on the ground, joining others that hadn't been swept up from the night before. There was a jukebox along one side, and I went over to see the selections. I put in some quarters but couldn't find anything I wanted to hear. They had old Elvis songs, Chuck Berry, Motown.

Pete came over, and I told him to choose. He punched in some Beatles. The speakers weren't great, and the room was too vast to hear anything. It was noise.

A woman walked out of the bathroom. I hadn't seen her go in, so she had been in there for a while. She wore a Northern sweatshirt—green with gold trim—and jeans. She walked over to the corner at the end of the bar, a few feet from where I was drinking my beer. I was curious. She had some things set up on a bar stool there: an empty glass, a cassette player.

She stood looking around the bar like she was going to do something, then crossed over to the jukebox and pulled the plug. Back in her spot, she pushed on her cassette player. A song played. It was too early for Christmas carols, but that's what it sounded like. Instrumental, no lyrics, not something you would dance to—there wasn't any real beat.

I cracked a peanut but tossed out the insides and put the shell in my mouth. It was all salt. I watched. The others hadn't noticed. Not yet.

She started moving her hips as if the song had a good beat, when there wasn't one at all.

"Oh my god," I said. I couldn't help it.

She was taking off her clothes.

Finley came over. "Don't stare," he said.

"I'm not staring."

"You are too," he said.

So what if I was? That's why she was there. So that we would watch her dance, so that we would watch her take off her clothes.

She was not an attractive woman. Her hair was brown or, rather, brownish, a grown-out perm where the curls had loosened into frizz.

The guys were talking, eating peanuts, and playing pool. Without the jangle of the jukebox, the bar got quiet, and they might have noticed that first. Then they saw. She had her sweatshirt off. She was moving her hips back and forth. Her bra was off-white, the band thick for support.

She took off her jeans after a bit of a struggle. She turned them inside out at the ankles, using one foot to step on the legs and then pulling them off like that. She moved around in her underwear and her white athletic socks. The bar floor had to be cold. It was hard to look.

I did.

The bra was off. Her breasts were cowlike—so heavy, the nipples dark and pimply. She stood in one spot and shook them—back and forth, back and forth. Another minute and she stopped the cassette player in the middle of the next song. She turned her back to us and put on her clothes. Right there in front of everyone. She dressed slowly, like she was bored, like she had all the time in the world. Once dressed, she went to the end of the bar and lit a cigarette. She drank Coke from a can. Five cents if you recycled it.

She went to the bathroom, and I relaxed. Several minutes later, she was back.

Back to her corner, she flicked on the cassette player, and "Dream Weaver" started up again, those same notes. She stood in her spot and moved her hips, back and forth, back and forth. Her sweatshirt went over her head.

It was all seedy and uncomfortable.

I couldn't stand it.

I went over.

"You don't have to do this," I said.

"And you don't have to be talking to me," she said. "No one asked you to open your mouth." She didn't spit at me, but she seemed close to doing just that.

"I mean, you don't have to dance for us." I said. I was being nice. I wasn't the problem. I stood there, thinking of ways to express myself. "It's just that we're a class. We've been to see the wildfires, and we got hungry." It seemed important that she know we weren't there for any other reason. I didn't think the others could hear me, and I didn't want them to.

"Get out of my face," she said.

I wasn't anywhere near her face until right then, when she put hers up to mine. She was so close I could see the cracks in her dry lips. She had put on lipstick, but instead of coloring her lips it had stuck in the dry parts, little balls of pink.

I stepped back. "I'm just saying if you don't want to, you shouldn't," I said.

She put up her hands as if she were a boxer and was going to punch me. "Are you the one writing me a paycheck?" she asked. "Are you the one giving me tips? No, I didn't think so. So now you can go fuck off." She jabbed her fist towards me, trying to get me to leave her alone.

I wasn't going to let her punch me. I went back to the bar. Finley came up beside me.

"You two have a nice conversation?" Finley asked.

"It was great," I said. "Very nice."

"That's funny," he said. "From here, it sounded like she was telling you to fuck off."

"Let's go," I said. The place felt grubby, and I wanted to get out.

"We can't leave without eating. That's the whole reason we came here," Finley said.

The bartender was bringing out the burgers. They were in red woven plastic baskets. He put them down in a line on the bar, one after the other. The guys pounced.

I grabbed my burger, wrapped it in a napkin. I would have to leave the fries. "I'll wait out in the van."

"Settle down," Finley said, and that got under my skin as if I were an overexcited child.

I pulled away from him.

But he held tight. "It's cold out there. Don't be an idiot."

He had a point. I was hungry. I didn't want to be cold. The guys were drinking beers. There was no telling how long I would be out there.

He was looking at me, standing too close, but at least the others couldn't hear. "What are you now? A women's libber?"

"That's not a thing," I said.

"It is," he said. "Women who are anti-men? That's a thing."

"No one said anything against any men," I said.

I had been thinking about what I was feeling in the van, sitting next to Jon, his body pressed up against mine. The way he had licked my face. That was gone. The naked dancing woman had killed that. Right then, sex seemed sordid, and I felt gross having thought about it on the drive there.

"You going to become an Amazon now?" he asked. "Complete with your man-hating diatribes?"

"What are you talking about?"

"One of your tribe women?" He was whispering but right at my face. "Running around the forests being strong women together."

"A what?" I asked.

"You know," he said. "Your one-breasted women's club? The ones who hated men. Went around with swords looking for men to kill." He was ranting, just this side of yelling at me.

"Bows and arrows."

"Does it matter what weapons they used?"

It was the reason they cut off their breasts. I thought it mattered quite a bit. Their breasts wouldn't have presented much hindrance with swords.

"They were real," I said. "I didn't make them up."

Shane must have told him. I didn't think it was something Finley would know on his own. So Shane must have been listening that night. He had repeated the facts, all the details included, exactly as I had described.

"People always get that wrong. You don't have to be anti-men to be pro-women," I said.

"You are heated up," he said. "I'll stay out of your way."

"Do that," I said.

He was allowed to be moody—let's-not-have-all-your-questions-today moody—but not me.

"You know, maybe the problem is that you've never been to a strip club before," Finley said.

For someone who was going to leave me alone, he was doing a terrible job.

"This isn't a strip club," I said.

It was a nasty, dirty bar with an old woman dancing in the corner for an old man bartender and some college kids who just wanted to eat some burgers and drink some beers because it was late Sunday afternoon and the dorm cafeteria closed early.

"You have no idea," Finley said.

"That's what you always think," I said. "That I have no idea. That I don't know anything. That I came from a different planet. So, you just go right ahead. You think what you want."

I was rattled and angry—a bad combination that made me want to lash out at anyone, but especially Finley because he was making fun of everything. I had to cross my arms to keep from hitting him.

It was time to go home. The others were done and ready to go.

We left.

I had been to a strip club before. Once, only one time, so I wasn't an expert. But I had gone for my cousin's eighteenth birthday. She had dragged me and three of her friends to a male strip club in Windsor called Pierre's.

Every guy I knew in Detroit went to a female strip club called Tracy Starrs. They almost all went on their eighteenth birthday and then talked about it all the time, like it had been life changing.

My cousin wanted to do the same thing. "Why should they have all the fun?" she asked.

Women couldn't go to Tracy Starrs. At least, I didn't think they could.

She had an even better idea.

It didn't sound like it would be any fun, but that's what she wanted, and I couldn't say no.

We drank beers on the way over, and I tried to make it fun. But I dreaded the night. We had to stop at a McDonald's to pee, and my cousin said she was already getting drunk. "Sure you want to go?" I had asked.

We cleaned the beer cans out of the car because we were going to cross the border at the tunnel. When they asked us why we were crossing into Canada, my cousin, buzzed and talkative, said we were going to visit our aunt. They asked where she lived, and I told the truth. He asked for our licenses, and I thought we were going to be turned back, but he waved us through.

It took us a few minutes to find the bar. I had been expecting something more like Las Vegas, but the club was really dark, with a string of Christmas lights—those thick multicolored bulbs—hung around the door. We got carded. It was the first time my cousin had been legal, and she told the doorman she had finally thrown away her fake ID. "This is me," she had said. Again, not something I thought he had to know.

It was all women—the first and probably only time I had been in a bar where all the customers were women. There were huge groups of women sitting at picnic tables—I had been expecting little tables for two, but the women came in gangs, all drinking pitchers of beer, being served trays of shots. The place was loud with laughter.

The guys were all French-Canadian. Most of them were trained dancers. They had costumes and routines, like a dance studio's spring recital. They came out fully dressed and danced and eventually stripped down to glow-in-the-dark G-strings. Then they were naked; you couldn't really see their genitals in the shadows. But the women howled and begged for more.

There was nothing raunchy or salacious about it. It had been fun, as if the mission was to make sure everyone had a good time. The dancers wore Barry Manilow shirts, shiny and unbuttoned, colors from the largest box of Crayola crayons—teal, azure, lime green. Some of them had elaborate headdresses.

The dancers' bodies had been sleek. Oiled. Muscular. They pointed their dancers' toes and sweated out their turns and kicks. The guys were gorgeous, mostly gay—maybe all.

My cousin wanted a lap dance. The guy took her to a dark corner of the room, where he caressed her face and told her she was beautiful. "You're going to make someone very happy one day." She cried. He told her he had never seen such gorgeous tears. Her friends and I were standing nearby, hidden in the shadows. We heard the whole lap dance. I wanted to cry too. It was that sweet.

I think that's why I told the woman to stop dancing: The old cassette player, the tinny speakers, the corner where she had been dancing with the overhead fluorescent light. The white crew socks, the way she danced; it was like she couldn't hear the music or didn't know how to move to it with any rhythm, almost as if fighting it. It was the exact opposite of the club I had been to in Windsor. It was about as far from that as you could get.

She wasn't having any fun. She wasn't the least bit sexy. I don't know what the guys thought, but they had stood and watched.

Looking at her had made me feel pathetic. She had nothing to do with sex or desire. I wanted the guys to know this.

She made me feel that the world was a sad place, and I felt like I was the only one who felt that way. She made me think that life wasn't fair and that romance and love weren't important to many people. It wasn't nice. It wasn't even something you could make fun of.

It had made my skin crawl to watch her.

The difference between men and women.

16

The snow started that night. In memory, it ended a few months later, falling from the sky like it never meant to stop. Ever.

It was my first Lake Superior snowstorm—strong and complete—the winds coming in quickly across the open waters from Canada. Everything was covered in white, most things covered in layers and layers of white.

I couldn't sleep. I sat at the end of my bed and watched the storm. Hours passed.

Janet was breathing heavily, snoring but nothing that loud. It was just her presence—being so close to someone who I didn't care about—was getting on my nerves.

The day before—the afternoon at the refuge, then the few hours at the Crossroads, the drunk drive with the Sues—had me rattled. The whole day had seemed off. From the start.

I wanted to go back to the parking lot of the Crossroads and make us drive somewhere else. It wasn't the only bar in the UP that served frozen fries and hamburgers on a Sunday afternoon. There had to be dozens. I especially wanted not to have seen the woman dancing in the shadowy corners of that dingy place. Most of all, I wanted never to have spoken to her. I wanted a time machine to take me back to yesterday morning, restart the whole day.

I wanted to go back to the Seney Wildlife Refuge and talk to Dr. Robinson and not say stupid things about poetry. I wanted him to think I was smarter than I had seemed. I wanted to tell him that all the things he told us were better than poetry. The things he said mattered more than lines in a book.

I wanted to live up to his standards. To be a real steward of the world. That's what I wanted more than anything else. I did not have his telephone number, but in the agitated state I was in, I would have called him and asked how I could change. I wanted to do better. I wanted things to be better.

I had a purpose. I just didn't know how to realize it.

I burned with the sense that I was letting time go by. That I wasn't doing enough. I was wasting my time in bed, fighting with Janet, walking around waiting for someone to tell me what time to be at the protest, only to discover that it had been canceled due to lack of interest. The world was going to end if I didn't do something. The destruction we had seen at the refuge was my warning. I had to act, and I had to act fast. Enough sitting around.

I wanted to start connecting what belonged together. The dying planet, the sleazy bar, Dr. Robinson, the Crusoes. The pieces of my life. I needed to bring them together. It was up to me. I had to do it.

The snow fell.

I got out of bed as soon as the sky moved from black to gray. I dressed, in the same clothes from the day before, the ones piled at the end of my bed. I found a hat, gloves, a scarf. They were dry, and I wrapped up, ready to brace the cold day.

There's a silence after a snowstorm. As if the snow has stunned the animals and trees, as if nature needs to take a moment to adjust. That was what it was like that morning. The world felt like it was resting after an attack.

I made my way up to main campus. The evergreen trees shifted, dumping their branches clear of snow, and that fluttered about. I was the first one to move through the snow. It crunched, so heavy for something that weighed nothing when it came from the sky.

I trudged along—taking my time, making plans for what I would do next.

First Finley. I would explain why I had been so upset at the bar. He might not understand, but at least he would hear me. Next, I would ask him to tell me what was bothering him. He had been in a bad mood all that day, and I had basically ignored it. I liked Finley. He was my friend. He was nice to me. I didn't want there to be any weirdness with us.

That's where I would start. The rest I would get to later.

Campus was completely empty—no one was around. Just me and the snow crunching so loud it felt like it would wake everyone.

I walked up the campus, past the library, Jamrich Hall, past the art building and then the theater, crossed the road that made a ring around campus. No one was around. No one.

Not until I got to their dorm.

She was coming out the side door—the one by their room, the one no one used except Shane and Finley.

She stepped outside, standing right in front of me, zipping up her ski parka. She was holding onto something woolen in her mouth.

It took her a minute. She didn't see me right away.

I stood there—not putting it together. Not at first.

She looked up and saw me. If she was surprised, she didn't show it. All cool. "Virgin snow," she said. "It's fresh and beautiful. But never lasts for long."

It was pristine, the courtyard with a foot of white sugary snow. The sun started to rise over the trees. The morning clouds were leaving the sky.

"Just like women," she said.

I didn't get what she was talking about.

"Virgin women?" she said, then laughed as if she was making a joke.

I didn't find her funny.

I doubted she remembered me. I had only met her the one time, and she had been drinking wine. Homemade wine made from wildflowers.

But she did. "I know you," she said.

She had met me; we had talked. She hadn't been that interested in me.

"But I can't remember from where," she said. The woolen thing was a gray cap. She put it on, pulling it over her ears.

"I'm in his class," I said. Then, just to make sure she knew who I meant, I clarified. "Dr. Robinson's."

Her lips were thin, but she could make a large smirk. "You're in his class?" she asked.

"Yes," I said.

"You're in his class?"

I thought we had established that.

"Of course you are. Isn't everybody in this godforsaken hellhole?"

The class was full, and there was always a waitlist of students who wanted to get in, but there was a cap because of the field trips—only so many people could fit in the van. Dr. Robinson couldn't allow everyone in who wanted to take it each semester. We were a select number—mostly majors.

"Not everyone," I said. "Not by a long shot."

"He's not normal," she said. "Don't ever make the mistake of thinking he is. It's not right to care so much about trees and animals. He doesn't need people. He only cares about the planet. Everything on it except for human beings."

She said the word with contempt. She seemed drunk—too loud for so early in the morning, and she kept running her tongue over her lips as if trying to get at something that wasn't there.

"He spends days watching bears and beavers have sex," she said. "That's what he cares about. The dating rituals of the animals that live in these woods."

I think she got that wrong. Animals didn't date. They mated but didn't have relationships.

"So you tell me. Who cares if it's an evergreen or a pine tree?"

She definitely got that wrong.

"A pine is an evergreen," I said.

"Oh my god," she said.

I knew we weren't really talking about tree identification, but I thought I'd set her straight. At least for future reference, so she wouldn't sound stupid. I was a Crusoe. I could imitate the lecture style of Dr. Robinson with the best of them.

"It's like asking the difference between a dog and a poodle," I said. "Most evergreens are conifers. The conifers include the blue spruce, the hemlocks, your red cedars, and pine trees."

"And that matters?" she asked.

"When you are on a farm, do you want to call everything an animal?" I asked. "A chicken, a horse, a cow, and a goat. They are all animals. Most people want to make some sort of distinction."

"More like a funny farm," she said.

"You have a variety," I said. "Out at your house. You have variety of conifers. Several kinds, in fact. I bet by now I could identify all of them. When I was there, I was still learning, but I know my trees now."

"It's a loony bin up here," she said. "I live in the middle of an insane asylum."

I watched her walk down the path, through the unplowed snow—it was a bit of a struggle to stay upright—and disappear around the corner of the student center.

I stood there, in the snow that I had ruined with my footsteps.

I had a hundred thoughts, everything coming to me, all at once. My head was a mess. Maybe Dr. Robinson's wife had been an apparition, something

I had made up. Maybe she had not been there at all. Maybe it was all in my head.

I could feel my cheeks tingle with cold. It was time for answers.

I went inside.

The room to the left was their TV room, even though there was no TV. It had been stolen the first week of the semester. The RA posted a note on all their doors: *BEWARE! I will start searching your rooms. Every room will be checked! I will find it, and you will be in BIG trouble.* There had never been any room searches, and Finley thought the RA had taken it himself and was only blaming them to deflect. Either way, there was no TV.

I looked in and saw Finley's hat on the table, his mukluks next to the couch. He was sleeping on the couch, under a sleeping bag, dead to the world. His socks were on the low table, next to his green parka. The fake fur collar was turned up, looking like a sleeping fox.

There was a paperback book open near his feet. It was Jack London stories, which he told me he had loved as a kid. I guessed he was rereading it.

I moved the book and sat down.

My thoughts had gone haywire. I couldn't even think them. My head was in complete chaos.

I put my hand on Finley's leg and pressed down as hard as I could. He woke at once.

He looked at me, without understanding. He looked around the room, then sat up, curling his legs under him as if to get away from me. "Molly," he said. "Jesus Christ."

The room was overheated, the radiators blasting hot air. I unzipped my ski parka, pulled off my hat and mittens.

"What?" he said. "What are you doing? What's wrong?"

"Tell me," I said.

He sat up, swung his legs around. He was dressed: pants, white fisherman's sweater—the one he had been wearing for weeks now.

"Jesus, how long have you been sitting there? What time is it? What are you doing here?"

"Tell me," I said again.

"You scared the shit out of me," he said. "Heart attacks run in my family."

"Can you hear me?" I asked. "When I talk, am I making sound?"

"I can hear you," he said. "You shouldn't talk so loud. You're going to wake the whole floor."

"Let's not have all your questions today," I said. "Don't speak unless you're giving me answers. One after the other."

I was on the precipice of some real destruction, like I wanted to throw something across the room. I wanted to rip his face off. I strained to control myself.

There were two or three bright orange milk crates in the corner. They were turned on their sides like bookshelves and were stuffed with clothes, shoes, books. I went over and picked up Finley's graph notebook, the one we all used for ecology. I flipped it open. He was a terrible notetaker. He drew in the margins, submarines and birds. Pictures instead of words, like he had listened to entirely different lectures. I tossed it back on top of the pile of crap.

"You've given up your room and moved in here?" I asked.

The room smelled like his dorm room—pot and Glade, socks and perspiration.

He told me to be quiet, which was not something I was going to do.

"You're living in the lounge?" I asked. "Is that why you're never around when I call your room?"

"Shut it," he said. "Don't talk." He put his hand up in front of my face.

"I saw her," I said. "I even talked to her. So don't try lying."

"Oh shit," he said. "Shit, shit, shit."

"I know," I said.

He grabbed my arm and pinched his fingers into my skin until it hurt. "Don't say another word. I don't want anyone to hear us."

He went down the hall to the bathroom, coming back with a toothbrush in his mouth. He picked through the piles of clothes in the corner, then spit the toothpaste into a towel.

"That's gross," I said.

He put on his boots, searched through the stuff on the couch until he found his coat. "Let's go," he said.

"I don't want to go anywhere," I said. It was cold. There was too much snow. "I want you to tell me what's going on."

"Come on," he said. "I don't want anyone to see you here."

"I'm not the problem," I said.

He walked out, giving me no choice but to follow.

We used a broom to clean off his car. There was more than a foot of snow on top. The more we worked, the angrier I got.

Campus was coming awake—not students but others. A giant snowplow came through, moving the snow from the road to mini hills on either side of the road. Two or three cars went by, driving slowly, then several cross-country skiers, skiing quickly over the fresh snow.

After all that work clearing the car, it wouldn't start. We had to push-start it to get it going. It had happened before, so I knew what to do. Finley would push from behind while I held the steering wheel. Once the engine turned over, I would put it into second gear. That morning, I wanted to do something physical, so I told Finley I'd push. The car wasn't that heavy. You only had to get it rolling to get it going.

It didn't take long.

I ran alongside the car, he slowed, then when I had hold of the door frame, I jumped into the passenger seat.

"Tell me," I said.

"Give me a minute," he said, though he wasn't the one out of breath.

"Unless you're wearing a wire, no one can hear us," I said.

"It's morning, Molly," he said. "This whole thing has fucked me up, so maybe you could just cool it for a minute while I try and wake up."

"It's got you fucked up?" I asked.

One thing after another, things that were hard to believe.

"I mean it," he said. "Not another word."

He stopped at the diner downtown and got two cups of coffee and some Danishes. I had to balance everything between the dashboard and the door, trying not to spill.

We drove up the hill, out of town.

"How long has it been going on?" I asked.

Dr. Robinson's wife and Shane. It was unbelievable.

Silence.

"Start there," I said.

He pulled over. There was a scenic overlook directly across from the prison. The parking lot was on the far side of the gift shop. He pulled the car in so that we were facing Marquette across the bay, the best view of the city. You could see the iron ore docks and the hills dotted with houses, the church spires, the buildings downtown.

"No one was supposed to know," he said.

"Then what was she doing in the dorm?"

"No one there knows who she is," he said. "Just another one of Shane's conquests."

That sounded horrible. I handed him one of the coffees and drank mine.

It was hot and tasteless. Without sugar or milk, it was like drinking a big cup of dirty hot water.

"I can't tell you much," he said. "I made a promise to Shane."

The last person in the world I cared about was Shane Lebarre. "Why would you promise him anything?"

"He's not a bad guy," Finley said. "No matter what you think."

"He's a creep who's sleeping with your professor's wife." I cared about Dr. Robinson. My compassion was limited to him in this situation.

"He's still my friend."

It wasn't like they were lifelong friends. They had known each other before the start of the semester, but Finley's loyalty bordered on irrational.

I ate some of the Danish. Finley had wrapped it in a napkin, which had stuck to the sticky parts on top. I ate around the napkin bits, or tried to, but I could taste paper. It wasn't much, so I just swallowed everything.

My world was all distorted and nonsensical now.

"Who comes to someone's dorm at 6 in the morning?" Finley asked.

"It was 7," I said.

Shane was gross, and the whole thing made me sick.

I hit Finley. I didn't know what else to do. I punched his arm. He pulled back as far as he could go, but we were in a car and I could easily get to him.

"You've ruined everything," I said.

"I haven't done a thing."

"But you should have."

"Done what?" he shouted at me. "What should I have done?"

"You should have stopped him," I said. "Now it's just as much your fault as his."

"That doesn't make any normal person sense."

"You know it's wrong," I said.

I wanted to say more, but I was lost in my own misery. I thought of Keith and how he had slept with the art teacher and how I felt the same kind of rage. People did something so wrong and yet thought they could get away with it.

There was someone at my window. A huge face, pressed right up to the window, their mouth on the glass, their eyes peering in. It was a woman, and she was knocking on the glass.

I tried to roll down the window. It was stuck and took me a few turns. Her face loomed into the car.

"I just wanted to tell you that the gift shop is open," she said.

"What?" I asked. I blew my nose into my mitten, then shoved it into my coat pocket.

"I saw you parked here when I walked in and assumed you were waiting for us to open?"

I wanted her to go away, to get out of our business. I started to roll up the window to get rid of her big face, but I wasn't rude like that. "Thank you," I said.

Her name tag, pinned just below her collar, was blank, as if she didn't have one or had forgotten it.

"Lots of nice things," she told us. "Souvenirs you'll like." With that, she went away.

Finley had his head down on the steering wheel. I took several deep breaths and got control of my tears. The headache was immediate.

Finley sat up. "I don't control Shane. I'm not his mother. I'm not in charge of him. Girls fall in love with him. I told you that. In fact, I think I said it several times. You just don't listen."

"Oh stop," I said. "He's not some rock star."

"You don't know," Finley said. "It's like they're all under his spell."

Shane was not that special.

"That's bullshit," I said.

"You should know," Finley said.

He had to be kidding. Either that or out of his mind. "I was never under any spell. I kissed him."

"Which proves my point."

"We had come from a party. We were drinking. I would have kissed the man in the moon."

"That's just you," he said, dismissing me like I was the annoying one.

"That's a lot of people," I said. "You ever notice that in the morning in the cafeteria when everyone's drinking coffee and eating cereal, there's not a lot of making out going on? But go to a party, add some spiked punch, and suddenly everyone's got their tongues down each other's throats? Let's see why that is."

"Oh, shut up," Finley said. "Can you? Can you ever just shut up?"

I didn't think my talking too much was the problem we were dealing with. "What does Dr. Robinson think?"

Finley didn't answer, as if this would make me shut up. I asked again.

"He doesn't know."

"What do you mean, 'He doesn't know'? He must. He's not stupid."

I thought back to the afternoon in the hospital after the midterm exam. He had said something about Shane. I remembered. I wasn't sure if it had been going on then? Could it have started before then? I thought back to yesterday at the Seney Wildlife Refuge: Dr. Robinson asking where Shane was. He definitely knew something. And the talk about love and poetry. It must have been connected.

"He might know that his wife is cheating, but he doesn't know she's cheating with Shane," Finley said. "I guess she wanders a bit."

"Having sex with a college kid isn't wandering anywhere. It's just gross. It's awful." I got stuck on that word because suddenly it seemed exactly what I wanted to say about everything. Everything was awful.

Shane was going to ruin everything. The whole semester. The Crusoes. The field trips, our mission to be stewards of the planet. All of it would be ruined. Secrets about sex never stayed secret for long, and everything would blow up.

Dr. Robinson might kill Shane when he discovered the truth. That was a possibility.

My mind was going too fast. It wasn't smart to think like that. I ranted some more. It didn't help, but I had to get it all out of my head.

"Stop talking. Stop making everything into a soap opera," Finley said. "I can't handle you freaking out. Besides, it's over."

"What?" I asked.

He made it sound like they were dead.

"They're not seeing each other anymore."

"Since when?"

It was 9 a.m. She had left his dorm room two hours ago.

"Shane promised," Finley said. "That was it. The last time."

That seemed about as far-fetched as anything that had happened.

"And you believe him?" I asked.

"I do," Finley said. "He knows it's dangerous. And he swore this would be the last time he was going to see her."

"What does he have on you?"

"Why do you think you know everything?"

"He must have something. You act like you're afraid of him. Like he's made a deal with you."

A deal with the devil, an evil sort. That's what I thought: just bad news, all around. Though he bragged about women falling in love with him, I didn't see the attraction. He was the least likable person I knew. Compared to any of the other guys, he was boring and mean. Mostly mean but not at all interesting either.

"Leave me alone."

"Is it because of the CIA?"

"I should never have told you that."

"But you did, so now I know, and you can tell me the truth for once."

"Shane was in the service."

"I know that. We all know that."

So do you ever think that maybe he knows something about the U.S. government?"

"No," I said. "I don't. I don't think he knows anything about anything. Not anything important."

"You always act like you know everything," he said.

"Are you in love with him?" I asked. "Is that it? I could understand that."

"I'm not talking to you. Not when you're being like this."

"Then don't," I said. "Don't talk to me. See what I care."

I had to get out of the car. I had to get away from his excuses. I had to get away from my thoughts. I wanted to throw myself into the lake, my whole body. I wanted to feel the cold, to feel nothing but cold water all over my body.

I got out and walked over to the gift shop.

The person who had come to the car was dusting the objects on the shelves. It was a long, low building, with shelves on the two long walls.

"Here we are," she said.

I felt sick—a crying headache, the horrible coffee, the sweet Danish. I felt like throwing up.

"Yes," I said. "Here I am."

"What are you looking for?"

It was odd to think that people came into a prison gift shop looking for something. I said I was just looking. I looked over the packed shelves. There was a lot of driftwood, painted with brightly colored animals. Turtles and fish. Cats were a popular subject. There were small boxes made from cheap plywood. Some were painted; others were plain, simple boxes with gold locks.

Bells rang as the door opened. I didn't have to look over to know that it was Finley.

"You coming?" he asked.

I picked up a flat, black rock. *Marquette*, in bright yellow paint, was written in script. It cost a dollar, and the proceeds went to help fund the prison's softball team.

We left.

Overhead, two planes flying in formation moved across the sky. They were from the Air Force base. A commercial jet would have been slower and would not have flown so close to another plane. The things I had learned since coming to Marquette. Then suddenly, that sound—the one I hated. The boom of them breaking the sound barrier.

The shattering crack of noise. I could feel it move through my body. Always frightening, always made me think that something was wrong: this time, that was true. I leaned over behind the car and threw up everything I had put in my stomach that morning. Then, just bile.

I went back to the dorm and slept the rest of the day.

17

I went to the bar that night. By myself. I wanted to be alone. I went up to Third Street and went into the first place I saw, an Italian restaurant. I sat at the far end of the bar, away from the door, so I wouldn't be cold if I took off my coat. The hostess seemed confused and came over a few times to ask if I was joining a party in the restaurant.

I ordered a vodka gimlet because I heard the waitress order one for a customer. I could see myself in the mirror behind the bar. It seemed a funny thing to do, watch yourself drink—watching yourself get drunk.

I didn't look bad, but that's how I felt. Like I had done something wrong.

I thought about my purpose, something that had fallen by the wayside. I needed to change that, to be more active. I wanted to be smarter, to know more about the world I lived in. If ELF was really dangerous for the region, I should know why. I didn't like being in the dark, feeling helpless, feeling like I was just going through the motions. Right then, I was definitely feeling the vodka.

A bit later, the place got more crowded, which made me feel better; there was more to distract me from my overthinking. The bartender, who had been talking to me, got busy. The lights had dimmed, and I couldn't see my reflection that clearly anymore.

I went home.

Janet was waiting for me, looming inside the door. She scared me.

"Your friend's been here," she said.

I didn't want any friends that night. "Thanks," I said.

I didn't have to ask. It was Finley. That week, he seemed to be the only friend who ever came around.

"I'm going to bed," she said. She had showered. She used baby powder, leaving white streaks on her dark towels.

I didn't like the smell, but she put it on every time she showered.

"Good night," I said.

We didn't usually give such detailed accounts of our movements while in the room together.

"I think he's still here," she said. "I saw him. He's in the TV room talking to some girls."

"It's okay," I said. It would be better for me if she would stop talking.

"How?" she asked.

"What?" I asked. I wanted the world to be quiet, for everything just to go away. But it wouldn't. I closed my eyes and tried to make Janet disappear. I didn't care where she went; I just wanted her gone.

"How is it going to be okay?"

"He'll go away eventually. Just ignore him. That's what I'm going to do."

I took off my boots and got in bed with all my clothes on.

I closed my eyes and willed sleep to come to my room. I was impatient, which never helps when you're trying to drift off.

Finley walked in. Our suitemates had let him in, and then he came through the bathroom.

"Get out," Janet said.

She never bothered trying to be nice, never cared about hiding her feelings. That night I didn't care. I was tired of Finley. Tired of the whole thing. I pulled the pillow over my head but could still hear everything.

"I just want to talk to Molly," Finley said. "It won't take long."

Janet stood, not at all happy, and went to the bathroom. She locked the door. She turned on the faucet, most likely brushing her teeth again. She did that when she got frustrated. She had very clean teeth.

"What?" I said.

"Where have you been?"

"Why?"

"Just checking," he said.

"On what?"

"I wanted to make sure you're alright."

"I am," I said. "Go away."

"Tell me where you went, and I'll go away."

"I went out," I said.

He didn't look good. He hadn't shaved, which on some guys might look good. On Finley it looked like he hadn't washed his face. His little hairs were gray and shadowed around his chin.

"With the guys?" he asked. "Which ones? Pete? Charlie? Jon?" He went through the list of Crusoes.

"I have other friends."

"Who?"

"Friends you don't know," I said.

"No, you don't," he said.

He was right. I didn't have any other friends. But that seemed wrong. I told myself to start making new ones. Anyone. Anyone who didn't know Dr. Robinson or Shane or anything about rocks and plants and the marine life of Lake Superior. Someone who cared about happy hour and smoking pot. I was going to find a whole new group of people to hang out with. I had been limiting myself. There were other people on campus. It was time I got to know them.

"I went to the bar," I said.

"Which one?"

"The one on Third Street," I said.

"There are twenty bars on Third Street."

That seemed an exaggeration.

"The Italian one," I said.

"Father's?" he asked.

It seemed like an odd name for an Italian restaurant, but I wasn't going to argue. It didn't matter where I had been, not to Finley. He had no right to ask me questions, not now. Not after what he had done.

"I had two vodka and lime juices. I talked to the bartender who told me that he grew up next to a cranberry farm in the lower peninsula. He hates the taste of cranberries and thinks he may even be allergic. He can eat oranges and apples but not cranberries. He offered to buy me another drink, but I said no because it was getting crowded and I didn't have anyone but him to talk to and he got busy, and I left. I walked back. I was a bit buzzed, so I didn't really notice how cold it was, but it was cold."

Finley's face was next to mine. I could smell his breath. It wasn't bad. It was just his.

"That's all?" he asked.

I thought that was a lot. It had been more interesting in the retelling—a boring night, but I had passed the time. There had even been moments when I had not thought about Shane or Dr. Robinson or his stupid wife—not many, but there had been some.

"And you're okay?"

"I'm the same as I always am."

Janet was back. She stood in the doorway of the bathroom and coughed. A long, continuous eruption of noise. I sat up and flicked off the light. I didn't wait for her to start her complaining. That was enough conversation for one night.

"I'm going to bed. He's going to leave," I said.

Finley zipped his coat. His red knit cap went in his mouth while he pulled on his gloves. He went to the door, no *good night* for me or for Janet.

"Hey Finley," I said. "Are you still thinking of getting a dog?"

"It's all I ever think about," he said.

I was glad to hear that. But it couldn't possibly be true.

18

I was nervous to go back to class, knowing what I did. I dreaded seeing Dr. Robinson. I thought he would take one look at me and know that I hadn't lived up to his expectations. He would think me a disappointment. That's how I felt, like I was the one who had made this trouble. I felt, and was therefore acting, guilty.

I had told Finley to wait for me in front of the library and walk in with me.

"What's that going to do?" he asked.

"I'm afraid I'm going to break down and tell Dr. Robinson," I said.

"You can't act all crazy-like," he said. "If you do, he'll know something is up."

I wanted to go back in time, snap my fingers and go back to the start of the year so I could get rid of Shane or even go back to when I didn't know him. Ignorance was better. So much better.

We ran into Jon and Pete walking across campus. The four of us walked into the building together.

"Do you guys believe in ghosts?" Jon asked.

"Not this again," Pete said. "You're an annoying broken record."

"I believe," Jon said. "I don't see why you have such a problem with that."

"I don't believe in all that shit," Finley said. "It's you. Being afraid of everything."

"No one does," Pete said. "Except you, so shut it."

"Molly?" Jon asked.

We were at the classroom. I saw Shane sitting at the table. It was where he usually sat, but I noticed for the first time that it was the furthest place you could be from where Dr. Robinson stood. I guessed now that it was on purpose.

"I'm not sure," I said.

"I'll take that as a yes," Jon said. "See?"

"It was a maybe, at best," Pete said.

"What about your grandmother?" I asked. "I thought you were going to introduce me to her."

"She's dead and in heaven," he said. "She's not a ghost."

"Sorry," I said.

The Crusoes loved to talk. They had their stories, and Jon had one that morning about his hike on Saturday.

"Early in the morning. Over near Wetmore's Landing." He had hitch-hiked out. He went by himself. It was a great walk. He saw a wolf. "Then I saw something strange."

We took off our coats and piled them on the hooks by the door. The guys took off their boots. I kept mine on. I didn't like to sit in class wearing my socks. That was too casual.

Jon was still talking. "It was all wispy-like. Like thick, thick smoke. It was a ghost, I'm sure of it."

"Did it go *boo*?" Pete asked. "Boo!"

The other guys looked over.

"It might have," Jon said. "I was so scared. I ran like hell back to the road. Just about had a heart attack when I got there and put out my thumb. I thought she'd come after me."

"It was a woman?" I asked.

"I think it was," Jon said. "It seemed female."

"You watch too much TV," Pete said.

This was the way they talked. Normally, I found it fascinating. That day, it made me nervous. It felt like endless bickering.

"I never watch it," Jon said.

"Then you should start," Pete said. "And stop with the ghost stories."

"See, you're scared too," Jon said.

"You're an asshole," Pete said.

"Maybe," Jon said. "Doesn't mean there aren't ghosts out there."

All that seemed normal enough. Typical Crusoe behavior. Jon had told me before that he had seen ghosts. They were always kidding him about it. I thought it was sweet. There was something old-fashioned about seeing a ghost in the woods.

I told him I believed that he had seen something. "Next time, I'll come with you," I said. "I want to see what you see."

"I want you to see it too."

Dr. Robinson came in and went right to the board. Trying not to be too obvious, I watched him. He began writing, putting terms and statistics on the board.

He turned, said hello, wiping the chalk dust down both sides of his navy sweater. That was normal; he was always doing that. But I felt a frisson of tension. Something seemed off-balance. I found that I was holding my breath. It made me dizzy, and I let it go and tried to relax.

He took out his notes, asked if we were ready. He started the lecture.

We were studying Lake Superior.

Limnology Dr. Robinson wrote on the board. Then he explained that no, it was not the study of tropical fruits, of limes and lemons, but the scientific study of inland aquatics and ecosystems. We were going to focus our studies on the biological, chemical, and physical geological characteristics and functions of Lake Superior.

"The largest freshwater lake in this hemisphere, the most beautiful body of water on the entire planet. Truly superior," Dr. Robinson said.

I was on high alert throughout the lecture. Every time Dr. Robinson said something, I felt like I was going to jump out of my skin, but he kept on.

Then he gave us the data—numbers we recorded in our graph notebooks: Lake Superior was 31,700 feet at the deepest point; there were 78 different species of fish. 350 shipwrecks—10,000 dead. And 300 streams and rivers empty into Superior. Then fun facts, like that Lake Superior contained as much water as all the other Great Lakes combined plus three extra Lake Eries. Superior held so much water that it could cover the entire land mass of both North and South America with 12 inches of water.

"That's amazing," Pete said.

"That's Superior," Dr. Robinson said.

We learned that dead bodies normally come to the surface once they've drowned in lake waters. Bacteria will bloat a body with gas, causing it to float to the water's surface. But Lake Superior is too cold and doesn't allow for any bacteria growth. Dead bodies in Superior sink to the bottom and rarely surface.

It seemed like he was talking to Shane. I thought it might even be a warning. I watched Shane when I was sure no one was looking at me. He was the only one not taking notes. And once I started thinking that, I couldn't stop. I forced myself to stop watching him.

"Long, cold winters bring whale sightings once spring comes. The waters are cold enough. It's not impossible."

"Have you ever seen one?"

"I've seen photographs," Dr. Robinson said.

"I don't believe that," Pete said. "Whales aren't found in freshwater lakes. Not unless they're really lost."

Dr. Robinson didn't argue. "There have also been shark reports. Rare ones but nonetheless."

The class laughed.

"I'm telling you what I've heard," Dr. Robinson said. "All sorts of stories about different kinds of sightings."

"Big lies," someone called out.

"Maybe," Dr. Robinson said.

No one was taking notes anymore. This was just Dr. Robinson talking and wasn't something we would get tested on.

I relaxed and spaced out for a few minutes. When I zoned back in, they were talking about boats adrift in Superior. People surviving on nothing but what they could fish out of the lake.

"It can be done in the summer months. Winter brings a whole other story."

Dr. Robinson came around the front of the conference table, and I got nervous again. I stopped listening and waited for something to happen. I was sure it would.

"It's an incredible story of survival. A tale of strength and unbelievable courage."

He was on a tangent, Lake Superior forgotten. I knew he'd return to it, but for now we had moved away from the lake.

That felt safe enough. It didn't sound like a lead into something personal. It didn't sound like he was going to start yelling at Shane, accusing Finley and me of covering things up.

"Molly?" Dr. Robinson said.

My name out of nowhere. The hairs on the back of my neck went up. I turned to see if someone had opened the window.

"Excuse me?" I asked.

"You'll be glad to know it's the story of a woman," he said.

"It is?"

I knew he suspected something. Why else was he telling us about this person at this time. I felt the sweat on my stomach. I pulled back from the table and saw my palms drenched, dragging across the dark wood.

"We don't get many of those, do we?"

I didn't trust myself to say anything more. I nodded. I didn't like him singling me out like that, though as I looked around, no one was paying me much attention. Except Finley who was staring at me with a blank expression on his face.

"Angelique Mott," he said. "Ever heard of her? Do you know who she is? It's a name that should be better known."

We learned that she was an Ojibwa who lived in the nineteenth century. She was from Sault Ste. Marie and was hired by the mining companies to help find copper in the Upper Peninsula.

I took notes furiously. I wrote everything he said, missing words but getting most of it.

Class was half over. It seemed like we had been there for days.

Then Dr. Robinson came around to the other side of the table. He pushed his papers aside and pulled up his legs. He sat cross-legged, his hands on his knees, and spoke as if telling us something he hadn't told anyone before. I didn't see the connection between copper and me. I didn't know anything about copper. Except I had a copper bracelet, a band that I wore every once in a while.

"This was during the copper boom. Copper was gold up here. It was making them rich. Everything was copper, and the world looked to the Keweenaw. They used the Ojibwa, who knew where to find the copper veins. They sent Angelique and her husband to an island in Superior one summer afternoon. Isle Royale. They dropped them off. Told them to mark where they found traces of copper. They agreed to pay them for a week or two of searching for their precious metal. Then for some reason, most likely because they didn't care enough about two Ojibwas, they left them there. Never went back to get them. No supplies, no weapons, no boat, nothing."

He waited, then finished the story.

"He died. She survived. The entire winter. Alone. With nothing."

He was speaking in his best lecture voice, low and calm, making the story seem dramatic by the way he said the words.

"Never underestimate the strength of the female," Dr. Robinson said. "She'll survive. Watch that, men."

I felt like he was trying to tell me something—like he was speaking in some kind of double-talk.

"Women are strong, gentlemen. We have to know this to appreciate it."

That's how he ended class.

"More on Lake Superior on Thursday,"

Then he was gone, all his things packed up during the lecture. He left in a hurry, as if he had somewhere else to be, the chalk dust still clinging to his sweater.

A reprieve.

Finley walked out with me. "Don't do this," he said. "Don't ruin everything. I've been keeping it together for months, and you can't start fucking things up now."

"That was weird," I said.

"It wasn't," he said.

"You heard him?"

"I saw you, scrunching up your face, staring at Dr. Robinson. You looked guilty."

I wasn't sure about that. It was just Finley overreacting.

"He was talking about women, talking about their power and their strength. He said the word courage eight times. I think he knows that I know."

"He always talks like that."

"No, he doesn't," I said. I wasn't wrong. At least I didn't think I was. "All that talk about women being so strong? You don't think he was trying to tell me something? Like giving me a secret message?"

"He told us about Angelique Mott," he said. "That had nothing to do with you. So cool your Frankenstein routine and be normal."

"Frankenstein?" I asked.

He took a few steps like a robot, not bending his legs or arms. "That's you being all strange. Just be normal."

"I am normal."

"Go back to the way you were," Finley said. "Or everyone's going to know something's going on."

"I can't," I said.

Maybe it had just been a lecture on a woman who had survived a brutal winter on Isle Royale. Isolated and alone, without help or any means to feed herself except her bare hands. I didn't think so. The story may have been true, but there was something behind his telling it to us—rather, to me—on that particular day.

I was late for French class and had not done the homework—conjugating a list of verbs into the future tense. I hadn't even started it. I'd answer everything in the present tense, which felt like something that would need to change—conditional. Some things needed time. Some things needed reflection before they could be answered. Madame was sure to disagree—the future.

19

Madame asked me to stay after class. I didn't think I had done anything wrong, but Madame and I were rarely on the same wavelength.

"How are you feeling?" She asked me in English, so she must have wanted to make sure I understood.

It felt like a trick question. Those kinds of things were usually said in French, and she expected a response of more than one word, which is what we tended to give.

I gave it a go. "Fine," I said. I smiled. That had to count for something.

"No more accidents?" she said.

"Accidents?"

"The hospital?"

That's what she was talking about. I breathed out.

"I already got the stitches out," I said.

I held up my chin, but she didn't look.

"Would you like to go for a drink?"

"What?"

"A drink?"

"With you?" I was surprised when she nodded. I looked around just to make sure this wasn't some sort of English-French prank.

Madame didn't rush my response. She was used to waiting for students to answer her questions.

"Okay," I said.

"How about tonight?" she asked. "I have a favorite place. Somewhere I like to go when I go out." She talked in English like she spoke French: fast, with no breath between words. "The Ramada Inn. Do you know where that is?"

"The hotel?"

"I guess that's what it is," Madame said. "7 p.m.? It's very private. We can talk."

I thought she was going to ask me about Dr. Robinson's wife. I was sure that's what she wanted to know. I tried to think about how to tell her that I had changed my mind. But the words didn't come. Maybe she would speak in French and I could tell her I didn't know what she was talking about, which would be true. I didn't want to talk to her about Dr. Robinson's wife.

I got there first.

The guy at the reception desk asked if I wanted a room.

"A drink," I said.

The bar was just off the small lobby. I went in. The guy followed. It seemed he was also the bartender.

The place was completely empty. No one. I had never been in a completely empty bar. The lights were too bright, and the tables and chairs were the same ones my mother had in our kitchen.

On the back wall was a painting of a tropical beach, and as you moved around the room, the trees seemed to sway—*a trompe l'oeil*. French could be useful.

"Can I get you something, or are you just going to stand here all night?"

I could see why it wasn't a popular place. He wasn't good at either of his jobs.

"I'm waiting for someone," I said.

"Okay, but I'm not going to make ice-cream drinks for you and your underage friends."

I didn't have a problem with that.

He was watching himself in the mirror behind the bar. His reflection seemed to fascinate him. Even with me there watching, he preened.

I would give her until 7:15, and then I would leave, I decided. I continued to stand, pretending to be fascinated by the scene of the beach.

Madame came rushing in about half an hour late. I had finished the bowl of pretzels. I stood. The bartender/receptionist was sleeping at the front desk, head down in his arms, not trying to hide or to disguise what he was doing,

"Let's sit in a booth where we can have some privacy," Madame said.

Maybe she didn't have the best eyesight. We had the whole bar. How much more privacy did she want—and why? The guy came to take our drink orders.

"You know what I want," Madame said.

I didn't know what to order. A beer made me seem too much like a student. And I didn't want to order vodka, in case she thought I was an alcoholic. I hesitated, and Madame suggested I try her drink. I was relieved not to have to decide.

"Sounds good," I said.

The drinks were made with ice cream, and the light in the booth made me think that they were green.

"It's called a grasshopper," Madame said.

"That's funny," I said. "Because it looks sort of green."

"It is green," she said. "That's why they call it a grasshopper."

"*Vert*," I said. I didn't know the French word for grasshopper.

The drink was delicious. Ambrosia. I remembered the word from high school literature class—it was what the Greek gods drank. I thought it would taste like that. I would have ordered ten of them, but that seemed extreme. I watched Madame sipping hers and thought I should have gone slower.

"Is everything good?" Madame asked.

"It's delicious," I said.

I held up the glass. The sides were sticky, and then my fingers were. I knew better than to lick them, though that was my first impulse. I wiped my hands down the sides of my pants, but that didn't really help.

"I meant about your life," Madame said.

I didn't quite know where to look. We were sitting across from each other; the booth wasn't that wide. Her face was right there. I could see that she wore foundation and that it was otherwise perfectly applied, but I could see where it splotched on the sides of her nose.

"I understand you're in Matt Robinson's famous ecology class?"

I was pretty sure Madame knew that already, so I didn't know what she was expecting me to say.

"It's a great class," I said. "I love it."

"More than French?" she asked.

I liked it so much more than French, but I wasn't going to say that. I started to protest.

She shook her head. "Don't mind me," she said. "I'm just having some fun."

I didn't see the fun in that, but maybe this is what happened at university. Maybe professors took you out and talked about other classes to see how they compared. Maybe there wasn't any real reason for getting together. I started to relax.

"Are you in love with him?"

I felt like she had pushed me to the edge of a cliff. I held on tight. I was so sure she was going to ask me about Shane and Dr. Robinson's wife, but she seemed clueless about that.

"I don't think it's a good idea," she said and then clarified in case I hadn't heard her the first time. "You don't want to be in love with him."

Flashback to Shane and that night after the bonfire. People telling me not to love. It was weird.

I knocked over my glass. It wasn't all my fault. The glass was top-heavy but thick. It rolled, and the leftover drink dribbled across the booth. I took my napkin and mopped it up. Then, not wanting to have a dirty napkin on the table, I shoved it into my coat pocket.

I wondered if that's what happened in the UP. People just fell in love. Maybe it was an epidemic that everyone knew about except me. Maybe it was the water. Maybe you liked your professor and thought that what he was teaching you was important and then people thought, *Oh, they must be in love.* Maybe you walked home from a party and had a stupid conversation with a guy you thought was cute, and then you fell in love even though he was an asshole. Maybe that's how love worked that far north of the forty-fifth parallel.

"Don't look at me like that," Madame said.

I was definitely not looking at her.

"You don't have to be embarrassed," she said. "You should never be embarrassed to love someone."

I felt backed into a corner, into a tight place, somewhere I did not want to be. "I'm not any of that," I said.

"You're so young," she said.

"No matter how old I am, I'm still not in love with my professor."

Madame wouldn't stop. She was like that in class, pressing us for answers, even when we said we didn't know. "A crush, then," she said. "There's nothing wrong with a harmless crush. Believe me. I've had thousands in my life."

I didn't like Madame right then. She was butting in where she didn't belong. Her nails bothered me. They were painted. Perfectly pink. Perfectly prissy. Perfectly perfect.

I shouldn't have come.

"He's a good man," Madame said. "I've known him for a long time. He's passionate and charismatic. But he's also foolish."

I was done. I reached into my back pocket and pulled out the money I had brought. A twenty dollar bill. "Can I give this to you? Thanks for having me to the bar."

"Have I upset you?"

I considered the question and went for the truth. "Yes," I said. "You have. I thought we would be talking about other things." For all I knew she was going to call me a slut next.

"Let me give you some advice," she said.

But I had learned a thing or two about advice. Especially when I didn't ask for it. I wondered if she was in love with him. Maybe that's what this was all about. She was warning me off because she wanted him for herself. Maybe I could give her some advice.

"Dr. Robinson says that the young aren't very good at taking advice," I said.

"He's right about that," she said. She took her finger and ran it around the rim of the glass, then put it into her mouth. She was a grown woman licking her fingers to finish her drink.

"He says it's not a bad thing," I said.

"That's probably where we part ways," she said.

"He says the young should be rebels," I said. "It's the only way we're going to get what we want from this world."

Madame was smiling at me. A tight pleased smile that didn't have anything to do with what we were talking about.

"He says we have to throw off the status quo, to get rid of authority that rules us. We need to clear a path to get what we want. It's the only way." I was improvising at that point. "Otherwise we're doomed. We'll fold under the powers of what has always been. We'll live in a world we don't want, with rules that aren't ours. We can't think someone else will do it. We have to do it ourselves. We must keep watch on the planet. We're like lighthouse keepers. That's what we are—the lighthouse keepers for the future."

I knew I was repeating myself. But I didn't care.

Madame tried to interrupt, but I was on a roll.

"The gift of freedom is not ours by right. It will always be a fight. There is always the struggle to achieve our destiny. We must be the keepers of the light."

My hands were on the table, and I made two fists and hit them together. I no longer knew what I was arguing. Madame grabbed my wrist.

"He's trained you well," she said.

She made me sound like a dog. I looked over her shoulder. Staring at the palm trees, seeing them sway in the wind that wasn't there.

"I'm not here to upset you," she said. "I'm sorry if you've taken this the wrong way."

She handed me back my twenty dollar bill. "It's my treat," she said.

"Thanks," I said. I was glad to get the money back. I didn't have much and didn't want to spend it all on one drink—even if it was that good.

I felt better when I was no longer sitting across from her being accused of things I wasn't feeling.

I wasn't sure I had ever been in love. It was a strong emotion, and I would let others know when I was experiencing it, rather than the other way around.

I didn't like that a female professor was trying to make me admit to something I didn't feel. A male professor wouldn't have done something like that. They wouldn't have overstepped my emotions. I think that bothered me the most. I thought she should have been more on my side. But she wasn't.

The next morning, I was late to French class. On purpose. Madame was writing on the chalkboard with her back to the class. She glanced over at me. She wore orange that day, which made her look like a flamenco dancer.

"*Et voilà, voilà. Elle est ici. Le gardienne de phare pour le futur. Notre gardienne de phare!*"

Words not in my vocabulary.

I had no idea what she was saying, but I pretended I did and smiled.

After class, I asked one of the hockey players to translate it for me. He was from Montreal but didn't know the word in English. He wrote it down, so I could look it up.

Lighthouse keeper.

She was making fun of me.

Maybe I deserved it after my outburst at the bar. But I could have made so much more trouble. Madame didn't understand that. She didn't understand me or what I knew. She had no idea.

I tried to avoid Madame after that. I sensed that she knew this and found it amusing.

She was off base, so far from the truth it wasn't worth bothering with.

THE MINING JOURNAL

Letter to the Editor—

Those protesting the installation of PROJECT
ELF think they're doing something good for the
planet, but what they're doing could get all of
us destroyed. They don't care about the future—
what could happen—but live in an idealized past.
They're like ostriches with their heads in the
sand, pretending that the world doesn't have
nuclear weapons. They can only be ignorant for
so long. But when the Russians attack, we'll all
be blown up.

Donny Kukla
Skandia, MI

20

Pete was playing with his band over at Vango's, a pizza place not far from campus. He announced the gig in class.

"If you're not doing anything, come on over. We're on first—around 8 p.m." He told us not to be too late. "I don't know how long we'll play for. There are a lot of bands."

I knew he played music but didn't know he was in a band. It sounded like fun.

"It's not rock and roll," he said. "So don't expect Bob Seger."

"You only wish," Charlie said. He had a good laugh, infectious.

I liked that he wasn't mean about making fun of the others. They all seemed to be in on the joke.

"We're just starting out," Pete said. "Who knows where we'll end up."

"Think I can make a guess," Jon said.

I told Pete I'd be there.

The other Crusoes acted like they were going even though they were ragging about having to pay for their own drinks, something Pete had made clear.

"Doc?" Pete asked Dr. Robinson, who had been standing at the board, reading through his notes.

"I just might surprise you and show up," he said and smiled.

I spent much of the class looking at Shane, who seemed tired and out of it. Dr. Robinson seemed professorial. I took both as positive signs that things might be okay—at least for now.

Finley followed me out of class. He had been doing that every day since I found out about Shane. Always the same questions. He wanted to know what I was doing. Where I was going. Who I was doing it with.

"You don't have to keep tabs on me," I said.

"I need to be careful," he said.

He was being more than that. An albatross around my neck, being around him felt heavy and depressing. He was all doom and gloom. I wanted to get away from him.

I wasn't the one he had to worry about.

"I don't think you should go to the bar to hear Pete," he said.

"Why not?" I asked.

"You might get drunk," he said.

"I might not," I said.

"You'll be in a bar," he said. "You'll have drinks. You'll start talking too much, and then you'll drink more and start wanting to kiss everyone."

He had nerve. He really did.

"You know I'm telling you the truth," Finley said. "It's what you always do." Like I was a despicable person who did terrible things. He was always quick with the put-downs.

"I'm going to go," I said. "Everyone is."

That was what he was afraid of. I wasn't going to ruin my life because Shane decided it was a good idea to sleep with the professor's wife. That wasn't on me.

"Do you expect me to stay in my room the rest of the semester?"

"It'd be easier on me if you would," he said.

He was having a rough time. I knew that, but deep down I blamed him. They were roommates and friends. He could have stopped Shane from sleeping with Dr. Robinson's wife. He should have locked him in the laundry room—he could have at least tried. But I don't think he did any of that. He indulged Shane. Anything Shane wanted, Finley thought it was okay. So this was his mess. I wasn't in it with him, and I was not going to help him clean it up. I wasn't even going to make things easier for him.

I went over to Vango's early.

I sat at an empty table. The Crusoes came and crowded around it. Jon and I shared a chair, but he kept pushing back, and I got tired of trying to hold my legs steady to keep my balance, so I gave it over. The place got so crowded they pushed the tables to the side, and then the chairs were in the way. After a while, we all just stood together, all mushed into the space.

There were three guys and a girl singer. Pete played the banjo and the harmonica; the others played guitars and dulcimers. They called themselves High Lonesome, which I thought sounded so romantic. But one of the guys said it meant being completely dead-drunk. They didn't seem like the right words to express that. They played songs I had never heard before. It was great. I had been to see rock bands in bars around Detroit, but the music was so loud you didn't really listen to it or care about the words. It was just there to get drunk to.

After a long set, they took a break, and I went to get another drink at the bar. Hot toddies were the special, one dollar until 10 p.m. The bartender told me to keep a spoon in the glass when I poured in the hot water. "It'll keep the glass from cracking." It was warm and tasted of fire—something earthy.

Finley came up. I hadn't thought he would come. But I guess he thought he had to babysit me. I held up my drink and took two or three long swallows, taunting him like a petulant child.

"They're awful," Finley said.

He had come with Shane, who stood by the door, looking bored, like he was enduring something painful instead of being at a bar with drinks and music.

"You should leave if you don't like it," I said. The tea and whiskey were making me happy.

The band started up again, and I went back to where I had been standing with the other guys. Pete held a banjo high in his arms, and he was so close to where I was standing that I could have reached out and touched him. His eyes weren't closed, and he was staring behind us, maybe beyond us.

I didn't know the songs. Some weren't in English, but the singer explained what they meant. Old Scots. She said they were about love and loss. Mostly about loss because that's what you got when you've had love.

I thought it was beautiful.

I had my winter jacket, the pockets stuffed with mittens and a hat, a long knitted scarf. There was no place to put it, so I tied it around my waist, holding onto my drink as best I could. More people packed in.

I lost track of the others. It was just music and bodies, but after a few hours, I was drenched with sweat. I couldn't breathe and went outside to get some air.

Just my luck, Shane was there, standing outside the bar smoking a cigarette. A little storm cloud following me everywhere I went.

I put on my jacket and zipped it up to my throat. I was still sweating, my shirt sticking to my skin. I gulped in the cold air as if I was afraid of drowning.

"You're leaving?" he asked.

What did he care?

"Maybe," I said.

I wanted to punch him. I wanted to physically hurt him to make sure he knew that there was someone in the world who didn't think he was God's gift to all women.

I was sure he knew that I knew about him and Dr. Robinson's wife. Finley would have told him. I didn't want to talk to him about her and about them. I thought it might have given him some satisfaction. He was twisted like that. I didn't want to give him that opportunity. In fact, I didn't want to talk to him at all.

"You alone?"

"I guess so, Shane."

That was already too many words between us.

"Too bad for you," he said.

He had nerve. Incredible nerve.

More and more people were coming out. The show was over. Then I saw Pete and called him over.

"That was great," I said.

I gave him a hug. We were both sweating, which felt strange in the cold night air.

"You liked it?" Pete said.

"Yes," I gushed.

I didn't care if I was being obvious. It was suddenly important that he know how beautiful I thought it had been. I wanted to kiss him but didn't want to do it in front of Shane. I thought he might want to kiss me too, and that felt great.

Our breath came out like smoke. The steam came off our bodies like we were burning.

He had his banjo and his backpack. I offered to give him a hand.

"You heading down to the dorms?" he said.

"Yeah," I said.

"You coming, Shane?" Pete asked.

There was no reason to. I crossed my fingers. I was wearing mittens, but crossed on both hands—*Don't let him come,* I wished. *He'll ruin everything.*

"I'm not going anywhere," he said.

He could stay there all night for all I cared. Out there in the cold, without a coat. He wasn't a kid. He knew what a winter night was like.

"He's good," I said. I didn't want to be near Shane. He felt tainted, like it was bad juju being near him. He could be left behind. "No one has to worry about him."

We walked over to campus. It felt late, but the academic buildings were all lit—night classes were ending. There was something wonderful about the night, the lights, the dark shapes of the students moving around us.

I fawned without caring how I sounded. "It was really beautiful. I've never heard anything like that."

"My parents both play," Pete said. "They've got relatives from Appalachia. That's where the music comes from."

"It's so cool to have a talent like that."

"I don't think the Crusoes liked it all that much," Pete said. "I heard some of them say that it was church music."

"That's just Finley. You shouldn't care what he thinks," I said. "He doesn't like anything."

I wanted to tell him that it *had* reminded me of church, but instead I told him I got goosebumps on the back of my neck.

"That's really nice."

"I'm a fan," I said. "Let me know when you play again."

"I'm glad you liked it," he said. "Did I interrupt you and Shane?"

"Shane? No, why would you say that?"

"I always thought you two kind of went out," Pete said.

"Never," I said.

Our feet made that crunchy sound on the packed snow, like walking on Styrofoam.

"Just making sure," he said. "I guess I thought he liked you."

"I don't think he likes me at all."

"I thought maybe you two were sneaking around. Didn't want the rest of us to know."

"Never," I said. "I think he's seeing someone else."

"Who?" he asked.

"Not sure," I said. "I don't really know. Don't even know why I said that."

The whiskey made me talkative, and I could have dumped the whole story right then. Finley had reason to worry. I did get careless about secrets when I drank. I stopped myself from spilling the whole Shane saga. Pete would tell the other Crusoes, and that would be bad for Dr. Robinson. Really bad. More than anything else, I wanted to protect Dr. Robinson from knowing that his wife was cheating on him.

That was enough thinking about Shane. The guy took up too much space in my head, took up way too much time in my life. I didn't want to talk about him. I wanted to talk about me and Pete and just leave everyone else out of our conversation.

"Hey, we could go to my room and get a drink if you want," I said.

I wouldn't bring him to the room, but we could sit in the lounge. I thought we had something to mix the alcohol with, 7UP or Coke. If not, there were machines for these kinds of emergencies.

"Okay," Pete said.

There seemed to be some hesitation, which wasn't good. Then he said something about running *these things* up to his room. He was talking about the instruments. I handed him his backpack.

A girl walked out of the dorm. She came right over to us, which I thought unnecessary. The sidewalk was paved; there was plenty of room.

"There you are," she said. She put her hand on Pete's shoulder.

They knew each other. I took a step back.

"You didn't make it," he said.

"I knowwww," she said in that way that made that one word sound like it went on for days.

"What happened?"

"You knowww," she said. Again, the word went on way too long. She stood in the pool of light cast by the dorm's two main spotlights.

"What was more important?" he asked. He was irritated.

"I tried," she said. "I really did want to see the show."

Pete introduced us. "Molly, this is Jeanne."

The tea and whisky I had been drinking at the bar were warm in my throat and in my stomach. I was at once both totally awake from the caffeine and dreamy from the alcohol. I understood why people drank that. I wanted to dream Jeanne away. I didn't want to see her blonde permed hair, her light blue puffy ski coat, her big teeth making that wide grin.

I said hi. She looked at me without saying hi back.

She became busy, putting her hands inside his jacket.

"You're all wet," she told Pete. "And you smell." She put her nose into his chest. It felt like she was doing this for my benefit, showing ownership.

"Molly's in my eco-sci class," Pete said.

"Oh yeah?" She wasn't the least bit interested in me.

"You should have come," he said. "They all did. The place was packed. Standing room only."

"All those Crusaders?"

"Crusoes," Pete and I said at the same time.

He punched me and called out *jinx*.

She didn't find it as funny. "Are you a member of this secret club too?"

It wasn't a secret club.

I didn't say anything. I didn't want to be talking to her. I didn't like the way she was mocking me.

"Can she talk?" she asked Pete.

"Why are you being like this?" he asked.

Girls like her bothered me. I thought of them as the Alibi chicks—groups of them went to the Alibi for happy hour on Friday afternoons. They got drink deals: two-for-one beer, wine, and rail alcohol. They danced to bad disco music, not caring who they danced with. They got smashed and then came back to the dorms yelling and puking in the halls before 7 p.m.

I was feeling left out and suddenly sorry for myself. Pete and I had been having such a good conversation. I should have realized those guys weren't just hanging around being single all the time. But I had never seen Pete with anyone.

"Yeah, Molly's one of us," Pete said. "She's the only girl."

Jeanne didn't look impressed, but I was momentarily happy. I would have been happier had she never shown up, but now I knew that they considered me part of the group—I was a Crusoe.

"You should do more recruiting," she said. "Sounds to me like you need more members."

"It doesn't work like that," Pete said. "The class is the class. We've been together since the start of the semester."

I think she was trying to be funny, which was pissing me off even more.

It was awkward standing out there in the cold. My reason for hanging around was gone.

"Really good show," I said. "It was beautiful."

I turned and walked away, and he called after me, "Thanks so much!"

"It was great!" I called back.

I had come. She had not. So there.

The last person I wanted to see was Finley, but there he was. Standing in front of my dorm, smoking a cigarette.

"I've been looking everywhere for you," he said.

"Are you following me?" I asked. "I can't go anywhere without you tagging after me."

I pulled out my lanyard and opened the door. Finley came in after me.

I stopped in the small space between the two double doors. He didn't have to come in. This was far enough.

"Where's Pete?" he said.

Shane must have told him I walked back to the dorms with Pete.

"You can't tell him," he said. "About Shane and all."

"That's not what I was planning to do with him," I said.

"I mean it. You can't tell one of the Crusoes. They talk. Dr. Robinson will find out. Is that what you want?"

He was riding my last nerve.

"I'm not telling anyone anything, so stop the lecture."

"Do you like Pete?" Finley asked.

That was none of his business.

"I don't not like him," I said.

"He's taken," Finley said.

"We're freshmen," I said. "How taken can he really be?"

"I mean it," Finley said.

"You mean what?"

"I don't want you talking to him when you've been drinking."

"Go away," I said.

"When you get drunk, you say stupid things." He wore his red knit cap, which had moved down his forehead so far that his eyes were partially covered. It made him look like a gumdrop.

"So do you," I said. "So does everybody."

"Stay away from the Crusoes," he said.

"I don't have to do anything," I said.

He pushed me up against the wall. "You have to keep your mouth shut."

I thought he was going to hit me, and I ducked and moved away from him. I searched in my pocket for my lanyard with the door key. It took me a minute.

"I'm sorry," Finley said.

"Don't touch me. Don't ever touch me like that again."

"It's just so frustrating." He stomped, one foot after another, back and forth, as if beating up the pavement beneath our feet. "I wish you had never found out. I wish you didn't know."

"But I do," I said.

He had hurt me. My shoulder felt bruised, and I felt like crying. Not from pain but because I liked life better when I didn't know about Shane and Dr. Robinson's wife. I liked things much better before the morning I saw her walking out of the dorm.

"Go home," I told Finley.

I was tired of him. It wasn't any fun being with him anymore. That had changed. I was angry at Shane for that too. What he had done had changed my friendship with Finley.

The days got colder. The snow piled up. The semester ended.

NOW

We thought our protests were against something tangible. Something we could win. We were teenagers of the seventies. Our ambitions were muted, defined by the generations before us. Post-Vietnam, we wanted something new, something unexplored and undiscovered, never understanding that our desire to be different was what made us unoriginal—exactly like all those who had gone before us.

I didn't realize we were playing with fire. Our emotions were too high—everything was personal. It was hard to see the forest for the trees. That would take some time. Retrospection doesn't occur while you're living it.

Not that it mattered. We were part of the generation that didn't do much more than float, doing this, then doing that. It was what most everyone did—floated around. Jobs seemed like they were for other people, not something we had been trained for. It took me a few years before I went back and got my teaching certificate so I could teach in the public schools. But like everyone in that decade, I drifted from one thing to the next, not feeling any pressure because there were no jobs. That's what we were told, and that's what we believed. It felt okay to be doing it in Marquette. I wasn't alone. Everyone I knew supported themselves with part-time work. No one did anything too ambitious or professional. It might have loomed on the horizon of the future, but it didn't seem important or vital to our lives. I liked living where I did. That seemed important. I let it be.

21

I was so glad to be back on campus after winter break.

I had spent three boring weeks in Detroit. My parents took off from work so we could spend time together. We ate three meals together every day for all that time. We ran out of things to say and finally agreed to watch television, and then we just talked about what we were watching.

I had missed Marquette. I had really missed the Crusoes—kept thinking about how much more fun they were having. Most likely winter camping, walking in the woods, doing stuff in the UP together. I worried about Dr. Robinson and kept my fingers crossed that he was okay.

I tried calling Finley, but every time I called his house, his mother answered and told me she hadn't seen him. I called Pete, and his little brother answered the phone and told me Pete didn't talk to girls. I wanted to call Charlie. But couldn't. I liked him too much to call him.

I tried to take walks. But the roads were wet with dirty slush. There weren't even sidewalks, just the sides of too-busy roads. I hung out with Keith, who talked about his new friends at Wayne State, and I told him I loved Marquette but it seemed far away. He called it the middle of nowhere, and I let him think that. I didn't see why I should try and change his mind. He was never going to see the UP. That was his loss.

I took the Greyhound bus back to Marquette. It was filled with students, but with all the stops and the bad roads, it took us seventeen hours.

Ecology was a year-long course. So were French and sociology—though for soc we got a new professor, one who didn't tell us about the differences between men and women. I started a mini course in ornithology and a literature course, for which the first book on the syllabus was *The Sun Also Rises*. She never once mentioned that he had spent time in the Upper Peninsula, and when I brought it up in class one day, she said that she preferred to study the text and not the author, so I didn't elaborate about the rivers and the fishing spots. Pete and Charlie were in my bird-watching class. I had assumed we would go on field trips and look at the birds, but the teacher said it was the wrong semester for that. We studied slides. It was dull, and we all had a hard time staying awake once the lights went down.

The Sues were no longer in the class. Dr. Robinson announced their absence the first day we were back. He didn't give a reason, and I assumed they were busy with their nursing schedules at the hospital, but later that week I ran into Sue 1 at the student union and she filled me in.

"The old gal is knocked up," she said.

"What?"

That was a total shock.

She was talking about the other Sue—Sue 2. "She's pregnant and keeping her baby," Sue 1 said. She laughed at my surprise.

"Why?" I asked.

It seemed a strange choice, not something anyone I knew would have done.

"Waited too long," Sue 1 said. "Thought she could get her boyfriend to fork over a ring, but he said he's too young to be tied down with a woman and kid. She's at her parents' place in the Sault."

"That's too bad," I said.

"Don't let her hear you say that," Sue 1 said. "She's acting like this is the best thing in the whole world. Being a mother all by herself. Maybe her mother will give her a few bucks, but I doubt it."

It sounded dismal.

There was more.

Sue 3 was also gone. Her boyfriend got a job in Duluth, and she had quit school.

"Three years in and she just gives up because her boyfriend wants to leave the UP."

Sue 1 laughed, but I could see she was pissed that they were gone, no matter what the reasons.

"They're both fools," she said. "Big ones."

"I guess, yeah," I said. I felt sorry for them. It seemed like a lot of change in the middle of the winter.

"We'll get drinks," Sue 1 said. "You can tell me about dreamy Dr. Robinson. We were all in love with him."

She wasn't kidding.

"I thought you told me that was a cliché," I told her.

"Can't help it," she said. "He's the best thing up here."

She wrote my telephone number on her hand and said she'd be in touch. I wasn't sure what we'd talk about. But she seemed enthusiastic to get together.

"Invite some of those cute boys," she said. "Always good to have some eye candy handy." She laughed at her own joke.

Now I was the only girl left, which should have been great but somehow wasn't.

Sex—saving the planet. I was stuck at a crossroads. Two things I wanted more than anything.

At the time, it seemed that one got in the way of the other. Like with Shane and Dr. Robinson's wife. His sleeping with her had probably ruined my chance to find a group that would help me save the world from overpopulation and water and air pollution.

My wanting to sleep with one or two of the Crusoes was another problem. I wasn't sure if I liked them because they were passionate and had the same goals as me or because I liked their long, shaggy hair, the way you could see their collarbones under their flannel shirts when they wore ripped T-shirts underneath. I liked the way their jeans smelled of dirt and fires and the way they all wore leather bracelets as if that was a mandatory part of the uniform that they had all been given at the first of the year.

I pondered this problem at the start of the second semester.

We were still studying limnology, but Dr. Robinson gave us a quick detour into the history of forestry in the Upper Peninsula. He called the logging in the area brutal. He wrote the word on the chalkboard and underlined it.

"It was done without any thought to anything but money," Dr. Robinson explained. "They wanted money and were willing to do anything in the world to get what they wanted." He was fired up that day. Using words like evil and vile. "I call them the soul eaters."

I liked the description, and I wrote it in all caps on my graph paper and then circled it several times in blue ink.

"We're talking the end of the last century and the lumber boom was like nothing anyone had ever seen before. There were acres and acres of forests. Beautiful trees. And they destroyed everything."

He had some old photographs of the lumber mills, the logs jammed across the water's surface. The sepia-colored prints showed the men who worked the camps. If there were any women—and there had to have been some—they were not in the photos.

White pine was in high demand.

"Everyone wanted it. It was like gold," Dr. Robinson said.

White pine because it was strong for its weight. It floated high in the water and moved easily in the lakes and streams over to the sawmills.

"Nineteen million acres of white pine forests were destroyed," Dr. Robinson said. "They clear-cut. Never replanted, never thought to rebuild the forests. So after a short time they were wiped out. Gone. What was left was barren land. Everything else was destroyed."

Class was just about over when there was a knock on the classroom door. Everyone turned as if there was something to see. No one ever knocked. If you were late, you walked in. Or didn't come. But you didn't knock. We looked at each other.

"Yes?" Dr. Robinson called out in his lecture voice. "Hello?"

The door opened. There were two policemen. Not campus security. Not Dr. Robinson's friend from the protest. They looked timid and out of place in the doorframe.

"Dr. Robinson?"

The class went dead silent. We were all watching Dr. Robinson. He was in charge of the classroom, but we could feel the shift. Something was happening.

"Can I help you?" he asked. He was cool. Or playing cool.

"Could you come out here?"

The slightest irritation. "Out where?"

"We'd like to talk to you." They were calm but serious.

"I'm in the middle of a lecture," he said.

"It's important," one said. He stepped into the classroom, and Charlie, the tallest of the Crusoes, stood up like he was going to fight them. "We wouldn't be here if it wasn't."

"This is important too," Dr. Robinson said. "I've got students here." He said it as if they might not have seen us. He motioned for Charlie to sit down. "Are you arresting me?" he asked.

He was playing with the chalk. It broke in two, and the white dust caught on his dark blue sweater. He wiped it away, or tried to; he had more on his hands and made it worse, large streaks of chalk dust all over his sweater.

"We'd like to talk," they said. "Let's start there."

This made the class crazy. It sounded like a line from a TV show.

"About what?" Dr. Robinson didn't seem worried.

"We have some things we need to discuss with you."

"How long will it take?" Dr. Robinson asked. He stepped away from the table, ready to leave the room.

"You should bring your coat and things."

Dr. Robinson stopped. "Again, let me ask you. Are you arresting me?"

"Just bring your things," they said.

Dr. Robinson took his time packing up his bag. There were several pieces of broken chalk on the table, and he shoved those in too. So maybe he wasn't as calm as he was pretending to be.

Finley snapped his fingers at me. "Molly, give him your trail mix."

It was a class joke that I always carried gorp. I did. It came in handy. I had to buy more and more nuts and raisins and oats. I kept it on the top shelf of my closet and double bagged it because I worried about mice. I took the bag out of my backpack. When Dr. Robinson passed me, I held it up. He took it.

They left. We could hear them moving down the hall.

We waited a few minutes. Total silence. Then everyone started talking at once. The room buzzed.

"That was quite a show," Shane said. "He should be ashamed of himself."

"What are you talking about, Lebarre?" Charlie asked.

"What kind of lesson is that?" It was Shane talking. "To be arrested in front of the whole class."

"We don't know that," I said.

"We don't know what?" Shane did not look at me but spoke to Charlie or Pete, who were sitting over by him.

"That he got arrested," I said. "They didn't say that. Not exactly."

I thought Dr. Robinson had acted admirably. He had been calm. He had not fought or yelled or acted out.

Pete was sitting next to me. He put his hand on my shoulder, then said it didn't look good. "I mean, the police took him down to the station. Chances are he's getting arrested," Pete said.

"But why?" I asked. "What did he do?"

I thought they were all being children—doing nothing while something important was happening right there in front of us. It was stupid. We were activists. Trained activists. When one of us got in trouble, the rest of us should have sprung into action.

"We have to help him," I said.

No one disagreed except Shane, who said he didn't think he had to do anything for anybody.

"Alright," Pete said. "What should we do?" As if I was the only one with the answer to what to do next.

Charlie had a copy of the day's edition of *The Mining Journal* and began flipping through the pages. "Here," he said. "This might be it." He turned the page around and pointed to an article in the lower right corner, not that any of us could read it from that distance. "Antinuke protestors causing trouble out in Republic this weekend. They were seen near the power station. It looks like they cut down some power lines."

I had thought the communications lines were to be installed underground, which is what would make them so precarious for the wildlife. Charlie said no, they were testing lines both above and below ground.

"Antinuke," Jon said. "That doesn't sound like Dr. R."

"And some environmentalists,'" Charlie read.

That sounded like Dr. Robinson.

"They cut the wrong wires," Charlie continued. "They took down telephone lines."

We were starting to understand now.

"That's got to piss everyone off."

"Michigan Bell guys are probably going crazy."

The Crusoes were getting ready to leave—notebooks away, coats on—not moving quickly, but they were definitely not doing anything about Dr. Robinson.

I rushed ahead. "I think this is great," I said. "It shows us that our professor isn't just some mouthpiece, reciting words from a dusty textbook. He shows us what he wants and why it's vital if we are going to save civilization. Otherwise, we're all doomed. We don't do anything, and it will be the end of the world."

I had been stumped in grade school. Overwhelmed by a problem our teacher thought no one could solve. But Dr. Robinson had shown me that it was possible to be aware of the doom and ruin waiting for the world and that there was a way out.

"We are not without choices," I said. "But we have to act."

"She does have a way with words," Jon said.

"She, at least, has a lot of them," Charlie said.

"Go ahead and make fun of me, but I still think it's a sign of a great teacher," I said. "He's doing what we should all be doing. He's following his heart. He's got beliefs. He's at least doing something, and now we have to help him."

"I got thrown in jail for drunk driving. Do you admire that?" Pete asked.

"Were you driving to a demonstration against overpopulation or pollution?" I asked.

"I think I was coming back from the bar."

"Then no," I said. "I think we should go down to the jail. It's not like anyone is going to know he was arrested. What happens if they're not allowed to make phone calls?"

"No, they have to do that," someone said. "It's your civil right to make one phone call."

They all watched too much television. I think they relied on cop shows to get most of their information.

I insisted that we go. "But he's not prepared. Maybe they allow him to make a phone call, but he can't—he doesn't have any change," I said. "Did you ever think of that?"

That got them talking. There was no shortage of their thoughts and opinions.

"He'd be the first one to the jail if one of us got arrested," I said.

"Because it would be his fault, dragging us down to all those demonstrations," Shane said. He wasn't looking at me when he said that, so it didn't count.

"She's right," Jon said. "Molly's right. We should at least go check to make sure he's okay."

In the end, five of us went down to the station: Charlie, Jon, Pete, Finley, and me. Shane said he had better things to do, and I was glad he wasn't coming. It was easier when he wasn't there.

We stuffed ourselves into Finley's VW. It would have been easier if there hadn't been so much trash, and the guys complained about the garbage all the way downtown.

The day had become so much more interesting. Things I liked best: being with the Crusoes and fighting for our cause. We were going to rescue our leader. I felt like a warrior, the five us going to set the world straight. Dr. Robinson was going to be proud.

Once we got there and piled out of the car, Jon, Pete, and Charlie didn't want to go into the station.

"Cops don't like crowds," Charlie said. "Feels like a riot."

"Yeah, some of us should wait out here," Jon said.

"We don't want to piss them off," Pete said. "Do they still have someone following you and Shane?"

Finley was messing around with the car. He didn't hear, or he wasn't listening. He kicked the blocks of ice from behind the tires. He tried, but he couldn't ignore them.

"Is the CIA still after you, Finley?"

"Is the government still spying on you?"

They couldn't let anything be, like dogs with a bone; once they got on something, they couldn't let go of it.

"They got a file on you?"

"Following you, taking photos? Getting into your business?"

"Who told you that?" he asked.

"Heard it through the grapevine."

"Not a good grapevine," he said.

"Then it's not true?"

They were relentless with him. He deserved it.

"I don't want to talk about it," Finley said.

"So, you're not being followed? The CIA doesn't have a file on you?"

He told them to fuck off. "You're all crazy," he said.

"Not sure we're the crazy ones," Charlie said.

I thought Charlie should go in. He was the tallest and, to my mind, looked the oldest.

"They'll listen to a woman."

I don't know where he was getting that from. The last person in the world anyone listened to was a woman. But I liked that he called me a woman.

We were wasting time. Finally, Finley and I went in.

The station was quiet, the halls dark and windowless. It was a formal, old building. We walked around. The place seemed empty. A very tall man wearing a mid-calf-length coat came out of the bathroom. We thought he worked there and asked him for help finding where they had taken Dr. Robinson.

"Don't ask me. I'm just using the john."

He stomped out of the building as if we had offended him.

The two policemen didn't know anything about any professor being arrested. They didn't know about anyone being arrested.

"You sure it had to do with ELF?"

We thought so.

"Maybe they were from K. I. Sawyer." He named the Air Force base. "Did they look like military?"

They had been in uniform. That's what we had noticed.

"Not us," they said. "Sorry. Can't help."

We moved away from the desk. I told Finley we should go out to Republic. We should go to the site and try and find Dr. Robinson.

He didn't think it was such a good idea. "It's a huge area," he said. "We could be driving around for hours."

I thought that would be great. The five of us going after our professor. I thought it seemed noble and exactly what we should be doing.

"It'd be a wild goose chase," he said.

"My great aunt uses expressions like that," I said.

"Like what?" Finley asked.

"Like that," I said.

He turned and looked at me. "Can you stop picking on me?"

I had been. I knew that. I blamed him for so much, but he was right. Despite everything, he was my friend, and I had to stop being so mad at him all the time.

"Yeah," I said. "Sorry."

"You told the guys about the CIA."

"I thought they should know," I said.

"I asked you not to tell anyone."

"I didn't know you meant the Crusoes," I said. "Why would they only pick you? Aren't we all being watched?"

"I specifically told you not to tell *anyone*," he said.

"I was worried."

"I never said CIA," he said. "You made that part up."

But he had. He had said government organizations—and what was there, beyond the FBI and the CIA?

"It was my problem, and I shared it with you. You didn't have to open your mouth and blab it to the whole world."

It still sounded far-fetched to me. We were so isolated, so far from any real city. The UP was miles from Washington, D.C. There was an Air Force base nearby. Maybe someone from the military was watching, but the federal government felt like a stretch, so hard to believe. Then again, Dr. Robinson had been removed from our classroom. There was a lot to consider.

Coming up the steps, a woman was wearing a short fur coat and a Russian mink hat. She looked strange, like she should be crossing the tundra. It took me a minute before I realized who it was. I should have known someone wearing something so ridiculous was someone ridiculous: Dr. Robinson's wife.

"You," she said. "The Crusaders to the rescue."

She had the earflaps pulled down; the hat was too big for her, and she looked like she was an animal hiding in its fur.

"Where is he?" she said.

Finley started to explain what we had learned, but she talked over him.

"I told him he should watch himself. These guys are not fooling around. He can't just do what he wants and think no one will stop him. But I've brought cash. The sooner we get him out of here, the sooner I can get back to what I was doing."

She was foul. I could barely look at her. Her pink shiny lips, her silly outfit, her self-importance. Her cheating on Dr. Robinson.

Finley finally told her what the police had told us. To this, she had a dozen questions, none that we could answer.

"He's probably out in Republic."

"So I've driven all the way to town and he's not here?"

Again, I didn't think it was up to us to explain what had happened. One, because we didn't know, but more importantly, because she didn't care about Dr. Robinson.

Not like I did.

"Someone owes me an explanation," she said. She continued up the steps and disappeared into the building.

I wanted to get away from her. Finley didn't say anything about waiting around for her, so I got the feeling he felt the same way. He couldn't have been a big fan of hers.

The guys were gone. A note on the windshield told us that they were walking back up to campus. *Free Dr. Robinson!* was the signature.

"I knew they wouldn't stick around. Not near a police station." Finley flicked the note off the car and let it fall into the street. "Guys are paranoid. Losers should have stuck around."

I picked up the note—no sense making trash like that. I guessed the guys had gotten bored—less paranoid and more tired of doing nothing in the dead-end street on that side of downtown Marquette.

"Who told her?" I asked.

"What's that?"

"Who told his wife that he'd been arrested?"

"How should I know?"

I looked at him. He stared back.

"What?" he asked.

"Well, think about it," I said. "It was in class. We were there. We came here right after class, and she's here. And she knows he's been arrested. So how did she know?"

"I'm sure the university called her."

"Who?" I asked. "Who would have done that?"

"How should I know?"

"There's only one person who could have told her," I said. "Only one."

"Who cares?"

I wouldn't get back in the car. Not until he admitted that it was true.

"It was Shane," I said.

"You don't know that."

"He called her. He's the only one who could have told her. The only one."

"I'm going," he said. "You can stay here for all I care."

"You know I'm right."

"I don't know anything."

"You say that way too often, Finley," I said. "What are you, some kind of fucking idiot?"

I wasn't pushing him off any cliff. He was doing that all by himself.

I walked away. I could hear him trying to get the car started. I would have gone back if he needed help jump-starting it. But it turned over, and he drove away.

I went up the hill towards campus. I didn't want Finley passing me and offering me a ride, so I went into the jewelry store on Washington Street. It was empty, and I interrupted the guy reading the newspaper in one of two comfy chairs that made the place look like a living room; the only thing missing was the fireplace.

The guy stood, the newspaper falling around his feet. He asked how he could help. I said I was just looking.

"You shouldn't be the one buying," he said. "Let them do it. It's the only way."

"I can't do what?"

He was rambling at me, all nonsense. "The boys," he said. "That's who I'm talking about. You should let them buy the gold and diamonds for you. Otherwise what's the point?"

I looked at the music boxes in the display case in front of me. They were old-fashioned, something that would have been in my grandmother's house. The one closest to me was painted white. I opened it, and a ballerina in a real net tutu started spinning in front of the tiny mirror. The song that played was "Strangers in the Night." No lyrics, just the melody. I watched her turn, her arms held over her head in a permanent pose. I shut the lid.

"Alright," I said. "I won't buy anything today." As if I had been planning to spend money.

The day had turned. Everything was gray; everything was bleak.

I knew I was right. Shane and Dr. Robinson's wife were still seeing each other. I didn't need Finley to tell me it was true.

Like the man said, what was the point? I knew.

22

I cut my hair. Had it all chopped off. It was halfway down my back, and when I had nothing to do, I would pull apart the split ends.

One day in class, Madame had come over and taken the hair out of my hand. "*Laisse, Laisse*," she had nagged, telling me to leave it alone. "You girls are like five-year-olds," she had said. "Playing with your hair to get attention."

It wasn't what I had been doing, and I resented her calling me out in class.

I had walked by a hair place often enough. I went down that afternoon, without making an appointment, and asked the woman working there to cut it all off.

"Are you sure?" she asked. "It must have taken years to grow this long."

It was time for a change—I was sure of that.

She pulled my hair back into a low ponytail right at my neck, then cut it off in one clip of the scissors. I cried.

"This is your youth," she said. "Go ahead with the tears."

She put the hair in a plastic bag and told me to keep it. "You can show your husband how young you were once."

She was more maudlin than I was. I left and stopped at the Togo's sub shop and tossed the hair into their garbage can.

My hair was just below my ears.

I looked different. Strange.

It was winter, and everyone was wearing hats and scarves, so I could hide it. It wasn't like anyone noticed.

A few days later, Pete came up behind me as I was walking up the campus to class. He pulled off my hat.

"What happened to it?"

"Cut it," I said.

"Why'd you do that?" he asked.

I shrugged.

"You look like a boy," he said. He must have thought it looked better long.

My hair was shorter than his. Shorter than most of the Crusoes. None of them had gotten haircuts since the start of the semester.

"It'll grow back," he said.

"I've heard that's what happens."

He put his hand on the nape of my neck. "It's different," he said.

I liked his touch. We stood there, letting the other students walk by.

"Yeah," he said. "I like it."

He pulled me in and kissed me. All toothpaste and Dr. Brown's liquid soap, the kind that didn't make suds or pollute the water. The guys all used it. That distinctive smell, not a fragrance, nothing flowery or soap-smelling. I had never heard of it until I knew the Crusoes. They used it for everything— shampoo, body soap, even to wash their dishes when they were camping.

It was morning. We were kissing on campus. Tongues in each other's mouths, warm and wet. Not what I had been expecting, but I wanted it. It had been a long time, and nothing felt better than what we were doing.

I opened my eyes, and there was Finley standing three feet away. Standing there—just watching.

Pete let go. Took a step back. "It's sexy," he said. He turned and walked into the library.

I walked over to Finley. "I've got study group. You coming? It'll be really boring, but you seem to like following me around, so let's go." I walked towards the main campus.

"He's got a girlfriend." Finley followed.

"Mind your own business," I said. "Stay out of mine."

The pine trees outside the student center were covered with the morning's snowfall. I stood there and watched the winds shake it free. Finley walked off.

It was exhilarating. After all those days of thinking about Shane and his stupid behavior, all that worry and nerves, to suddenly feel something so positive and fun was such a relief.

My study group was sitting on the far side of the room, away from the pool tables and the chessboards that no one touched.

I was late, but they had started working on the assignment.

We had to act out a scene in French. We could make it about anything we wanted. It had to include the past, present, and future tenses. We decided to make it about a woman—me—who goes into the grocery store to get things for a party the next night. Her last party was not a good one. The food burned; the guests got drunk. We made the hockey players write it. All I had to do was memorize my lines before class the next day. I didn't argue or add much to the assignment. I couldn't stop thinking about Pete.

I had liked the way he had touched me. The strangeness and surprise of the kiss, the way his tongue had pushed my lips apart.

It was such an attraction. I wanted to see him again. It was so much better than thinking about Shane and the stupid things he had done. It was so much better.

23

I didn't notice right away. Or maybe I did and just didn't care.

Janet and I were not friends, so it wasn't like I was missing anything.

Besides, I liked it. I liked coming home from class and not having anyone there. It was a relief to have the room to myself. I wanted time to think with no one else around.

I was also distracted by the Shane mess, and then I had the Pete problem—as in, was anything more going to happen, or were we going to leave it with that one kiss? There wasn't room for any other concerns.

So, if I had thought about it, I assumed she had met some friends or was studying or was doing whatever she was doing. I knew what I knew—she wasn't there very much anymore, and I was fine with not seeing her.

Then one afternoon, I was in the library, sitting sideways in my favorite chair, where I could shut my eyes if I wanted and no one would notice. I had my French book in my lap, but I was miles away from Marquette, even further from the French countryside, which was where I was supposed to be. Mostly, I was watching the snow on the evergreens outside the huge window. The winds shook it, and it would fall for several minutes as if it had stored buckets of snow up there on the branches.

Finley came in and stood too close to me, so I couldn't ignore him, which I tried to do. I waited a few minutes, then swung my legs around and sat up.

"What're you doing?" he asked.

"Playing pool," I said. "What are you doing?"

He didn't get my joke, so I held up my book. We were reading a novel for French class. It was difficult and slow moving: *Le Grand Meaulnes*. I had looked for an English translation, but there wasn't one. I had to read every sentence slowly and had a French-English dictionary to look up every other word I didn't know. I figured that would give me the gist of the sentence, and from there I would decipher the meaning.

Madame seemed to understand the level of difficulty and assured us that even in French it was a complex text. She would go over the pages with us, underlining the major points. "The satisfaction of a desire is often the death of that desire," Madame had said. "Remember that."

I liked that and wanted to see what desire died in the book, which was why I was taking so much care in trying to read it.

I turned the page. Finley stayed.

The library was full. That time of day when students came—many of them to sleep; others, like me, to be inside, somewhere warm, pretending to study. There weren't any empty chairs nearby. Finley shoved in beside me. It wasn't wide enough for two, and I would have left, but he had questions.

"Your roommate," he said. "What's her name again?"

"Why?" I asked.

I thought I might go through the next few chapters and underline the words—*désir et mort*—maybe, that way, I could just read the parts where it talked about desire and death. That's what I wanted to know about.

"You don't answer a question with a question," Finley said. "It doesn't get us anywhere."

I had thought he had come to bother me about Pete, but I didn't have anything to tell him on that—desire but no death. It was hard to find him alone; he was usually with Jon or with one of the others, like Charlie. I didn't want to seem too aggressive or too obvious, but I was hoping he would ask me to go somewhere with him or that I would run into him when he wasn't with the others.

"Why do you care?" I asked Finley. "Is that better?"

"It's still a question," Finley said.

His lips were chapped, dry and flaking off. He had some dead skin on the front of his sweater. I took out my Chapstick and handed it to him.

"What do I do with this?" he asked.

I made the motion of applying lipstick, and he handed it back. I took off the cap and leaned over. I ran it across his lips. He pulled away.

"It'll help," I said.

"I don't need help." He licked his lips, which would only make the chapping worse. "Is that cherry?"

I looked at the label. "Strawberry."

He took the stick and licked the open end. "That's good."

"It's not a sucker."

"It tastes like one," he said.

It did. I wiped it off and put it back in my pocket. "Janet," I said. "You've met her."

"She from downstate?"

"Again, why do you want to know?" I asked.

"She's from a small town—right below the bridge?"

"Pellston," I said.

The bottom line was I didn't really care. I figured he would tell me eventually.

"I think she's getting friendly with Shane," he said.

I was sitting so close to him, I could see the blackheads on the side of his nose.

"Getting friendly?" I asked.

Janet wasn't the sort to be friendly with anyone.

"Yeah," Finley said.

"Getting friendly like going out?" I asked.

"I guess that's what you'd call it," he said. His deliberate casualness was irritating.

"Shane and Janet?" I asked. I couldn't even see them in the same room, let alone going out together. "Is this your plan? Janet and Shane? Is that the best you could do?"

"I don't know what you're talking about," Finley said.

He smelled permanently like campfires. It must have been in his clothes. Either the fire smell didn't come out, or he didn't wash his clothes very often.

"Don't play dumb," I said. "You're not good at it. You know exactly what I'm talking about."

"I think he likes her," Finley said, but I knew it was a lie.

Someone like Shane was not going to like someone like Janet. Oil and water, they were not going to mix. This was Finley's doing.

I pushed him off the chair and got up. I had unlaced my boots and had to retie them before leaving. It wasn't a hasty exit.

Finley had time to protest my accusations half a dozen times. "This has nothing to do with me."

"You say that a lot," I said. "In fact, you say it too much. It's really your only response to anything that happens."

I packed up my books and opened my thermos. The coffee was cold. I had poured it that morning before classes.

"Where you going?" Finley asked.

"It's got nothing to do with you," I said. "Just like everything else that goes on around here."

She was my roommate. I owed her something. I had to let her know that Shane didn't like her—that this was just some sort of game he was playing. It was impossible to run on the icy path down to the dorms, but I did my best.

Janet was just out of the shower. She was standing in front of the mirror, wearing only a towel. The floor was slightly wet. I made it worse, tracking in snow.

"You're seeing Shane?" I asked.

"How did you find out?" she asked. Her cheeks pinked.

She really did look guilty, something I only thought happened in books. But Janet was a living picture of someone getting caught doing something they shouldn't be.

"So it's true?"

"He didn't want you to know," she said.

She stood in front of the mirror with her baby powder. It made her pale skin even whiter. She never used to do this in the room. She never walked around the room in nothing but a towel. She was no longer as shy about her body as she used to be, maybe because of Shane. But the two of them having sex was not something I wanted to think about. Poor Janet.

"You know he's not a good guy?" I said.

"That's what he said you'd say," she said. She went over to the closet and dressed. The baby powder was everywhere, like a mist that hung over the room.

"You've got to listen to me," I said. "I don't want you to get hurt."

"He warned me you'd go all *bizzarro* if you found out. I see he was right."

I thought I was far from *bizzarro*. "He's a . . ." I started to say but could not figure out how to explain him to Janet without telling her about Dr. Robinson's wife. "He's mixed up."

It was one way to describe him.

"He's the one who's mixed up?"

Of course she was defensive. She had been seduced by Shane. He was good-looking. I got that. Attractive people were given a lot of leeway, much more than average-looking people.

She said, "I think you're really mixed up."

"Listen," I rushed ahead. "Shane's a pretender. He acts like he's a great guy, but he's not. He's not that nice to girls."

That was true. I wasn't even exaggerating to get her to understand what I knew.

"You don't like him, so what?" She was angry, tight lipped and sour faced.

I wasn't her biggest fan, but I didn't want to see her made a fool. That was on him.

"I don't care how he is with anyone else." She was crying, mostly from her nose, snot coming out in big globs. Her tongue flicked across her top lip and caught one.

I turned away so I wouldn't have to see where it landed—either in her mouth or somwhere in the room.

"He's really popular," she told me. "You don't know how many girls like him."

I hated this conversation. There was no way I could tell her everything, and so there was no way she would understand what a creep he was.

"I was really surprised when he asked me to hang out with him. Even more surprised when he asked me again."

She was being used. Shane was a liar. Or worse, he made things up and believed them. I didn't think it was a random choice.

"I know you liked him too," she said.

"No," I said. "Never."

"He told me," she said. "He told me the whole story."

That's what it was—one of his lies. *A Story by Shane.*

"It's not his fault he didn't like you back," she said. "He told me how you chased him and how you went after Finley when you knew Shane didn't want you as a girlfriend."

Not at all what had happened. Not even close.

"Oh Janet," I said. "Don't do this."

"Leave me alone," she said.

She would be so hurt.

"Why do you even care?" she asked. "You don't even like me."

She had a point. I hated the smell of baby powder. I got up and went straight to Pete's dorm.

The door was open. His roommate was on the bed, shirtless, though the room was freezing.

"What do you want with Pete?" he asked.

He seemed more cocky than nice, trying to intimidate me with his bare chest, his attitude, like I should be afraid of him.

"I want to have sex with him," I said.

He was so surprised by my answer, he couldn't think of a comeback but simply stared at me, like I had told him I was going to blow up the world.

"So if you wouldn't mind, tell him I came by when you see him."

"What's your name?" he asked.

I didn't think that was something he needed. I left.

"I don't know your name!" he shouted when I was halfway down the hall.

"But Pete will!" I shouted back.

Janet was gone when I got back to the room. I took a long shower and played music so loud my suitemates came over and told me to turn it down. They were tired and wanted to take naps. I didn't know when or if they ever went to classes. I did know that they slept most afternoons.

24

Finley tried to tell me it was a good thing.

"Enlighten me," I said.

For Shane it might have been okay, but for Janet it was horrible. She was shy, awkward around people she didn't know, maybe even people she did know, but she was not a mean person. She didn't deserve to be treated like she didn't matter.

"Well, for one, she's his age," Finley said. He was pleased with himself, the happiest he had been in weeks.

"You're going to joke about this?"

"These aren't jokes. They're good reasons. She's eighteen. She's not married. She's not our professor's wife. You can't tell me those aren't good things."

"But why Janet? Because she's my roommate."

"That makes you sound conceited," Finley said.

I wasn't. Of all the girls on campus, did he have to pick someone like Janet? Someone with no experience with guys. Shane would destroy her.

"He should have left her alone."

"It doesn't work like that," he said.

"What doesn't?" I asked.

"Relationships," Finley answered.

"They're not in a relationship," I said.

"They are," he said. "And from what I can see, they're getting serious."

"You know they're not," I said. "This is a sham. He's not serious about anything except covering up what he's done. "

"You don't know everything," Finley said.

But I was right. I knew what Shane and Finley had cooked up. "You're the one who called her grim."

"I don't even know her," he said.

"You met her, and that's what you called her."

"Maybe Shane likes grim," he said. He must have heard how ridiculous he sounded.

I refused to even respond to something so stupid.

"For all you know, he's in love with her and planning to marry her next month."

"You think that's where this is headed?"

"A lakeshore wedding, bridesmaids, flowers, tons of champagne, crappy food."

"I've never been a bridesmaid," I said.

"And you won't be one this time. There's not a chance in hell she'd ask you," Finley said. "She doesn't like you."

Like he had hit me, I recoiled. He could turn mean so fast.

"Do you?" I asked.

"What?" he asked.

I put my face up to his, and he backed up, walking without looking until he hit a snowbank and stopped.

"Do you like me?"

He had three or four apples from the cafeteria stuffed into his coat pockets. No one ate them. They were shipped in from somewhere on the East Coast. They were mushy and might have been good for baking but not for eating.

Finley was the only one I ever saw eating them. He pulled one out and began to chomp on it like he was enjoying it, which I knew he wasn't.

"Are you my friend?"

"What?"

"I want to know," I said.

"What do you think?" he asked.

I wasn't sure—maybe at one time but not anymore. Now, I was someone he had to deal with. Not someone he wanted to be with—not someone he liked, not anymore. Maybe he never had.

Maybe that had been all me. I had wanted a friend. I had been eager and easy—always willing to do whatever Finley needed me to do. Not one of the guys—not a friend at all.

He was making me feel bad about being me. I didn't like who I was when I was around him: mean, nervous, suspicious. It wasn't any fun to be with him.

So I stopped. Until he stopped his games, I wasn't going to be his friend. I had my limits.

25

I didn't see much of Janet. If she was seeing or sleeping with Shane, they were doing it somewhere other than our room.

I spent time in the library, reading my French novel. But a claustrophobic feeling set in. Winter was tiring. You could only be indoors for so long.

Jon, Pete, and Charlie invited me snowshoeing one afternoon, and I jumped at the chance. It became a thing. We went out to Presque Isle Park and went on the paths the cross-country skiers had packed down. They were easy to follow and almost every day there was clean, fresh snow that made it feel like we were trekking someplace new.

Those were the best days—the bitter, cold winter afternoons, the difficulty of keeping up, the way Presque Isle looked in the late day sun. The sky was so brilliantly blue you wanted to hold it. The ice floes formed in the lake, waves stopped in midmotion.

Pete never said anything about my coming to his room. I didn't either. Something had changed. Or maybe I felt I had been given a warning. I didn't want to lose them as friends, and I thought I would if I slept with one of them. I had a bad feeling about that—I knew, at least, that it would change everything. And I didn't want anything to change.

I think it was then that I began to think of Marquette as a verb—*to be Marquette* was to be rid of the person I had been and to embrace someone completely different.

I was no longer from Royal Oak. I had rejected that life. I had rejected downstate. At times, I felt like Dr. Robinson and I would have eagerly signed a petition to blow up the Mackinac Bridge. I never wanted to go back to Detroit. I especially never wanted to live there again.

Marquette meant that the future was possible, that somehow we could turn back time and undo all that had been done to the planet. I was a realist, though I wanted to be a romantic. These were fantasies, but as long as I was in Marquette, they existed. They felt like a life I could actually have. Dr. Robinson had given me that hope. I believed it.

Up there, I was a different person.

In Marquette, I was a steward of the earth. Everything seemed possible. Up there, I lived so close to the natural world—up there, I lived so close to beauty. I couldn't let anything change my new way of thinking.

MICHIGAN'S MOOSE POPULATION

From Michigan's Department of Natural Resources

Moose is a species native to Michigan, but their numbers declined substantially during European settlement. By the late 1800s, moose had disappeared from the lower peninsula and only a handful remained in the Upper Peninsula. In the mid-1980s, the DNR translocated fifty-nine moose from Algonquin Provincial Park in Ontario, Canada, and released them in Marquette County. The goal of the moose reintroduction was to produce a self-sustaining population of free-ranging moose in the Upper Peninsula. Moose are currently found in two areas of the Upper Peninsula: the reintroduced population in Marquette, Baraga, and Iron counties, and a smaller remnant population in the eastern UP, found primarily in Alger, Schoolcraft, Luce, and Chippewa counties.

The department conducts an aerial moose survey onIy every other year in January. The survey involves flying systematically at a low altitude over parts of Marquette, Baraga, and Iron counties and recording how many moose are seen. Although conducting the survey in the winter helps our trained spotters to see moose on the snow-covered landscape, it is still impossible to count every moose, so the counts are corrected with a statistical model to provide an estimate of the actual population size. The statistical model was derived from running experimental trials on radio-collared moose.

The estimated moose population in the western Upper Peninsula was 323 animals. This indicates a decrease, compared to the 1980 survey results of 433 animals. We will continue to monitor future survey results for changes in the population.

26

When we had finished snowshoeing, we would stop at the North End Bar for a drink, or a burger if we were going to be late for dinner. There was a pool table there, and we played if no one else was using it. None of us was very good, and when someone challenged us, we lost quarters.

I didn't want to lose the afternoons spent on Presque Isle. A few miles from campus, it had started to feel like something precious. It was beautiful, covered in snow. Almost no cars drove out there in the winter, maybe a few on the weekends, but we had the place to ourselves. The views of the lake changed depending on the cloud coverage. Sometimes we could see the brilliant blue expanse on the horizon; sometimes there was nothing but the long white of the snow-and-ice-covered shore.

It felt magical—at least spiritual. And even then, I could feel that it would not last.

Janet was waiting for me one night. She got off the bed as soon as I walked into the room. She stood there, watching me while I took off my wet things. I hung them from the shower rod. She stood in the doorway, her face twisted in worry.

"What?" I asked.

"Shane's acting weird."

I knew they weren't going to last. There was no chance of that, and my first impulse was to say, *I told you so.* But I couldn't do that. She hadn't done anything to deserve Shane. That was just rotten luck.

"I'm sorry," I said.

"You have to come with me," she said.

I didn't see that happening.

"Please," she said. She was begging. "Walk up campus with me. To his dorm. He won't answer the door."

"Maybe he's not there."

"He is," she said. "I just know it."

I had no intention of getting involved in their mess. "But if he doesn't want to see you—" I started to say.

She had no interest in what I felt about the situation. "I just have to talk to him."

I felt sorry for her. Her distress got to me. "First let me take a shower," I said.

She stood in the doorway and bit the skin around her nails. She spit the piece out between her lips. I got dressed quickly, best to get it over with as quickly as I could.

She worried the entire walk to his dormitory. "What does Finley say?" she asked.

"About?"

"Me!" she said. "What does he say about Shane and me?"

"I try not to listen when he talks," I said.

"This is serious. I need to know. Is Shane going to break up with me?" she asked. "I'm afraid he is."

I wanted to hurry this along.

The dorm was loud with kids partying—music and yelling, all that shrill laughter, like everything in the world was just funny, funny, funny. Card games and bongs. The smell of pot was everywhere.

I knocked. No answer. I knocked again.

"I know he's in there," Janet said.

"Really? How?" There was too much noise to be able to hear anything from inside the room.

Still, we waited another few moments.

"Okay? Now can we go?" I asked. I had done what she had asked.

We were halfway down the hall when the room door opened. Janet turned and ran back. But it wasn't Shane coming out. It was a man. It was hard to tell how old he was because he wore a ski jacket with the hood pulled up over his head. Finley followed.

They passed us.

"Not a good time," Finley said.

"Just looking for Shane," I said.

"Go away," he said.

It was not a bad suggestion.

Janet went into their room. I guessed she was going to check under the bed to see if Shane was hiding

There was an envelope with Finley's name on it. Typed.

"He's not here," Janet said. She opened the closet.

Finley came back. "Get out." He grabbed the envelope from me. "Why are you touching my things?"

He was in a mood, for no real reason. Unless I was missing something. Then it hit me.

"Hey, who was that guy?" I asked. Something about the way he was acting got me thinking.

"Who do you think it was?" he asked.

"Was he from the . . . " I asked. I didn't say the word, not in front of Janet. I had that much discretion.

"Get out of my business," he said.

Janet was watching us. "What?" she asked.

Finley shook his head. "I'm done."

Janet wasn't ready to go, but I dragged her out.

"Tell me," she said. "You have to tell me."

"It's not about you," I said. My mind was spinning, one thought coming faster than the next.

She kept bugging me. So many questions. So many questions about Shane. I had had enough. We were halfway to the lower campus, halfway to the dorm. She kept stopping and trying to walk back to Shane's dorm. I pulled on her coat sleeve, dragging her back. But she kept stalling, and I—finally pushed to the brink—told her.

"Shane and Finley are being followed by the CIA," I said.

"That's a lie," she said.

I didn't think it was. That guy had definitely been CIA. I could tell by the coat. That's what they wore. Long, dark blue jackets with hoods lined in fur. The buttons were wood, and there were several pockets.

"I don't believe you," she said. "You're making that up."

"Why would I do that?" I asked.

"Because you hate him."

I was done. Back in our room, I got into bed with all my clothes on, trying to get warm.

Janet wasn't done. "Call their room," she said. "Please?"

There was no reason for that.

"I just want to know he's there," she said.

I didn't know what that would prove.

"Please?" she asked again. "Do it for me?"

I dialed a number. Not Finley's. I held out the phone and let her hear the ringing. I was lucky. It was someone's dorm room, and they were out. No one picked up.

"Okay? Now can I get some sleep?"

She waited ten minutes, then asked me to call again.

I should have moved rooms after she called me a slut. I should have requested a single. I could have told them I had a medical condition. A girl in my sociology class lived alone. She had told the university she had alopecia, and when they had asked her for a doctor's note, she showed them some wigs she had. She was a theater major, and they were costumes. I couldn't have told the same lie, but I could have come up with something creative, like I needed sleep and privacy and not to be involved in other students' problems. That would have been the truth.

The lights went out. I heard her in the bathroom. She was there for a long time. I fell asleep, and when I woke, the light was on over her bed. She had her books out, but she wasn't reading.

"I should never have gone out with him," she said.

Shane was a dark cloud. It was hard to get away from him. I had spent the semester trying.

"You've got to stop thinking about him. Don't give him so much power. He's a guy. I've told you; he's an unbelievable jerk. You're better off without him. If he's going to break up with you, then there's nothing you can do."

"I could change his mind," she said.

"You can't make people like you," I said. "You definitely can't make them fall in love with you."

"But I do. I do love him," she said.

That could not be true.

"I'll die if he's got someone new."

Pillow over my head, I tried to sleep.

"You made up that stuff about the government because you know something."

"I don't know anything."

"You do," she said.

I was caught. Trapped in my own honesty—or maybe my own confusion. There was no choice. I exploded.

"Shane's not in love with you. I'm not sure he ever even liked you."

That ended the discussion—and my relationship with my roommate, the one I had thought would be trouble-free if only I could try to ignore the petty things.

Janet never spoke to me again.

She did, however, take her revenge.

27

It was the middle of the afternoon. I had skipped all my classes so that I could I sit on my bed and watch the snow fall outside my window and had fallen asleep. When my RA walked into my room, I woke at once.

"Looks like someone's in trouble," she said.

"Why?" I sat up, and the world went black for an instant. "What's going on?"

"How am I supposed to know?" she asked.

She was no longer so friendly with me. Her enthusiasm had waned completely. I think she realized we weren't ever going to be friends. I wasn't ever going to go with her to the Alibi. We would not drink happy hour half-priced drinks or go sledding on cafeteria trays.

"Then why did you say that?" I asked. "Why are you here?"

"I was told to bring you downstairs. Those were my directions. The dorm director wants to see you. Now."

There was no reason for her to be so bossy.

The bumblebees with our names were gone from the door. The leftover pieces of the sticky tape I had used to adhere them to the door were still there, and she peeled them off with her thumbnail.

That annoyed me too.

I got up and walked downstairs. She followed, though I was pretty sure I could find my way all on my own.

The dorm director was standing by the mailboxes in front of the cafeteria doors. "Molly Grey?"

"That's me," I said.

She reached into her back pocket and pulled out a comb. It was yellow with large teeth, a few of them missing.

"You look like you just woke up," she said. "Do your hair."

I didn't take the comb but ran my fingers through the ends. A few minutes before, I had been dead asleep, having a dream about being in a zoo. I remember standing in front of dirty glass, looking at the penguins.

She inspected me. "Better," she said. "Don't be nervous. Just tell the truth."

"About what?" I asked.

"About everything," she said.

"Who am I talking to?" I hadn't done anything wrong, so I wasn't worried. I was curious but not nervous.

"It's not a joke," she said. "This is serious."

I wasn't aware that I had said anything to give her the impression I was joking.

She led me into the cafeteria, where three men in suit coats sat at a table, and made some introductions. Like she knew me, even though that wasn't true. I said hello and stood looking at them. They told me to sit.

"Why?" I asked.

They were sitting at the same table where Pete, Charlie, Jon, and I had sat during the windstorm blackout. It's funny how time and people can change a place. It still smelled like fried fish, but there was nothing fun about this meeting.

I got nervous then. It was the dark suit coats, something no one wore up there—not the professors, not anyone I knew. They looked like undertakers, and I thought something had happened to my parents. I welled up anticipating the news of loss.

"We're going to ask you some questions," they told me. "And we want you to answer them honestly."

It didn't sound like they were talking about my parents' deaths. I didn't think three of them would come, and the one wouldn't have needed a notebook to tell me that my parents had been killed in a car accident.

"The thing is, you have to tell us the truth, no matter how much you don't want to."

"About what?" I asked.

"About what we're going to ask you."

"Which is what?"

"Sit down, and we'll get to it."

"What did I do?" I couldn't think what I had done wrong.

"You're an impatient girl," the one man said.

I didn't like him. If I had come there to be criticized and to have my personality discussed, then I wanted to leave. I stood behind the chair, all of them motioning me to sit.

"I'd like to know why I'm here," I said.

They ignored this request. "We want to talk to you about Dr. Robinson."

That wasn't good—he was the one thing I didn't want to talk about.

I sat.

"I'm not sure I'm the one you want to talk to," I said.

Finley should be here if they wanted to know about Shane and Dr. Robinson's wife. I wasn't the one who had the information.

But that wasn't why they were there, not why they had asked me to come down to talk to them.

"We want to make sure Dr. Robinson has been acting appropriately."

"Has he what?"

The cafeteria kids were on shift. They moved around the dining room setting up for dinner. A radio played. One of the men asked them to turn it down, and they did—but not right away and not all the way down. We moved to the far corner, and the sound of plates and silverware in the serving station got louder.

"We've had some reports that he's been less than professional with you."

"With me?" I asked. "Dr. Robinson?"

Not this again. Too many people in the UP thought the same way, like they were all reading the same romance novel. They needed to have bigger imaginations.

"Yes," they said. "Calm down. There's no reason to yell."

It seemed an exaggeration to say that I was yelling.

"You're wrong," I said. "I don't know who's feeding you information, but you're way off base."

"That's your story?"

"It's not a story," I said.

It wasn't really even mine. It belonged to the whole class—all the Crusoes, everyone who thought saving the planet meant learning why and how it was being destroyed.

"Just trying to get to the bottom of things."

They had no idea what they were talking about. These guys were so far from the truth that it was funny, except I didn't want to laugh in front of them. They'd get that wrong too.

"He's a great professor. The best professor up here," I said.

"Why?"

"Why is he the best?" I asked.

"In your own words," they said. "Tell us why someone like Dr. Robinson is such a good teacher."

"He knows things," I said after a few moments of silence. "He knows what he's talking about."

"We hope all the professors you have know things," one said.

I could tell he didn't like me—or thought I was not worth bothering with.

"He knows things I care about."

"And that doesn't happen in your other classes?"

"Not so often." I could have clarified. For instance, I liked knowing that the town of L'Anse meant *bay* because there was one there and that the French explorers had named it aptly. That sort of thing was fun. But it wasn't something you'd get all passionate about. "He's teaching us to care for the planet."

"You can't do that on your own?"

"I don't know enough," I said. "Before I came to Northern, I didn't realize all I didn't know about the world, about nature, about how connected things are. The world is a delicate web. Everything's dependent on everything else. You pull on thread, and the whole thing will collapse. Eventually, of course. Not right away."

"And he does this by making you go to protests?"

"He doesn't make us go," I said.

"It's not a course requirement?"

"Of course not," I explained. "We have our own minds. We decide for ourselves what we do, what we want to do."

"You're anti-ELF?" they asked. "Is that what you're saying? You're against a government installation?"

"Yes," I said. I didn't hesitate. "I am very much against it."

"Any particular reason?" they asked. "We know you're from Detroit. How many people downstate even know what ELF is?"

"I don't think it's good for the environment," I said.

"But you don't know?"

"It doesn't sound like digging into the bedrock will be good for the wildlife in the UP."

They didn't have anything to say to that. They had other questions.

"Have you been having a relationship with Dr. Robinson?" They did not say sexual; there was no mention of that, but it was what they were talking about.

"No," I said.

They waited. It had been a yes or no question, and I had answered it. I waited too.

"Whoever told you that is lying," I said.

People could be so stupid. Thinking one thing when quite another thing was happening. They were clueless.

At first, I thought it was Madame. She must have said something to someone. I should have realized that night she took me out that she didn't just want to give me some friendly teacher-student advice. She was fishing, trolling for information. I had been too defensive, making her even more suspicious.

But it couldn't be Madame. She would never have done anything to hurt Dr. Robinson. She cared for him too much.

It was Janet.

This whole thing was her doing.

This was her revenge. She was getting back at me for telling her about Shane. She had made up this story about Dr. Robinson and me a few days ago and had gone to the administration with it. I knew it. I knew it was her.

The men asked me some more questions. I answered with either *yes* or *no*. I told them before I left that they had been lied to. I wasn't sleeping with anyone. I told them that.

Janet dropped out of Northern later that week. I assumed that's what happened. I was never told anything officially. Her half of the room was cleared out. Even the bottles of alcohol. I didn't imagine she and her father were back home in Pellston, in the new house, making Harvey Wallbangers—because I didn't think of her much after she left. She was gone. That was it. When I thought about her, I felt bad. She had been played by Shane, but she had blamed me.

I had suffered an hour of humiliation, a useless talk with men who had no clue about me or about what was happening on campus.

That was the reach of her anger. The end result of how Shane had hurt her.

28

After the university officials asking me about Dr. Robinson told me I could leave, I went upstairs and found Jon, Pete, and Charlie waiting for me. They were slumped against the hall outside my room.

"Hey!" I said, immediately happy and willing to forget the weird inquisition down in the cafeteria.

"Finally," Charlie said.

I grinned.

"So?" he asked.

"So?" I asked.

"Have you been expelled?" Jon said.

"Why would you think that?"

"The guys in suits don't come because they want to see if you're happy. They mean business."

Pete said they had seen me go in and had been waiting and worrying since then. "Tell us," he said. "What's wrong?"

I didn't think it was a good idea to talk there.

"It's that bad?" Charlie said.

"It's sort of bad," I said.

"Give us a hint. What's it about?"

"Me," I said.

"You?" Pete said. "What did you do?"

The girls on the floor were not my friends. I didn't want them eavesdropping on us. I'm sure they were already, in their rooms with the doors cracked open. Three guys who looked like these Crusoes had gotten their attention. They would listen, get the story wrong, and then repeat it to their friends, who would do exactly the same thing until it would be so distorted even I wouldn't recognize it.

There was some discussion about where we would go. They had something they had to do, and Pete said it was okay.

"Come on," he said. "Come with us."

It didn't matter where we were going, so I didn't ask.

Charlie borrowed a car from someone who didn't know he was borrowing it.

"Guy never uses it," he said. "Never seen him drive it anywhere."

I don't know how he got the keys, but he had them, and he drove us downtown to the Heritage House, a hotel on Front Street.

We went into the lobby. There was no one behind the desk, but an older woman sat in front of the fireplace. There was no fire. She had two rolls of toilet paper in her lap, and when we sat nearby, she put her arms around them as if we meant to take them.

Jon said hello.

She looked us over intently. "I am Irma," she said.

"Hello," Charlie said.

"I am," she said, as if we had accused her of being someone else.

"Alright," he said.

I appreciated that they did not laugh at her. But still, she was agitated and continued to clarify her name.

Two Air Force guys walked in. There was never any mistaking them—crew cuts, an attractive look. One of them approached Pete, and if I hadn't been watching the exchange, I would have missed it. The flyboys left.

There was some noise near the entrance, and I saw that the bar had opened.

"Just in time for happy hour," Pete said. "Let's get a drink."

I knew what I had seen. "You're selling pot to guys from the base?"

That seemed dangerous and really reckless.

"Pretend you didn't see anything," Jon said.

"They're soldiers," I said. "Aren't you afraid they'll turn you in?"

"Not really," Pete said.

"I would be," I said.

"No, I mean they're not really soldiers," Pete said. "There's no war. You have to have a war for them to be soldiers."

I wasn't sure that was true. "They're government employees," I said. "That's who they work for. Dealing drugs is a criminal offense."

"They like to get high," Charlie said. "We're just helping them."

"It's still against the law."

I wanted them to be safe. I didn't want to seem like a narc. I didn't think it was a good idea to sell to the guys from K. I. Sawyer, but it wasn't my business. They wanted to make money, and they liked taking risks.

"They're the ones buying it," Jon said.

"But you're the ones selling it," I said. I didn't want them to get kicked out of school.

"Hey," Jon said. "We're not the ones in trouble. That's you."

"Me?" I said.

"We're not the one getting questioned by old men in suits," they said. "That's you. You're the troublemaker."

"I haven't done anything wrong," I said.

"Then why did the guys in the suits call you in?"

"I don't have a clue," I said.

"You still have to tell us what happened," Charlie said.

"Nothing happened," I said.

"Right," Pete said.

He pinched my hip bone, and I slapped him away. It was hard to say if they were kidding. I didn't want them to get in any trouble. I was nervous around drugs, maybe too naïve. I knew the CIA was nearby and thought drugs would only make things so much worse.

The bar had a popcorn machine that the bartender said he had just turned on. "Give it twenty minutes."

We sat at the table by the window, and the guys polished off plates of mini hot dogs dipped in mayo and mustard sauce. Snow was falling—again—always.

Charlie took my drink and held it over the table. "Time to tell," he said. "No secrets between Crusoes. Tell."

"It's about Dr. Robinson," I said.

They weren't expecting that. "Do they think he's a bad influence on us?"

"Maybe," I said.

We were drinking fast, the salty food making us thirsty, which I guessed was the real point of happy hour. We got drunk.

Some time later, Pete went off with some guys from his band, and Jon fell asleep in the corner. I liked being there alone with Charlie.

"Should we take him home?" I asked, pointing at Jon.

"He'll be fine," Charlie said. "So?"

"So what?" I asked

"What's the real story?"

"I told you," I said. "It was about Dr. Robinson."

"That's it?" Charlie asked. "They accused you of sleeping with Dr. R., and you said *no way* and they said *okay, go away*?" His eyes squinted shut when he smiled.

"Basically," I said.

"You were there for almost an hour."

"They asked me what kind of professor he is."

"Why would they do that?"

"I guess they wanted to know if he's the kind of person who would have an affair with a student."

"And do you think he is?"

"I don't," I said.

I never got that feeling from Dr. Robinson. I didn't think Charlie believed that either. But he kept pressing me, question after question. It started as teasing, but then he kept pushing.

"But you know something, don't you?"

"Why do you say that?"

"I can tell," he said. "You're hiding something."

I didn't deny it. "I promised," I said.

"You can tell me," he said.

I wanted to. I had been wanting to tell someone since I first saw Dr. Robinson's wife walk out of Shane's dormitory.

I knew this about secrets: you tell one person, and they'll tell one person, and then it's all over the place before you know it.

But I was tired of keeping it to myself—or that's how I justified it. Maybe it was the alcohol, maybe it was being so close to Charlie, the way he held my hand under the table and brought his face close to mine, the way I could see the wisps of hair on his chin, his tongue licking the salt of the popcorn off his lips again and again. We went into the bathroom and kissed until the bartender came in and told us to get lost. When we got back to the table, the light had faded from the room. We went back to his dorm, where we got into his bed, and before we had sex, I told him the whole story. Everything I knew.

The world blew up after that.

29

It didn't take long. I should have known it would spread, but its speed was surprising—like a tornado had ripped through campus.

I told myself it wasn't my fault. I told myself it was inevitable. Sooner or later, it would have gotten out, even if I hadn't said anything to Charlie. My doing so might have hurried things along, but people would have found out eventually.

I was afraid to think anything else.

A graduate student from the science department came to our class. She told us Dr. Robinson was unable to be in class that week. We bombarded her.

"What's going on?"

"Where is he?"

"Why isn't he here?"

As far as she knew, he was ill. She was sure that classes would resume the following week, if he was feeling better. She had our assignment: a research project—we would have to go through old issues of *The Mining Journal* to find the answers.

"Any questions?" she asked. "About the project. I don't know anything more about Dr. Robinson, so don't ask me."

Shane and Finley also were also MIA.

No surprise there—about Shane at least. Finley, I thought, didn't want to face the firing squad of questions, which he wouldn't have answered anyway. Had he been in class, even on campus, he would have denied responsibility. He would have said it had nothing to do with him. It was partially correct but not altogether true.

I asked, but no one had seen them, which I thought strange. It was not that big a place, and I wondered if Finley was hiding, deliberately staying out of everyone's way. I had tried calling, but no one answered the phone.

We sat in the classroom long after the graduate student had gone. The noise level got so high—everyone talking at once—that the professor teaching the class next door came in and told us to quiet down.

"Where's your professor?" he asked.

No one answered. There didn't seem any reason to give out that kind of information. It wasn't against the law to be talking in a classroom. He stood there waiting for an answer, then gave up.

We shut the door after he left. We went back to debating whether or not Dr. Robinson would ever come back. Almost everyone thought this was it and that the university would fire him.

I disagreed. "He didn't do anything wrong. Why shouldn't he come back?"

It wasn't right. Dr. Robinson was 100 percent innocent.

"He's never going to live this down."

"What's he done? He's not the one who did anything wrong." I couldn't be the only one defending him, but I felt like I was the sole voice speaking up for him.

They also talked about what would happen to Shane.

"He'll be expelled."

That was the general feeling. Everyone was sure he was going to be kicked out.

"They're not going to let him keep taking classes."

That was a solution I could live with. We agreed it was probably a good thing. Get rid of Shane, get rid of Dr. Robinson's wife, and we could go back to before.

We could be good again. I wanted that. So did everyone else.

Campus was a minefield. It was impossible to go anywhere—besides maybe the bathroom on the second floor of the university center—without someone stopping me to talk about Dr. Robinson and/or Shane. Mostly, they just pointed or talked about us as if we couldn't hear them. I didn't realize other people knew us as the Crusoes, but they did. We had been in the newspaper for our participation in the Project ELF protests—and now this. They also called us the *nature kids*, *save-the-planet weirdos*, even the *Robinson groupies*, which made us sound like we were in a cult.

The next day, our class was taught by a graduate student.

He kept telling us that he had never taught before. "It's really nerve-racking to stand up here in front of all of you."

No one made him cry. He just did. He got worked up by his own confusion and nervousness. He'd leave the room on the verge, and then when he returned, he came back blowing his nose. So unless he was doing blow in the bathroom, he was crying.

In the middle of French class, Madame asked to speak to me. She spoke in English.

"Come with me," she said, and I followed her out of the room, down the hall, and around the corner.

"How long have you known?" She held my coat lapels and pushed her face into mine as if trying to get into my head.

I wasn't one for the truth. I could have told her that night we had drinks at the Ramada Inn, but it all felt so petty now.

"Why?" I asked. "What does it matter?"

"It does."

"I found out when everyone else found out."

That was safe—neutral ground. She couldn't be mad at me for that.

She motioned for me to lower my voice. That was senseless. It was the main topic of conversation everywhere on campus. There weren't any more secrets or things that weren't being said, so there wasn't any purpose in whispered conversations in empty corridors.

"I don't understand why Matt didn't confide in me," she said.

That was not something I could answer.

"Have you seen him?" I asked.

She hadn't. "I'm very worried about him."

"We all are," I said.

She looked at me. She wore foundation. It was an odd color, one that didn't match her skin tone. I could see the way she had applied it across her cheek bones; it wasn't blended in. Had we been friends, I would have told her to go fix it in the bathroom mirror. Instead, we went back to class, where she had us perform our skits. She didn't seem to enjoy them. She never laughed; she never corrected our badly translated French. She smiled, but it didn't seem like she cared at all about what we were doing, what we were saying, or how we were saying it.

NOW

It looked like garbage, like someone's trash bag had exploded. But it didn't move, didn't wash up to the shore. If you looked closely, you could see that they were flowers, corn cobs of yellow stems, then green buds, tons of them—the entire cove covered.

We knew algae sometimes infected the lower Great Lakes, but Superior had always been spared, most likely because of the winter temperatures. The average daily summer temperature was too cold for much pollution. That was changing; it was warming at an alarming rate.

It appeared in late August. Most people blamed it on the lack of rain; it had been a very dry summer. The strange-colored blooms covered the water's surface, and swimming was prohibited near the beaches in the city. Even wading was thought to be dangerous, and the greenish streak the flower blooms left in the water looked like toads' tails.

We were told the toxins the algae created were more potent than cyanide. Lake Superior was being poisoned by climate change. Even Dr. Robinson could not have foreseen or forewarned about this danger. The flower stems disappeared. The city made no statement on the safety of the water. I waited to swim. The best days for swimming, late summer in the early evening, were ruined.

30

I thought the world was coming to an end.

The first time I saw it, I had no idea what was happening.

The odd green light cracked the night sky, the strange colors shimmering and reflecting off the lake's surface. I was alone and thought we were being invaded. I watched and waited. It didn't last long, and when I tried to explain it to the guys, they laughed at me.

The aurora borealis.

"It's a trip, isn't it?"

Jon said the first time he saw it, he thought it was aliens landing from outer space.

"But what is it?" I asked.

Jon explained. Pete corrected him.

"Crazy, isn't it?"

I couldn't explain how scared I was, how the flickering lights had come up from the horizon, and I really did think something awful was happening.

"You ever seen anything so amazing?" Pete asked. "It's like God's talking to you."

The guys made fun of him for talking about God. He ignored them and told me he should write a song about it.

It would take me a few more times to appreciate the beauty.

It was so startling and so unexpected.

I never heard Pete's song. I wasn't sure he really did write it.

Project ELF Dead?

April 10, 1985

MARQUETTE, MI-When questioned about the implementation of Project ELF in Michigan's Upper Peninsula, Governor Milliken denied any knowledge about what happened. "I haven't heard anything on it at all. I think they've moved on." Asked to clarify, Millkien simply said that he did not know. "Given the silence, I feel like it's a dead-end project." He refused to elaborate, saying he had no more information.

31

Later that week, I went to their dorm room. The door was open; the room was mostly cleared out of anything personal that might have belonged to them. The mattresses were flipped up against the wall. The dressers were emptied, the desks cluttered with papers but no books.

A guy walked by. He stopped.

"They got kicked out," he said.

"They did?" I asked.

"Yep," he said.

"Both of them?"

"That's what everyone's saying."

They—meaning everyone on campus—were saying a lot of things. I heard rumors that Shane and Finley had jumped off the break wall in the lower harbor. That was the big one that week. There was no proof or even a sign that this had happened; the story hung on for months.

"Why?" I asked.

"Why are they saying that?"

"No," I said. "Why did they get kicked out? What did they do?"

"Who knows?" he said, as if they were no longer important. "Flunked out as far as I know."

He didn't know very far, and I didn't correct him.

The windows were dirty in the sunlight. I could see the dust caked on them. Someone's handprint was on one side, where they had pushed against the glass. Finley's student ID was on his desk. It was the surest sign for me that he wasn't coming back—not anytime soon anyway.

Spring came to the UP slowly, with some backtracking into winter, as if it wasn't sure it wanted to be there. There were some snowstorms that didn't last long, but the winds were brutal for late March and early April.

When it got warmer, the other Crusoes and I hung out at the lake. It became our ritual, McCarty's Cove after classes. We played Frisbee, we made fires, we drank some. We talked Dr. Robinson nonstop—almost nothing else, unless it was Shane and Finley.

The Crusoes had turned on them. They were mean, most of all dismissive. "We should have kicked them out last semester."

That would have been a great idea. If only one of us was clairvoyant. Had we had crystal balls or something, that would have worked just as well.

"Losers ruined the year."

I tried to stick up for Finley. But there wasn't much I could say in his defense.

We had all been cheated out of the year with Dr. Robinson. Shane and Finley were to blame—Shane because he had had an affair with Dr. Robinson's wife and Finley because he could have—and should have—stopped it. That was the consensus.

I didn't care about Shane. Now that he was gone, he no longer mattered. I was mad at Finley for leaving like he had—without a word. Weeks later, he still hadn't called or sent a letter. I blamed Shane for Finley's silence. It got to me. We had been friends. He owed me a phone call. He really did.

One afternoon, I was walking down to the lake to meet the guys. I was always the first to get there. I was always early—nothing had changed there. I had stopped at the corner store for some beers. The cans rattled in my backpack even though I tried to hold it still. They would explode open as soon as someone popped the tab. Spring in Marquette meant mud and rain and melting snow, but finally we were having warm days. The vistas had changed, the trees budding, the hues turning green and yellow.

It was early; the guys wouldn't be there for another hour. I walked the road following the shoreline. I liked being down there by myself before everyone arrived. I liked sitting there on the tree stumps watching the waves. I liked the reverence of the iron ore ships when they came into the harbor and docked. There was some sort of connection to the world when I saw them come in—a sense that we were all a part of something much larger. Living on the edge of a Great Lake did that.

A car stopped behind me. I heard the motor slow, and I turned, irritated that the driver couldn't or wouldn't go around me. The road was wide, with plenty of room for everyone.

It was a Jeep. I had been fooled before—every other person in the UP drove one.

But this time, it was him. It was Dr. Robinson.

"Molly Grey," he said.

I was so happy, I hugged him—wrapped my arms around him, inhaling the wonderful smell of Drum tobacco and detergent.

I apologized.

"I'm glad you've missed me."

I had.

"I missed you all too."

There was so much to tell him, so much I wanted to know. He didn't look any different. I had thought he would, with everything that had happened.

Dr. Robinson and I walked. He was closer to the water's edge. He wore boots that must have been waterproof; he didn't care that he got them wet. It was good to be there, listening to him, his lecture voice, telling me something he thought I should learn, things he thought I should know.

"I read a story in a magazine the other day. It was about a farmer. A simple farmer. I can't remember where he lived. Maybe France, maybe Wales. I've forgotten that part," he said. "The thing is, they wrote that he eats the same thing every day. The same meal. Every day, three times a day. Three hundred and sixty-five days a year. His entire life. Forty years."

I thought there might be a lesson in his story, a lesson that would connect his wife's affair with Shane to the farmer who ate the same thing every day. I waited for the connection.

"He works his farm. He eats his egg, pickle, and bacon sandwich. He drinks hot coffee in the morning, cold coffee at lunch from the same pot. In the evening, he drinks beers, two or three, almost never more unless it's a holiday like Christmas or his birthday. He listens to the radio at night. He was born there and has lived there his whole life. He's got a truck that helps with the farmwork, but he's never left. He goes to town for supplies, things he needs. But otherwise he hasn't ever been more than ten miles from where he was born."

I thought he was going to tell me that the man was dead. I thought that's where the story was going to end.

"I think he might be one of the happiest men in the world," Dr. Robinson said.

He sounded lonely to me, his life so unbelievably boring. Eggs, bacon, and pickles didn't seem like something I wanted to eat every day, let alone three times a day, forever. I didn't think that was the lesson.

"I guess he's not married," I said.

One guy might do something eccentric like that, but I didn't think he could convince someone else to live like that.

Dr. Robinson laughed. I hadn't meant to be funny.

"I was going to say how much I admire a life like that. Simple. Plain. Knows exactly what he wants."

I thought it sounded monotonous. It lacked any sort of imagination. I hated doing the same thing every day.

"I could live like that," Dr. Robinson said.

"Really?" I asked. That was a surprise. "Why?"

It was the life of a hermit, someone removed from society. It didn't sound like he had much of a social life—not many friends, no family.

"Really," he said. "That would be enough for me. To know what I have in my life and to love what I have in my life."

I wanted to talk him out of admiring this lifestyle. I thought he was just saying this because of everything that had happened.

"But no one wants to eat the same thing all the time," I said. "He goes to town for supplies. He could get other things besides eggs and pickles, bread, and beer."

"I think you're missing the point."

Then there had been a point. I had missed it. I hadn't been sleeping much, and I had been walking around campus in a cloud of confusion. It hung over my head and wouldn't let me go.

"But maybe you're right. Maybe you get the real point. One can live like that. But one would have to live alone."

The Crusoes were all glad to see him. He hugged them all, just like he had hugged me. Arms all the way around our backs. Holding us each for a minute. It got to me. Seeing him do that with all the guys, my eyes filled. I made sure no one saw, but really, I wouldn't have cared if they had.

He told us that he was leaving Marquette.

"Forever?" I asked.

He told me he could never do that. "For now," he said. "Just for a while."

That was a change I did not want.

He had a friend up in Houghton who was doing a study for Michigan Tech. They were going to spend time on Isle Royale and study the moose and wolf population, how one affected the other.

The guys said it was cool to be out on Isle Royale.

"Like Angelique Mott?" I asked.

"I hope things don't get that dire," he said. "But I'm glad you remembered her name. You should. One day, maybe you'll write about her so that other girls will know what strength can do."

"There are ghosts out there on that island," Jon said.

"I don't mind that," Dr. Robinson said.

"But you'll be back," I said.

It was not a question, and the Crusoes laughed.

"Time for some change," Dr. Robinson said.

I thought we had just discussed the opposite—that we were not going to change the world. I thought that had been the point of his story, that doing the same thing was alright if it made you happy. I didn't want to eat the same thing three times a day, but I didn't want Dr. Robinson to leave. It felt like he was abandoning us. It wasn't fair that he had to do that because of Shane Lebarre. I was sure that was why he was leaving. I was sure of that.

The Crusoes were loud with their protests. "You can't leave. You can't leave us here alone."

"You'll be fine," Dr. Robinson said. "I have faith you'll be alright. All of you here."

He didn't say anything about Shane. Or Finley. He did not say anything about his wife.

His voice caught, but he spoke anyway. "Don't stop asking your questions. Never, ever."

I wasn't the only one crying.

He hugged us again—one by one—and promised to be in touch. I didn't know how that would work. But I got a postcard just before the semester ended. It showed a large pole marking the snowfall in the Keweenaw Peninsula that winter: a record-breaking amount, 394 inches.

Don't give up. Mother Earth is depending on you. Hope you're happy and doing good work for our future.

Dr. Robinson

NOW

It's funny what you think about. What you don't.

You never really understood what went on. Or why. You were young. The world revolved around you and your emotions. You were sleeping with Charlie, and that was fun. For a long time, it was perfect. Then you had your futures. He got a job in Alaska, and you thought you'd follow him up there. But you didn't ever go. You never left.

People were always leaving Marquette.

From the start—the Sues, then Janet. Shane left, and that was no big deal. You hoped that was out of shame, but maybe it wasn't. There were rumors that he had moved downstate with Dr. Robinson's wife, but the story ended vaguely with names of cities—a whole list of them—in the lower peninsula: Flint, Bad Axe, Ludington. Dr. Robinson had gone to the woods. He had been seen in the Keweenaw—lots of people saw him. You thought he was up there in the woods embracing his solitude and the same meal three times a day, every day. But Finley? He disappeared. He went off the grid. Completely. You never heard anything from him again.

People you loved starting leaving.

The Crusoes—one by one—they left.

You always thought they'd come back. All of them, some of them—at least one of them.

Lots changed. All that trouble and then months of talking about what had happened. Endless talking really—all those theories, the suppositions, the countless questions and ideas about what went on, but no one knew anything for certain.

The answers never came. The questions and the concern—all that worry—somehow got replaced by other things.

It's funny. You're living your life, moving along. You start to feel like it's time for change—time for you to finally get up and do something, like maybe you're stagnating and too much time is passing. You remember that you once had a purpose, and you'd like to have that again. You can't go back in time, but you're nostalgic all the same.

And then.

I was reshelving books at the Peter White Library, one of my part-time jobs that year, when I saw the old copy of *The Mining Journal.*

There were always stacks of books and newspapers waiting to be put back where they belonged. This was on the top, so someone had been reading it recently, though the library was empty.

The headline was above the fold. I flipped it over, and that's when I saw the photograph: Dr. Robinson, the Crusoes. It took me a few minutes to recognize myself, but there I was. The first demonstration—my first one, anyway. It was September, and we had formed a line, our arms linked, a solid wall of anti-ELF. I was standing next to Finley. He was looking at the camera. I was looking at him.

There was a lot of hair and a lot of flannel, almost as if we were wearing uniforms. The guys all had the same haircut or the same non-haircut. They just let it grow. It fell to their shoulders. Mine was longer. We looked pleased with ourselves. I was quoted in the article. Something about nature and beauty. I thought it sounded sweet but misguided, like I was an idealist, not someone who had understood the issues at hand.

The head librarian was a nosy woman. I made sure she was busy checking out a stack of romance novels for a reader who came in twice a week, before I slipped the journal into my backpack, then left. I wanted to keep the photograph.

I went back to my apartment and reread the article. I read it over and over until I had it memorized.

It was good to think about those days, but seeing the old photo and reading the article got me feeling restless. It had been ten years since I was a freshman. Time lost, time gone. Back then, I had had a purpose. That had faded. Maybe a trace was left. I always hoped things would start up again. They seemed stalled.

I told people I was a high school teacher; in reality, I was a substitute. The principal promised me I was up for the next full-time position that became available. He thought one of the teachers would get pregnant and quit. That's what I was waiting for. "They're like rabbits," he had said. "Babies, babies, babies, all the time."

But no one seemed to be doing much procreating—they weren't asking for leave, in any case. I got days here and there but nothing permanent. I wanted my own class, my own lesson plans. Substituting felt more like babysitting than professional teaching, but I thought a full-time position would feel important and worthwhile.

In the summer months, I worked at my friend Terry's pottery shop out on Presque Isle Road. Anyone visiting the area stopped in. Terry crafted things out of wood and clay. The ones that sold the best were the little souvenirs he made in fifteen minutes. Things that said *Marquette* or *Superior* or *the Upper Peninsula*—cheap souvenirs that people wanted to buy but that Terry hated making. The people who came in were from different parts of the state, some from further away, but most had driven there.

We had an idea to start giving hiking tours of the area. We were planning that for next summer. I would lead the tours. They could be educational— identifying species of flora and fauna, which I still cared about. It also seemed like something I wanted to do.

Terry was a horrible stoner. He had two or three toddlers and a wife who was always after him to do things around the white elephant of a house they had bought on the north side of town. Terry never got around to doing them. I hoped this was the year we would get the tour company off the ground.

I waited for something to happen

I got by. I made enough money to support myself. I had a great third-floor apartment on Arch Street with a view of Superior. I loved being there and watching the lake. It always looked different. I had friends, but the sense that I was doing something important in my life was not there anymore. It wasn't like I could go back a decade in time. I had to live in the present. I missed the Crusoes. I missed Dr. Robinson. I missed the energy and focus we had had that first year in Marquette.

I don't know if it was the article or something else, but I had a strong sense that I was wasting my time. I felt lost and didn't know how to ask for directions or help because I had no idea where I wanted to go.

I put the article away, but it wasn't like I could just forget it.

A few weeks later, I was playing fetch with Doug's rescue dog. I had been dating Doug for about six months. Just after we met, he adopted the dog from a shelter in Gwinn. It was a stupid thing to do. He worked at the television station near the airport and was never home. So I got the job of taking care of the dog. The dog, still not named—Doug couldn't decide—yanked on the leash so hard it hurt my arm. Most afternoons, I took her to the lake. Doug didn't like that the dog came home wet. "She'll catch a cold," he complained. It was September—not warm, I wouldn't go that far—but we were not in winter yet. It bothered me that he cared so much about a wet dog. It seemed like chasing sticks into a lake was something healthy dogs did regularly.

I didn't see the guy in the dark blue parka until I was almost on top of him. I could say he appeared out of nowhere, but that would make it sound like something whimsical, like he was something I had conjured. And that's not what happened. More than likely, he had been standing there the whole time. I had been in my own head and just hadn't seen him.

But there he was—standing a few feet from me. "Hello, hello."

He had some stones in his hand. He turned sideways and tossed one out across the surface of the water. It skipped twice, then sank.

I backed away, apologizing for getting too close, invading his space, though it really did seem like he had just materialized.

"It sure is beautiful here," he said.

It was late in the season for visitors.

"The most beautiful place in the world," I said.

I believed that; my appreciation of Superior and Marquette had never wavered—it was probably the reason I had never left.

"Can't believe we almost lost all of this," he said.

"What's that?"

I wasn't in the mood for an odd conversation with someone I didn't know. I had just decided that if Doug complained about the dog when I brought her back, I was going to end it. Maybe I had even decided I was going to end it no matter what he said. I didn't like him enough; he didn't seem like he liked me enough either. And that really bothered me.

"If the government had had their way," he said, "all this could have been in peril."

It wasn't a word you heard very often. Not on the beach anyway.

He jerked his head towards the lake.

"Superior?" I first thought that his concern was pollution, that he was talking about waste in the water.

"Not just the lake," he said. "All of this. Everything."

I thought he was rambling nonsense.

He went on. "Retaliation is a bitch. Given the chance, they would have destroyed it."

That didn't sound like polluted lakes. I thought about the algae and how if it had come any earlier, it would have ruined the summer.

"You ever hear of Project ELF?"

I spun around. I looked at his face just to make sure he wasn't someone I knew. He took my silence for ignorance and began to talk. He knew his stuff, almost as if he had studied it.

"Project ELF," I said.

I wished Dr. Robinson would materialize there on the shoreline. I would have liked that.

"Have you heard of it?" The man in the blue parka wanted to know.

"Of course," I said.

I got nervous without understanding why. I didn't know him. He didn't know me. He wasn't familiar.

"The government thought it was going to be easy as pie," he said. "Simple one, two, three. Boy, were they wrong."

The dog came back and dropped the stick at his feet, not mine. The guy did not pick it up.

I wanted to hear more. "The government was wrong?"

"Couldn't have been more wrong," he said. "Way off base. Way, way off."

I leaned over and grabbed the stick. The dog wanted to play tug of war, and we wrestled for a second, but I sensed the guy didn't like talking to me when I was busy playing fetch. I grabbed another stick and tossed it as far as I could across the shallow waters. The dog ran off.

"They were stunned by the Green Peacer wannabes that were up here. All the back-to-nature kids living on and loving the land up here. Never counted on all that. Thought it was the boondocks. Nothing here but a bunch of stupid hicks."

A gut punch. These were things he couldn't have known.

"How do you know that?"

"Because I do," he said.

Like a ghost from the past.

"Think about it. All those young activists, those tree huggers trying to save the world from pollution. Charismatic leaders, like cults."

The dog was still in the water. I could see her head. I thought she might go under, then she came charging out and ran up the beach to the rocks where she collapsed in the sun.

I was the one who was cold. It was too much. First, the photograph from *The Mining Journal*—something someone had sought out—and now this.

"Were you here then?" I asked.

"Not me," he said. He moved his hand up and down, a childish gesture that had me guessing what it meant.

"Is that an airplane?" I said.

"I was in the Air Force," he said.

"At K. I. Sawyer?"

"Maybe," he said.

That wasn't an answer.

"I was in security," he said. "Still can't talk about what I was doing. But I was a bit further from home."

For someone who didn't want to talk, he had an awful lot to say.

"What I know is this. The government wanted that project installed up there. They soon learned that it wasn't going to be a slam dunk, but that didn't stop them. The government doesn't back down just because of some ragtag group of tree huggers."

A blast from the past—that word. Because people who cared about the planet were considered to be hippies looking for a cause.

He was a big know-it-all—but not big on answering direct questions. I asked him a bunch.

"Again, can't talk about any of the specifics," he said. "But I'm from Escanaba, so I got dragged into it. Someone who understood what or maybe who they were dealing with."

If we had been talking about anything else, I would have said it was a coincidence, but this was too close for comfort. He was scaring me.

"Escanaba?" I asked.

"It was the Cold War, and Russia was our enemy," he said. "They did what they had to do."

"Which was what?"

"That's the question, isn't it?" he said. "Think they chased them away. Got rid of them."

"Got rid of who?"

He was talking quickly now, as if he was running out of time. "We're talking years ago," he said. "The Iron Curtain was a bad enemy. No one had any idea what the Russkies were up to. But believe me, they were afraid."

I wanted to know more.

But he was giving me this weird smile. "Top secret," he said.

"Still?"

"What I know. What I heard. What I overheard and what I think I heard," he said. "Always best just to keep your mouth shut."

He mimed locking his mouth with a key and then tossed the imaginary key into the lake.

"Dennis Finley," I said. "Do you know him?"

"Doesn't sound familiar," he said. "Lots of Finnish in Escanaba."

Dennis Finley was the least Finnish name in the world.

"What about Shane Lebarre?"

"You going to ask me about every guy you've met from Escanaba?" he asked. "How long's this going to last?"

No, just the two. I only wanted to know what he knew about Shane and Finley. "So?" I asked.

"I don't know anybody anymore," he said, like he was being deliberately evasive.

I wanted to know about Dr. Robinson, but he stopped me.

"Think your dog's ready to go," he said.

The dog had wandered up to the parking lot. It wasn't safe there. I ran up to find him, and when I turned back, I saw that they guy had walked towards the lower harbor.

He couldn't have known who I was. It wasn't possible. And yet it hadn't felt like a random encounter.

I dropped the dog off at Doug's.

Then I went home and called Charlie.

His directive: *You need to find out what happened. They did sort of disappear. I can't. Too many holes in my head. It feels important. Even now.*

I was really the only one who could—the only one left up there.

I went back to McCarthy's Cove the next day to see if he was there. It was the only place I thought he might be. I wanted to know so much more; I had so many questions. He wasn't anywhere around. I walked up and down the shore for the better part of an hour but never saw him.

I checked at the Heritage House, the old hotel, now newly renovated. I didn't know his name and didn't want to seem creepy, so I just sat in the lobby and waited to see if he would come in.

The receptionist, a young girl with a high blonde ponytail, came out from behind the desk and picked up the dirty coffee cups and egg-stained plates from a side table. It was afternoon, and they looked like they had been sitting there since that morning. I didn't want to be obvious. She had already asked how she could help me, and I had told her I was waiting for someone.

"Hey," I said, like we had been talking. "Whatever happened to Irma?"

"Who?" she asked.

She was chewing fluorescent green gum. Instead of making bubbles, she flicked it out with her tongue, wrapped it around her index finger a few times, then sucked it all back into her mouth.

"An older woman. She was always sitting here by the fireplace."

The fireplace was lit. There were logs piled into the large metal crate off to one side. Someone had been tending to it. I doubted it was the blonde ponytail-green-gum girl.

"Was she one of the fossils?"

I might have called Irma that too.

"They let them live here until they croaked," she said.

She was young to be so mean.

I gave it a try. "I'm looking for a guy. About forty. Blondish. Wears a blue coat."

"I bet you are," she said.

"You what?" I asked.

"Not me," she said. "You. Looking for a rich guy from downstate."

Is that what I had communicated to her? Had she been standing closer to me, I would have pulled on that taut ponytail and told her to be nice to guests. Though I suppose she would have said I was technically not a hotel guest. I went outside and wandered around the hotel a few times. Besides the chains, it was the nicest place to stay in Marquette. He didn't appear. If he was staying there, I never saw him.

But my mind was in motion. Things from the past had been stirred up Disturbing memories that were like a jigsaw puzzle. As pieces, they didn't mean anything, but put together, they told me that something was wrong.

Charlie had said it: *They disappeared. They were there, and then they weren't. Gone.*

Looking back, I saw that that was exactly what had happened. They had disappeared. Not all of them—I kept in touch with Charlie, Pete, and Jon.

But Dr. Robinson had vanished. I used to think I would come across him one day. I hiked everywhere in the area—long walks in winter, spring, summer, and—my favorite—fall. I thought I'd see him. He'd be sitting in front of a campfire, and we'd talk. I waited for that to happen. I always thought it would.

Finley had also gone missing—evaporated into the stratosphere. I drove down to Escanaba that first summer. I had looked up his name in the phone book and found his address. I went to the house. It looked drab and empty. I rang the doorbell. No one answered. I drove around, wasted about an hour. When I went back, there was a truck parked in the drive. I rang the bell. A woman answered. I asked for Dennis.

She shook her head. "Finleys? That's who you're talking about? They're gone, girlie. Moved south."

The door closed before I could ask about a forwarding address. South could mean almost anything—south in the city of Escanaba, south like Wisconsin, or anywhere south of the UP.

I let it go. She didn't look the type to help. I should have been more persistent. I should have gone back and asked.

I always assumed I'd see them again. I just did. Then the years passed. Time started to add up.

I guess I thought it was what happened. You made friends. Things were transient. You weren't always going to be together.

But now, those sorts of vague wonderings about the past had changed. I was sure something had happened. It wasn't normal. They hadn't just gone on their way.

Now, it seemed it was something else

I spent the next few weeks at the library going through old copies of *The Mining Journal* and articles from other newspapers in the Upper Peninsula that had reported on Project ELF and the protests. Anything I could find.

"Are you working on a research paper?" The head librarian was helpful in showing me how to find articles but asked too many questions. "I thought you were a teacher," she said.

"I am," I said. "I'm just doing some research for someone." I tried to keep it vague, even when she pressed for more details.

She was a talker and had a reputation as a huge gossip around town. Her sister was a hairdresser over at Shear Image on Third Street, and the two of them hung out at the Crow's Nest Bar every Friday during happy hour. They drank the two-for-one drinks and ate the hot appetizers that were warmed in silver serving trays on Bunsen burners. I had sat next to them once. The gossip had been fast and complete. They covered the city in under an hour.

She didn't work on Thursdays, so that's when I did the bulk of my searching. I didn't want everyone in town to know that I was looking into what happened with Project ELF and those of us who had protested it in the UP.

The Mining Journal had documented those years well. Dr. Robinson was at every protest, all the demonstrations, the vigils, the marches, and the rallies over on Presque Isle. He was always being quoted, always giving some information. He had been arrested a number of times. I had only known about the time they had taken him out of class. So much happened that I hadn't known about. There were photographs too—a lot of Dr. Robinson. There was one of the woman who had dressed like Death, then some of the Crusoes and Finley and me. We had been busy that year.

We had protested, but the threat that ELF would come and ruin the landscape of our lives hadn't been something I worried about. It felt like a distant threat. The enemy seemed far away. I never thought the wilderness of the Upper Peninsula was ever in any real danger. As far as the communications lines with distant submarines—that felt something that might happen somewhere far away. It was just too far-fetched.

Another call to Charlie. Another message, this one long and detailed, ending with a request: "I need to talk to the Crusoes. Are you in touch with any of them? Call me back as soon as you get this."

I had let the years pass, always with the thought that we would have a reunion. I didn't want to leave Marquette. I didn't think the others would stay away as long as they did. I had this thought, always, that Dr. Robinson would come back and explain what had happened. I always thought that one day it would make sense and I would know.

In a year, I would be thirty. It felt like a goal line. By then, I used to think, I'd have everything settled. I thought by then I would have quit biting my nails. I would own a house. I did not have pregnancy dreams like a lot of my friends, but I assumed I would have someone major in my life, someone there. In reality, I didn't feel that much different. I was still me, still myself. I bit my nails. I slept with guys I didn't really like but who were fun for the night. I liked getting drunk and making out. I liked to walk in the woods. I liked to see the lake every day. I liked the soft hills and the streets where I lived. I held tight to Marquette. And I waited for an answer about what had happened.

✳

I drove up to Houghton to see if I could find Pete. I didn't think he was there. In fact, I knew he wouldn't be. Every six months or so, he sent me a letter he wrote from a bar near his house. He always wrote in pencil on legal yellow pads. He wrote like he talked, stream of consciousness, always changing the subject.

But the encounter on the shore had been a sign. It was an omen that I couldn't ignore. I went to Pete's father's house. He came back once or twice a year. He almost always got in touch when he came to Marquette. But this was important. I took a chance. I talked to his father, who was never sober. He seemed confused. "Pete's not here," he said. "He hasn't been here in a long time."

I would have been more surprised if he had been there. Another wild goose chase. Then another, when I tried to get in touch with Jon. I knew he had signed on with one of the shipping companies. He didn't necessarily work on the freighters, but he did every once in a while. He had called a few years ago and told me he had seen Marquette from the ship. "It was incredible," he reported. I told him to come visit. He was living in Duluth and said he would when he had some time off. The guy who answered the phone at the office said he'd try and get him a message if it was important. He couldn't tell me where Jon was, only that yes, he did work for the company and that he'd try and let him know that I had called. I phoned Jon's home number in Duluth. There was no answering machine. It rang and rang. I tried it at least once a day for the next few weeks.

Then, something happened that showed me I wasn't delusional. Something was going on: I saw Shane Lebarre. It was the first time in ten years.

I was at the Ultimate Frisbee Tournament outside of Munising. It was a big party on some guy's farm. There were a few hundred people there. Out-of-towners camped along the hillside, and the entire area smelled like hot dogs and campfires.

He was walking towards me, holding hands with a woman. I knew right away it was Shane. Then a bunch of people crossed in front of me, and I lost sight of him. I kept looking. It seemed he had disappeared—that felt deliberate.

I saw the woman he had been holding hands with waiting in line for a beer. I asked her what her boyfriend's name was.

"Why?" she asked.

"I think I might know him," I said.

"I doubt it," she said. "He's not from here."

"He's from Escanaba," I said.

When I said that, she took a handful of my hair and pulled on it. She did it so forcefully and so fast that I was shocked into tears.

"I don't want you talking to him," she said. She stepped out of line.

I retaliated by pulling on her thin wispy braid. It was a futile move. I got the bird feathers.

"He's supposed to be dead," I said. "He jumped off the break wall into Lake Superior in the middle of winter. Did he tell you that?"

"You're out of your mind," she said.

But I wasn't.

I followed her—stealthily—or as close as I could at a Frisbee tournament. They met up by the campfires, where people were roasting hot dogs over open fire pits.

I called out his name. He turned. I know he did. He saw me, looked directly at me. I ran ahead and then lost track of them, like they had run off to get away from me. That's what they did; they had to have. They were running from me—he was, at least.

If I had seen which way they went, I would have chased after them. But there were too many people, the area too large. I was sure he had avoided me. On purpose.

Seeing Shane was no accident.

I called Charlie as soon as I got back into Marquette.

I waited for all the beeps to finish, then left a message. "It wasn't a coincidence. Guess who I ran into today?"

He picked up. "Who?"

"Are you screening my calls?" I asked.

"Have to," he said. "The banshee is on the warpath." He was talking about the woman he lived with. "Shows up unannounced. Odd times. Out of nowhere."

"Like the peacocks?" I asked.

"The peacocks don't care who I'm talking to," he said.

I worried his girlfriend would cut us off just when I had something to tell him. "Shane Lebarre."

"No way!"

"See? The guy on the beach wasn't some random encounter," I said. "Not when, a week later, I run into Shane Lebarre—who, by the way, completely ignored me."

"I did always wonder about him," Charlie said. "There was something weird about that guy."

"Like what?"

"I mean, he was older than us. He had been in the service. I wasn't the only one who thought he worked for the government."

All part of the stories we heard, the rumors we repeated that first year in Marquette.

"It couldn't have been a coincidence," he said. "Think about it."

It was all I had been thinking about.

"You think they planned the whole thing?"

"I think something happened."

"Why?" I asked.

"Think of the money," Charlie said. "You know how much they were spending on the project? Millions of dollars. They weren't going to just walk away from that."

It was not something I had considered.

All this time I had been telling myself to believe the opposite—to believe that I had been exaggerating, that I had blown it up in my mind because I was young, because I was dramatic and wanted it to matter more than it did.

No longer.

Now I was dead sure someone was telling me something. I had a mission: to find out what happened. I wasn't going to brush it aside and wait for another sign. It was time to discover the truth. Finally, it was time to do something about what had happened back then.

His voice got muffled. He was talking to someone I couldn't hear.

Then silence, the connection ended.

I had a friend who told me her boyfriend was doing construction work out at K. I. Sawyer.

It was odd. People from Marquette never work on the base.

"It's closing," she said. "Or getting ready to close."

"The Air Force is leaving?"

"They're decommissioning the entire base."

"Why?" I asked. I didn't know they did that sort of thing.

"How should I know?" she said.

I asked if he'd let me tag along one day.

"What are you going to do on an Air Force base?" she asked.

She was the jealous sort and probably thought I was up to something fishy with her boyfriend. It wasn't me she had to worry about. We lived in a small town, and if you wanted to keep your friends, you kept your mouth shut. Besides, though I had seen him with other women, I had never actually seen him having sex with any of them. Flirting and drinking and maybe some kissing—but I wasn't reporting any of that back to her. She knew who he was. I wasn't a threat.

I just wanted to get onto the base. I didn't think I'd find a file that said *TOP SECRET—PROJECT ELF*, but I thought I'd get more information on my quest to find out what had happened.

He took me on Friday when he was only working half day.

"It's boring as shit out there."

"Don't worry about me."

"It's not like I can run you back to town," he said. He explained that they were remodeling the barracks out there. "It's a huge project, and I don't have enough workers."

"Making them into what?" I asked.

"Rentals," he said. "Long-term apartments and short-term vacation places."

The drive out was gray, the roads out there flat with nothing to see but brush. It did not seem like a place anyone would want to live—or visit for that matter.

"Who's going to stay out there?" I asked.

It was a drive into Marquette. I didn't imagine there was anywhere to work this far out.

"The rentals will be for tourists, I guess."

"Tourists are going to stay on an Air Force base? Why? What's there to see?"

"Nothing."

"Then why would people want to stay there?"

"Beats me," he said. "The whole UP's going to become a vacation mecca." I didn't believe that.

"They're moving the airport from Marquette out there," he said.

It seemed like an awful lot of changes for a place that didn't make them very often.

The base did not look how I had imagined it would, though as soon as I saw it, I wasn't sure what I had been expecting. It was flat and looked like an enormous airport tarmac—lots of runways, a few buildings, but not that many for the number of people who had worked there. No trees, no wildlife—not even grasses. Just barren and empty. Desolate, it was a wasteland of concrete that looked like it hadn't been used in years. *Dismal* was also a good word to describe it.

I spent the day wandering in and out of the buildings. Some were locked. Some were open, but the rooms had been emptied. There was dirt on the floor, pop cans, cigarette butts—not much more. There were no offices, no file cabinets. I was disappointed, so I guess I had been wanting to find a file with *TOP SECRET—PROJECT ELF* stamped on it and the answers to all my questions inside. I even had this strange thought that I might see Shane Lebarre out there.

I met Eric at his truck. I was exhausted from walking around, doing nothing all day.

"You find what you were looking for?"

"Not really," I said.

"Told you," he said. "Nothing here. Not anymore."

It was nothing but a large emptiness. Out of place in the Upper Peninsula. At one time it might have been beautiful, but that had been erased.

"What was it that you wanted to find?"

"Hoping to find out what happened to Project ELF."

"Nothing happened to it," he said.

"Well something did."

"What are you talking about? It's there."

"What?"

He jerked on the gear shift, three on the tree behind the steering wheel. "Right here. Where it's always been."

"It's what?" I asked.

"Republic," he said. "The site's been there for years."

That was impossible.

"That can't be," I said. I would have known if Project ELF had been installed.

"Top secret operation," Eric said.

I didn't believe it.

"They fought the residents for as long as they could. But they weren't going to do that forever, and they wanted the system. It was the Cold War. The U.S. had enemies. So they just installed it. In-the-dark-of-the-night sort of thing."

"Is that true?"

"Oh yeah," he said.

I wasn't sure how I could have missed that. I read the newspaper every day. I knew what was going on around town.

"Don't feel bad. It wasn't like they advertised what they were doing. Definitely done on the sly. I had some buddies working with Ma Bell out this way, and they knew about it—had to. They could see the lines. They were given bonuses—cash, I should add, to keep it on the down-low."

In-the-dark-of-the-night sort of thing. Without Dr. Robinson. Without his band of devout followers. They had made sure to get rid of the protesters.

The site was a large fenced-off area. There was a radio tower with telephone wires attached to telephone poles. It looked like nothing. It didn't seem dangerous. It didn't seem powerful. It didn't seem destructive.

I thought Eric had gotten it wrong.

"This can't be it."

It was supposed to be official. Enormous. It was supposed to be guarded. But this was underwhelming—a disappointment, not a threat.

"There it is," he said. "The million-dollar defense program. They tried to play nice with the locals, but in the end, they got what they wanted. Of course. Don't they always?"

"A million dollars?"

"More like five million," he said. "A drop in the bucket for the DOD, but they weren't going to let some leftover sixties protestors stand in their way. They had way too much riding on it."

Everyone agreed—and me, still clueless. I got that weird sensation. I felt removed, like I was looking down at myself sitting there with Eric in the truck. It happened every once in a while. I would be sitting somewhere, and then I'd go off. It felt like I was watching the whole scene from a tall tower, far above where I had been sitting. I could see myself. No one else knew that I had left, but I wasn't there anymore, but watching. That's what I did then. I could see myself sitting in the truck beside Eric, but I was looking down on us, like I was watching myself instead of being myself. I saw that Eric was freaked out because I was crying, but he didn't really care that much. I was his girlfriend's friend, and as long as I kept quiet about what I saw him doing when I ran into him at midnight at the bars, he didn't care what I did. Then I saw myself, a ball of confusion. I was all mixed-up and still didn't know what I was doing—or why. I needed some answers before I could do anything else. I couldn't go on without knowing. Not knowing was keeping me from getting to where I wanted to go. I saw that.

I told myself to stop it. To just stop it. Stop wasting time. As Charlie said: *It was important. Even now. It felt really important. Go find out.*

I even argued with myself: *I'm trying. I'm really trying here.*

The box was left on my porch. I hadn't heard the mailman ring the doorbell or knock, which was what he usually did when I got packages. They didn't come often. My mother sometimes sent me chocolate chip cookies. They arrived broken and in bits, but it was a way to connect and I appreciated that. My parents were not fans of the UP—the drive too long, most of the year too cold, and they didn't like being far from home. I made an effort to go down at least once a year, but I hated Detroit, hated everything about it. Phone conversations were good for us.

So the box was a surprise. Inside the layers and layers of bubble wrap was a wine bottle—empty—or so I thought, until I held it up to the window to see if the label would tell me who had sent it. That's when I saw the note.

Like most of what happened in the past few weeks, this was not what I had been expecting.

A message from Charlie: *I'm coming to help. It's obvious you can't do this alone. I'm done with the West Coast. Done with trailer parks and RVs and peacocks wandering around screeching shit at me. I'm coming back to Marquette. We'll find out exactly what happened. It was strange. Those guys did just disappear. Be there soon.*

NOW

Stewards of the Earth, keepers of the planet: that's what he believed about us. He told us Project ELF would ruin the beauty we loved, and we knew this to be true.

We had been charged with the task of saving the world around us. We thought this was possible. At the time, all things were possible but especially this. It was a challenge. But we thought we were up to it.

We should have done better. We should have stayed together. We should have done so much more.

We were supposed to rebel, to do something brand new, something different.

We should have tried harder to save the planet. All these years later, it's more of a mess than we could ever have imagined. We had done a terrible job.

We're doomed. People talk about the inevitability of what will happen. And guess what? They're right. We are never going to save the planet from destruction. Mrs. Jones was off by a few years, but ultimately, she knew what she was talking about. She had been right all along.

I can't think like that. I can't stop now. The satisfaction of a desire is the death of that desire, and I'm willing to get to the end.

I'm going to find out what happened. Somebody knows. Top secret doesn't mean anything—not up here in Marquette. It's an extreme place—every other person is anti-government. Somebody knows something. Somebody does.

I'm waiting for Charlie. Still waiting for him to make good on his missive in the bottle.

It's been a while since I heard from him. The phone number I had for him has been disconnected, so I have faith he's on his way. I just have this feeling. One of these days, he'll show up.

I'm not giving up. This is my purpose now. I've got to see it through.

I like to go to the lake at dusk—that time between wolf and dog.

I was down there just the other day. The beach was quiet—no one else was there—at least, no one I could see.

The winds were still, the lake completely calm. I walked the shore. Back and forth, keeping an eye on the horizon.

I wasn't sure, but then I was. I had heard something. Boom-boom, boom-boom, boom-boom.

This was no mistake. It sounded just like a heartbeat.

It wasn't mine. Someone or something was out there.

I could feel them.

I stood on the shore, feeling the sands, the coldness of the spring lake waters coming ashore. I felt the low vibration, then another and another, heartbeats coming at me, communicating as if code.

Am I making this up?

Maybe.

But it feels real. It feels very real.

So let's just say it is.

And it was.

So much appreciation to Heather McAdams, Tim Haggerty, Jen Bannan, and Connie Egan. Thanks to my ride or die, Mel Novak. To my lifesavers Connie Amoroso and Cynthia Lamb. And to Jerry and to getting rid of all the photos in the lounge.

In the UP: to Beth Veker, who was there and connected us all; to Julie Sport Spero; Todd Turnquist; Bonnie Lindberg, up in the Crow's Nest; to Toby Rose, who told me I could; to Keith-Henry, who went above and beyond. And to all of us, who like Rounds found the light on I-75 going north and never looked back.

And of course, to you, Donny Kukla, because you were right—we never should have left.